Chasing the Stars

Books by Melanie Hooyenga

The Campfire Series
CHASING THE SUN

The Rules Series
THE SLOPE RULES
THE TRAIL RULES
THE EDGE RULES

The Flicker Effect Trilogy
FLICKER
FRACTURE
FADED

Anthologies
LOVE ON MAIN
THE ART OF TAKING CHANCES

Left-Handed Mitten
Publications

CHASING THE STARS

Published by Left-Handed Mitten Publications
ISBN-13 979-8473954371

UPC

Book design, cover design, and ebook formatting by Left-Handed Mitten Publications.

Author website: melaniehoo.com
Email: melaniehooyenga@gmail.com
Facebook: facebook.com/MelanieHooyenga
Twitter: @melaniehoo
Instagram: @melaniehoo
Newsletter: www.melaniehoo.com/hoos-letter/

For Super Owen,
who brightened my life for twelve years
and left a furry hole in my heart

1

NAOMI

"So how can I tell if he actually likes me?" the high-pitched voice in my headphones asks. "That he's not just being polite because we're forced to work together for our class?"

Even though the caller can't see me, sweat breaks out over my lip and my brain freezes. The only sounds are the steady thump-thump-thump of my heart echoing in my ears. This is the third interview on this episode of Three Good Things and the first one who's stumped me. I can usually pull advice out of the air without missing a beat.

"Do you think it's hopeless?" she asks, defeat clear in her voice.

Theo, my seven-minutes-younger brother who's sitting across from the old desk that serves as our recording studio in the corner of our basement, gives me a stern look.

The silence drags on—something Theo will edit out in production—and I wipe my clammy hands on my jeans.

"Naomi," he whispers. I lock eyes with him and he makes a cutting motion with his fingers indicating we can edit this out later, then motions for me to continue.

The gears in my brain whir to life and the words tumble out. "It's all in the body language," I tell the caller. "If a person likes you, they find ways to make physical contact. And even when they don't touch you, they subconsciously keep their posture open to you."

The girl on the phone giggles. "Like he's coming in for a hug?"

Theo covers his eyes with his hand and shakes his head, his shaggy black hair falling over his fingers.

Research shows that people can hear a smile in your voice, and mine comes naturally. "Not that obvious. Subtle things." I picture my best friend Sage and her boyfriend Neb. From the moment they met, they seemed connected by an invisible string, always aware of each other's proximity and in a constant dance to be near each other.

Theo makes a show of crossing his arms and widens his eyes at me.

I mouth, "I know," then clear my throat. "Sometimes it's easier to explain how to tell if a person's not interested. If they avoid eye contact, or cross their arms, or if you're sitting near each other and they shift away from you, those are pretty good signs they're not into you."

"Oh." Her voice sounds farther away than it did a moment ago.

"But just because a person isn't interested now doesn't mean they never will be. Find ways to get to know them. Show them what a wonderful person you are." My shoulders relax and I exhale, feeling my rhythm returning. "Insta-love only happens in books and movies, so don't worry if you don't have an immediate love connection." I smile at Theo. "Real love takes time."

I wrap up the call, thanking the caller for her bravery in calling into the Three Good Things podcast and while Theo takes down her contact information, I toss my headphones onto the desk.

"Three good things *that's* over," Theo says.

"That was a train wreck."

"I said good things."

The premise of my show, aside from the advice I give, is to find the positives in every situation—even a dumpster fire like that interview. I tick off my fingers. "My guest was well spoken, I got to reiterate my stance that love takes time, and..." My eyes dart over the recording equipment in our corner studio to the worn couch and first generation flatscreen TV against the far wall. The scent of mom's lemon cleaner mingles with the musty odor that comes with living in a damp climate like Oregon. "And it's over?"

"I can salvage it in editing." He picks at a nick in the wooden desktop and lets his headphones settle around his neck.

"You always do."

We produce my weekly podcast every Wednesday, and despite the occasional misstep like what just happened, it took off faster than I ever dreamed. My friends not only blanketed the high school with buttons with the show's logo—*my show has a logo*—they pushed everyone to submit questions, and now underclassmen call me the Podcast Chick, which I love way more than I ever imagined. To anyone who asks, I insist I launched the show because I want to help people, but this little taste of fame has been pretty fricking cool.

Even Theo seems to enjoy the notoriety. I've heard him called the Producer Twin, and he beams whenever someone talks about the show. When he agreed to help, I don't think he realized how much work would go into producing each episode, and while moments like these are sometimes demoralizing, getting feedback from the person who knows me best in the world is easier than it would be from a stranger.

He types something into his laptop before looking up at me. "We've got enough to cover our trip, plus the week after that."

We double-booked the past two weeks because in two days we're leaving for a week of family bonding—in the form of camping, canoeing, and star gazing. While our mom has always enjoyed sitting around a fire in the backyard, in my seventeen years, she's never slept in a camper, let alone gone camping in the woods. And yet we're about to drive over six hundred miles to Salt Lake City, Utah.

Utah. To stare at stars.

All because mom's friend Margo has always wanted to visit a dark park and they thought it'd be fun for our families to vacation together.

"And you're sure it'll launch without you pushing the button?" So far, we've manually published each episode. This will be our first time relying on technology to launch my baby into the airwaves.

Theo shrugs. "I trust the technology. Worst case, we publish it as soon as we're back. But hey, we probably won't have signal so at least you won't know."

That sounds like pure torture. I make a mental note to ask Sage to text me when it's live. "But texts will still work, right?"

When Theo and I camped a couple months ago to see the eclipse with a group from school, the WiFi was nonexistent, but texts still worked.

"Sure?"

"I can't believe we're camping again," I say.

"Repeating your disbelief won't change it. I just hope this Hunter guy can handle the tents."

"Gender stereotype much?"

He flips his hair off his face and rolls his eyes. "As if. We know Mom's ability, and she said Margo has a fancy tent that basically assembles itself, which implies she doesn't want to deal with those bendy poles."

The summer trip proved neither of us is an expert with the bendy poles.

"Which leaves Hunter."

Margo's son, who we've never met.

"Hey, I put mine together okay," I say.

"Then you two are in charge." He powers down the recording equipment and stands.

"I should have interviewed Sage."

"You can't keep having your best friend on. She's amazing and I love her, but unless you're making her a co-host, you need to mix it up."

"There's a thought."

"What?"

"Co-host."

He presses a hand to his chest and feigns shock. "I'm not enough for you?"

"I meant you, ya goofball."

I reach for his hand and grab it. Our fingers look eerily similar—I can never decide if that means mine look masculine or his look feminine—and my twin-love thuds in my chest. Having him by my side makes life easier, and I couldn't imagine it any other way. But we're two months into senior year and, despite our tendency to overshare everything, we haven't talked about what will happen to the podcast after we graduate. For all I know, he's thinking it'll end once we go to college.

Either way, I'm gonna miss him. He's like an appendage I don't know how to live without. My heart's set on the University of California at Berkeley, hundreds of miles south of where we live in Oregon, and while Theo's undecided, I'm ninety-nine percent certain he's not planning to go that far from home. If he's even going to college.

Which means we'll be apart for the first time in our lives.

I hate that I don't know what he's thinking, so before I lose my nerve, I spit out the question I've been wanting to ask for months. "Hey, I've been meaning to talk to you about—"

"Maybe we should cut that last section from the show."

I drop his hand, the warm fuzzies evaporating along with my confidence. "Doesn't that feel inauthentic? We can't keep deleting the interviews where I screw up."

"What difference does it make?"

The difference is the email I haven't told him about. The one that has a contract that's due next week and represents everything I dreamed of when I decided to launch the Three Good Things podcast.

Not telling Theo could destroy his trust in me and ruin what we have before we get to college. Even worse, if I reply and it leads where I think it might—it could expose me as a fraud.

2
HUNTER

"Dude, you really have to go?" Darren, my fellow Media Studies major and the closest I have to a best friend since starting college, eyes me from across my cramped dorm room. The industrial beige walls are mostly bare, save the poster of an Underwood typewriter over my desk and another of the New York skyline over my bed. "This is like a once in a lifetime thing, man."

"Don't remind me." I shove a pile of T-shirts and my favorite UC Berkeley sweatshirt—the one I got at orientation over the summer and screams Go Golden Bears!—into my duffel bag, followed by enough underwear for a week. Because that's how long I'll be camping in Utah with my mom and sister and a family I've never met instead of listening to one of the top book publishing acquisition editors in New York, my idol Evie Monroe. My dreams of meeting her afterwards died when Mom insisted I come home today.

Darren slides a pile of books across my desk to make room for him to lean. His brown hair is cut in the same shaggy style as mine and we have the same slight build, but he's like a miniature version of me: he barely stands five foot five while I'm just over six. "Just show up a couple days late."

"My mom's not having it. She wants us to drive there together for family bonding." And something about my car not making the seven hundred miles across three states to Salt Lake City.

"You'll be well bonded after a week."

"Along with my mom's friend and her kids who I've never met." I grab my copy of *Into the Wild* by Erin Hunter and finger the worn edges before tossing it next to my bag. My twelve-year-old sister Melody and I haven't read together since I left for college and I'm looking forward to rekindling that habit. I drop to my knees and pull my sneakers from a tangle of clothes under my bed.

"You said they're seniors in high school? At least they're around our age."

Darren's the master of arguing both sides of a situation, sometimes even in the same breath. There are times, like now, that I don't think he even realizes he's doing it.

"Yeah, and I get to share a tent with the guy."

"Did you really think you'd get to bunk with the girl?"

The corner of my mouth lifts, telling him he should know better.

He holds up one hand and grabs the front of his jeans with the other. "I know. You don't have time for girls, Mr. I'm Gonna Graduate in Three Years Even if It Means I Die a Virgin."

"Hey!" I throw a balled-up sock at him and he swats it away, laughing. "I didn't swear off sex, but I also don't believe in screwing my way through college."

"Oh, so you *were* hoping for a little something something."

"Who's getting some?" Shawna, another Media Studies major, materializes in the doorway. She's got dark skin, braids halfway down her back, and a smile so bright I swear it's fake. And she's on the same three-year track as me. The three of us met the first week of classes and quickly became the Three-Act Structure. No one else calls us that, but I like it.

"Dude, I was joking when I suggested the no dating pact." Darren pulls himself onto the desk, his feet swinging against the drawers. "Date! Be free! Get some!"

He may have been joking about the pact, but it makes sense. Romance is nothing but a distraction.

Shawna's gaze settles on my duffel bag and the underwear hanging out of the top. "You're not gettin' some with those."

Heat flushes my neck and sweat breaks out on my upper lip. I've got mom's Mediterranean complexion, which means my embarrassment isn't usually telegraphed for the entire world, but Shawna has the magic touch. I shove the offending boxer briefs deeper into my bag. "What's wrong with my underwear?"

She strides across the room and swats away my hand. Darren snorts as she pulls out a pair and examines the navy cotton. "Nothing, really. But they look like they came from a five-pack at Walmart."

Which they probably did. New underwear appears in my drawer once a year. I've never questioned its origins. "And that's bad because..."

"Hunter, you're in college. Time to step up your game."

I wouldn't even know where to begin. I lock eyes with Darren, who's failing at trying not to laugh.

"Dude, she's not wrong."

I grab the underwear from her, and the cotton suddenly feels rougher than I remember. I imagine being alone with a girl and her... feeling it... and my face flames hotter. "My underwear is fine."

Shawna grazes a hand over my shoulder and sits on the end of the bed, picking up the book and idly flipping through the pages. "I haven't read the Warrior Cats series in forever." I want to snatch it from her hands before she teases me for my reading choices, but she tucks it into my bag and gives me a gentle smile. "We didn't mean to embarrass you. But at some point..." She nods her head back and forth. "I'm just saying there's more than one way to be prepared when it finally happens."

My head whips to Darren. The lasers from my eyes nearly set him on fire.

His eyes go wide, understanding my freak-out. "I didn't say anything."

"Would you chill," Shawna says. "Darren didn't out you on purpose, but he calls you a virgin all the time."

My glare stays locked on Darren. My lack of a sex life is a personal choice, but that doesn't mean I want it to be the center of the conversation.

"Seriously, your secret is safe with me." She takes the underwear from me, FOLDS IT, and puts it back in my bag. "At least until the lucky girl who sees those."

"Did you two need something—besides making fun of my life choices?"

Shawna tosses her braids over her shoulder with a flick of her wrist. "I was just *making sure—*" she rolls her eyes on the last words—"you're really missing Ms. Monroe. This is a once in a lifetime opportunity."

"You two tag-teaming me isn't going to change anything." No matter how badly I want to stay, when my mom makes up her mind about something, there's no changing it. Just ask my dad, who moved across the country after she filed for divorce. "I'm surprised she hasn't checked in yet to make sure I've left."

As if on cue, my phone buzzes with a text. But it's from my sister Melody, not Mom.

Melody: promise me you'll listen to her podcast on ur way home

"Speaking of tag-teaming."

"Do tell." Shawna leans against my arm to look at my phone. "The podcast girl?"

I throw even sharper daggers at Darren. "Is nothing sacred?"

He pushes off the desk and approaches the bed, looking stricken. "I didn't know some random chick you haven't met was a secret."

"Hunter, is something else bothering you?" Shawna asks. She has a knack for cutting through my bluster and seeing what's really going on. I both love and hate it about her.

"No, sorry," I say to Darren. "I'm just on edge about missing Evie." And spending a week with total strangers. I thumb out a reply to Mel.

Me: won't I hear her enough camping?

Melody: duuuuuuude trust me
Me: I'll think about it

The little dots bounce as she types, and types, and types.

Melody: but you'll need to download it before you leave so ur not scrolling and driving because that's as bad as texting and driving and even though ur annoying sometimes I love you cuz ur my brother
Me: punctuation, I beg of you
Me: and I love you too
Melody: please Hunt, just listen to it
Melody: (curtsey for punctuation)
Me: I'll think about it

I stand and slip my phone in my back pocket. "If you two really want to help me, there is something you can do."

"Name it," Shawna says.

"Record Evie's presentation?" Because I'm not letting this vacation get in the way of my dreams to be an acquisitions editor for one of the big publishers in New York.

Learning from a successful editor is the first step to the rest of my future. To avoiding the mistake my parents made of getting married too early and divorcing too late.

This trip is just a bump in my plot. It won't change anything.

3
NAOMI

"When you first met your boyfriend in person, you'd already been texting for months, right?"

Sage bites her lip. "It was a few weeks, so—"

I swipe my hand across my throat to cut her off. "So you'd already gotten to know each other. You weren't complete strangers."

Sage's smile falters and guilt pummels me. She was so nervous to meet Neb after texting for weeks—not months—and I'm erasing that excitement for the sake of my podcast. "Yeah, I knew we got along." A spark twinkles in her eye and her smile returns. "But we agreed not to exchange pictures, so I had no idea what he looked like."

Theo pumps his hands over his head and silently chants, "Insta-love! Insta-love!"

My professionalism slips and love and happiness and all the gushiness that I've yet to experience for myself courses through me. Seeing Sage happy means everything to me and I know better than to diminish that for ratings. "That's really sweet," I say.

Theo throws his head back in exaggerated frustration. He met Neb before Sage and I did, and he bore the brunt of our interrogation about Neb. Including countless questions about his appearance.

A soft smile lights Sage's face. "Sweet, but nerve-wracking when we finally met in person. I really liked getting to know him without the pressure of appearances, but all the insecurities about whether the person you like will be attracted to you were made even bigger at the reveal."

Theo snorts and jumps away before I can smack his arm.

The moments leading up to when Sage and Neb saw each other for the first time rank as one of the top climactic love scenes in real life—at least that I've witnessed. And even though it felt a bit like insta-love, it most definitely was not. But how do I express that to my listeners without stomping all over Sage's feelings?

Sage continues, saving me. "On the outside, it might have looked like insta-love. I mean, I definitely had an O-M-G at first sight moment." She giggles and her face reddens. "But once we got past the initial awkwardness of finally seeing each other, we fell back on the friendship we'd already established."

Yes! I pump my fists above my bobbling head, my red curls falling in my face. We wrap up the interview and leave Theo to do his producer magic. Once in my room, we flop onto my bed and I hug my pillow to my chest.

"Thank you for being on the show again."

"I'm happy to help."

"But you hate being interviewed."

"Okay, yes, but my help makes you happy, therefore it makes me happy."

"Theo worries about having you on too much."

Sage sighs. "He's probably right. It's not like I'm a co-host."

I don't tell her that's exactly what Theo said. "I can't believe I have to leave you for a week."

"It's not like you're going to Mars. We can text."

"What if I don't have a cell signal?"

"I am proof you can camp without a cell phone." Sage broke her phone on the eclipse camping trip and, despite some serious withdrawals, did survive without it.

"Yeah, but I was right there the whole time."

She waggles her brows. "Not the whole time."

I roll onto my side and push her away. "You weren't gone long enough for me to miss you."

"And you won't miss me on this trip. You'll be too busy ogling the Sherpas."

"I'm sorry, what?"

Sage waves her hands. "The Sherpas. The guys who help you hike? Don't they carry all your crap and lead the way without oxygen while you ride a donkey or something?"

"What the hell trip do you think I'm going on? We're not hiking a mountain, we're camping and canoeing and stuff." I pause. "And you know we're not supposed to use that word? It's offensive to the people whose only option for work is carrying things up a mountain for rich tourists."

Her eyes go wide. "You're supposed to tell me these things!"

"I'm telling you now! But I don't even know if there are guides on Lake Powell."

"So back to my point. You'll be too busy to miss me."

"Impossible."

A knock on my door makes us both look up. Mom's leaning into the room, her red curls piled on top of her head like mine, except hers are somehow held up with a single pencil—a skill I've yet to master. "How'd the episode go?"

"It was great," Sage says before I can open my mouth. "I'm so impressed with what Naomi has done with her show."

A twinge of guilt makes me clench my lips. While Mom knows about the life-changing email, I still haven't told Sage. Or Theo.

"I wouldn't expect anything less from my brilliant daughter." A smile dances on her lips and I hug the pillow tighter. That look means she's excited about something that I most definitely will not be excited about.

"What?" I ask.

"Have you checked your email?"

"Not since yesterday, why?"

Mom's smile grows bigger, and she gestures at Sage and me. "I took a page out of your playbook."

"We have a playbook?" Sage whispers.

"Please don't encourage her," I whisper back. Louder, I say, "And what page might that be?"

"Having a group text before we camp together. Except Margo and I decided on email instead of text." Mom seems pleased as punch, as she likes to say. 'This way you kids can get to know each other before we get to East Canyon."

"Mom, no one emails for pleasure."

Her smile doesn't falter. "We do, so please reply." She turns her attention to Sage. "Are you staying for dinner, dear?"

"Yes," I answer for Sage. "I need all the quality time I can get before we leave."

"It's only a week," Sage says at the same time Mom says, "You're so dramatic," and walks away.

"I get that from you!" I call after her.

Sage rolls closer so we're hip to hip. "Read the email so we can stalk him."

My brow quirks. "Oh, now you're all for checking him out ahead of time? What happened to keeping it a mystery? Getting to know the guy without the pressure of appearances?"

Sage bumps her shoulder against mine. "Check your email." She drags out her words until I open my email app and click on the message from Mom titled The Stars at Night, Shine Big and Bright.

"She is so embarrassing," I say.

"You know you get that from her."

"Ugh, stop."

"Read it out loud."

I clear my throat and use my podcaster voice, which Theo insists is my attempt at being sultry. Really I'm just trying to sound professional.

Greetings Thompson and McGinnis families!

As we pack up our gear and make final arrangements for our trip, Margo and I thought it would be fun for the kids to get to know each other before we arrive. We know instead of thinking this is super cool, you'll roll your eyes and think this is super lame and old-school, but we're your moms and you should be used to this by now.

Please answer the following questions by the end of today:

"Oh my god, there's a written test?" Sage asks.

I hold up a finger as I read ahead. "Do they seriously think we're going to do this?"

Sage leans closer and reads the questions aloud.

What are you most looking forward to on this trip? What are you dreading? What is one thing everyone should know about you?

I interrupt to read the last question.

What will it take to make this is a successful trip for you?

"Wowwwwwwww," Sage says.

"This is what happens when you bring two self-help-obsessed women together."

"I've never been on a vacation with homework."

"I can't imagine anyone else will answer these."

"Forget those for now," Sage says. "Let's stalk—" she swipes my screen to the top to see Margo's son's name—"Hunter Thompson. Can't be more than a dozen of those."

I switch to Instagram and type his name in the search bar. Only six exact matches appear. Two are too old—fathers with pictures of their toddlers—and one is a page dedicated to a famous writer from the 1970s by the same name.

"That's bizarre," says Sage. "I wonder if he's named after that guy."

"Do people actually do that to their children?"

"People continue to surprise me."

I swipe down the screen. The other three Hunter Thompsons could all be college freshmen. At least from the quarter-inch profile pic. I tap on the first one. "The Thompsons live in California, so the New York guy is out."

Sage peers closer. "So it's either the guy wearing the flag like a cape or the group photo in what seems to be... a library?"

"It's gotta be the group pic because why would anything be easy?" I click the picture and three people are indeed standing in in front of bookshelves in what looks like a library. The Black girl in the middle seems to be corralling the two guys—a short white guy with shaggy brown hair and a taller version of that guy but with black plastic-framed glasses. She's the only one actually looking at the camera. The short guy's studying the hem of his T-shirt and the tall guy's looking at something in the distance, a playful smirk lifting the corner of his mouth.

"I vote that it's him," says Sage, tapping the tall guy's face. The picture zooms and we squint to get a better look at the pixelated image. "Try his other pics."

We scroll for a full minute but there's not a single picture of his face. "Why are boys so frustrating? This is completely unhelpful." I say. "His feed is nothing but books and hikes in the woods. And a couple of his shoes."

"Books and hikes? Sounds perfect to me." Sage flutters her eyelashes and rolls onto her back, pretending to swoon. She and Neb love being outdoors almost as much as they love books. It's one of the bazillion things they have in common.

"You would live inside a book if it were socially acceptable."

"Take me for a walk once a day and I'm set." She flips back over. "Try his tagged pictures."

I click the icon and a dozen little Hunters fill my screen. "Jackpot."

"Holy uncurated aesthetic." The pictures are a jumble of him eating, studying, and hiking, so not much different from his feed except we can actually see his face. He's cute in a geeky, nerdy way. The smirk from his profile pic is repeated in most of the pics, like he has a secret he doesn't want to tell but can't keep inside, and he looks comfortable in his own skin—even in the pic from a football game where he looks wildly out of place in a button-down shirt.

Sage nudges my shoulder. "Maybe it's time to answer those questions."

"Hmmmm. Maybe." Because if this is who I'm spending a week with, vacation just got a lot more interesting.

4

HUNTER

"Explain why I couldn't have met you in Utah. It's four extra hours of driving for me."

Mom gives me The Look—brows raised, lips pursed—like she's saying just because I'm off at my fancy college doesn't mean she's no longer in charge.

I soften my tone. "Why is it so important that we drive together?"

She paces the length of the kitchen. "We have to drive together because I don't want your car breaking down in the middle of Nevada, and I would appreciate the help on the ten-hour drive. But most importantly, we've missed you since you left for school and it'll be nice to have some family time before we meet up with the McGinnises."

Guilt sweeps through me like the hot Santa Ana winds that ravage our town every fall. Familiar, yet it carries a sense of uneasiness because I never know if these feelings will rush through me, fiery and destructive, or simply pass through like a gentle breeze. "How's she doing?"

"She misses you. I do, too. It's not the same without you around, but you know it's different when you're younger."

That's an understatement. I was the same age Melody is now when Mom and Dad split up, and while I had friends whose parents divorced, I wasn't prepared for the emptiness that filled the quiet corners of our home. The fact that I've made Mel feel anything similar is like a dagger in my heart.

The squeal of air brakes from the school bus outside interrupts my thoughts, and thirty seconds later, Melody bursts through the front door. "Is he here? Are you here?" She rounds the corner into the kitchen, cheeks flushed, hair the same color as mine tied into a high ponytail, mouth open in a smile wide enough to swallow me whole. Her bag lands on the floor with a thud and she leaps into my arms.

"You're getting too big for the Flying Thompson." I laugh into her hair. She smells like strawberry shampoo and grape gum and home.

"Never!"

I lift her into my lap, and she wraps her arms around my neck. Melody invented the Flying Thompson before she could walk. It involves launching herself off any surface into my arms, usually with a running start for maximum impact, and the full trust that I'll catch her.

Because I always do.

"How long have you been here? Are you excited for this trip? I'm so glad you're home!" She tucks her head against my chest and gives me another squeeze.

I chuckle, and an unexpected lump catches in my throat. "About an hour. Yes. And me too."

She pulls back to look me in the eye, and I'm startled by how grown-up she seems. "I thought you're pissed you had to miss the fancy New York lady."

My eyes dart to Mom, who shrugs. "I can be pissed about one thing and excited about another. Spending time with you and Mom is worth missing what may have been the singular opportunity to meet someone who could open doors for my future."

Melody bites the side of her lip.

"What?"

"I don't remember you being so dramatic."

"Away with you!" I shove her off my lap and she runs to the stairs, her giggles filling me with joy.

"Backpack!" Mom calls after her, and Melody jogs backward in slow motion, grabs her bag, then continues upstairs. Mom looks at me. "There will be other opportunities."

My knuckle grazes the edge of the counter. I know she's right, but I'm not agreeing that fast.

"Hunter." She waits until I meet her eyes. "You've got almost four more years of college—"

"Almost three." I wish I could fast forward through college and get on with my life.

"Almost three," she repeats. "You are the most determined person I know, after myself." She gives a mirthful smile. "Berkeley has guest speakers every week. There will be someone else from the publishing industry. Maybe someone even bigger than Emmy Monroe."

"Evie."

She rolls her eyes. "You understand my point."

I nod, but I avoid her eyes. Because I haven't told her the one thing that could change the future for all of us.

Before I can consider sharing my thoughts, Melody bounds down the stairs and runs directly to the refrigerator. She emerges with a cheese stick and an apple, then takes the seat next to me.

I raise a brow at her selection. "What happened to granola bars and drinkable yogurt?" Her afternoon snack of choice since she was old enough to have an opinion, which in her case was before she could form complete sentences.

She shrugs, but her eyes gleam. She's pleased I noticed. "Things have changed since you left, big bro. I'm not a little kid anymore." Her eyes widen as she levels her gaze at me. "Do you *know* how much sugar is in granola bars?"

Mom slides a paper towel in Melody's direction and folds her hands on the counter, a smile playing on her lips. "There is one other thing I want to talk to you both about."

"Are you getting married?" Melody bounces in her seat, a thread of string cheese dangling from her lips. So not *that* grown-up.

I laugh but Mom rolls her eyes. "What is your obsession with me getting remarried?" Mom asks.

Suddenly Melody's question takes on new meaning. "Wait, is there something I should know?" I ask.

"No," Mom says. "She's been bitten by the romance bug and—"

"Mom deserves happiness as much as the next person," Melody finishes.

My head tilts in mock concern. "Who are you and what have you done with my sister?"

"Can I please finish?" Mom says.

Melody takes a bite of apple. Juice dribbles down her chin and she swipes it with the paper towel.

My heart relaxes a bit more. She's still my little sister.

"Nancy and I started a group email so you kids—well, all of us—can get to know each other better before we arrive in Utah. I'd appreciate it if you can reply tonight."

"That's weird." Melody looks at me. "Can't we just text?"

I ruffle her hair and she jerks away. "The olds still rely on the archaic form of communication that requires complete sentences and proper punctuation." I pull out my phone to check my email, and sure enough, there's a message from a Nancy McGinnis called The Stars at Night, Shine Big and Bright.

Melody leans against my arm to look over my shoulder and her mouth falls open. "We have *homework*?"

"I can help you if you want," I say. Writing's like breathing for me, and helping others fine-tune their thoughts is what gives me purpose. It's what I've wanted to do since the first time I helped a friend edit his essays sophomore year of high school.

"By the way, I brought *Into the Wild*. Thought maybe we could start reading before dinner." I was obsessed with the Warrior Cats series around the time Dad left, so even though the books were too advanced for Mel, reading them together became our thing. Books saved me that first year and now I hope being an editor will allow me to capture the magic I felt when I got lost in books—to be part of that experience for other kids who need to escape reality.

"Let's look up Theo and Naomi instead."

My gaze drops and I ignore the twist in my gut. She's probably just distracted right now. We've got all week to hang out.

"Haven't you already done that?" Mom asks.

"Well, yeah. But this is for Hunter." She winks at Mom and does a little shimmy.

Alarm bells clang in my head. "What?"

Melody smiles sweetly. "Nothing… except I told you Naomi has a podcast and it's really cool and you need to listen to it. Like now. Before you answer any weird questions Mom and Mrs. McGinnis came up with."

I look to Mom for help, but she backs away from the counter, distancing herself from whatever has Melody practically bouncing out of her skin.

"It's called Three Good Things and she talks about how you can always find something good in even the worst situations. People call in and ask her questions and she helps them."

"So she gives advice."

"It's more than that. She really helps people." She scowls. "If you listened like I asked you to, you would understand."

I shake my head. "You mean you told me to."

"Yes, so why didn't you?"

"Isn't she a senior in high school? What does she know about helping people?"

"Dude, just listen to it. If you do, I'll let you help me with my questions after dinner *and* we'll read the first chapter."

My head snaps back. I'm being manipulated. By a twelve-year-old. I give Mom a questioning look.

She holds up her hands and laughs. "This is between the two of you. But if you want my advice, withhold your judgment until you listen to an episode. Naomi is quite captivating. And I obviously think her mother is fabulous, so I'm sure her children are as well."

"And she's pretty," Melody adds.

"I'll think about it."

After dinner, I follow the link Melody texted me and pick an episode at random. But I don't hit play. Mom and Melody talked this girl up so much at dinner that she's sure to be a disappointment. Not that it matters. I'm set on my goals, and it'll take a more than a pretty smile and generous spirit to distract me from that.

I fall asleep reading in my room, trying not to overanalyze the fact that Mel ran off to her room without mentioning the book. On the surface, we've fallen back into our usual routine, but something feels off. Like when I was six and my goldfish died, but instead of telling me, Mom and Dad bought a new one and hoped I wouldn't notice.

It took me a couple days, but I noticed.

Just like now.

— **5** —

NAOMI

"Theo, stop!" I elbow him to the backseat, away from the dashboard. In the five hours we've been in the car, he's hijacked the music no less than a dozen times. It's not that our musical tastes are that different—it's just that I prefer to be in control. "You're in charge of the music when it's your turn to drive."

Mom sighs from the passenger seat. "I thought you two outgrew this."

"I did. He didn't."

Theo knees the back of my seat in response.

Moments like these make me think it won't be so bad to go away to school, but no matter how frustrating he can be, I will always adore my brother. We're almost always in sync and it's rare that we don't know what the other is thinking, which is why it's so unsettling that he keeps avoiding talking about the future. And why it's killing me to keep the offer a secret. I mentally fire questions at him, urging him to share his thoughts, but he's staring out the window.

As the miles slip by, my mind wanders to the email thread. Everyone dutifully answered the questions, and as much as I hate to admit it, I feel like I know Hunter and Melody enough that it won't be completely awkward when we meet in person.

Since I haven't seen a picture of Melody, she's a faceless yet insightful seventh grader who seems like she's ready for an adventure, but Hunter's thoughtful reply combined with that smirk from his picture has my insides doing backflips. It's not that he said anything particularly profound, but his outlook feels refreshing after being surrounded by guys who are more focused on being kings of the school than, you know, educating themselves so they can be productive members of society.

My eyes roll at myself. If Theo could hear my thoughts, I'd never hear the end of it.

His head pokes between the front seats. "Whatcha thinkin'?"

"How do you do that?"

"After almost eighteen years, why do you still question my powers?"

"It's creepy." Especially since my ability seems to be lacking.

He presses the side of his head against my shoulder and whispers, "I saw you roll your eyes. So whatcha rollin' about?"

"Your answers to the vacation homework."

He gasps in fake horror.

"A little over the top, don't ya think?"

"That's kind of my brand."

"But iambic pentameter? You wrote your answers in iambic pentameter."

Mom snorts and quickly covers her mouth with her hand. "I wasn't going to say anything."

"Mom said Hunter's studying to be an editor or something. I didn't want him thinking he's sharing a tent with a caveman."

"You definitely accomplished that."

"You're just jealous you didn't think of it first."

A sigh escapes me, and I admit, "Maybe." Because while I firmly believe in not making an ass of yourself to impress the person you like—not that I'm saying I like Hunter, because hello, I don't even know him—but amplifying aspects of your personality are completely within reason. Not that I'm good at poetry, but I could have put a little more effort into my answers so I didn't come off so bright and shiny.

Theo pokes my shoulder. "Quit stressing. Your answers were one hundred percent representative of you."

"Thanks?"

"Kids, this was supposed to be a fun way to get to know each other," Mom says. "No one will make their final judgement on your character based on this."

"Okay, whatever," I whisper. But I don't believe her. Because I've made assumptions about Hunter based on his reply. When we switch drivers somewhere in Idaho, I snuggle into the backseat and reread Hunter's email.

Hi everyone, I hope you all feel as weird and exposed as I do. Without further adieu, here are my answers. Make of them what you will.

1. What are you most looking forward to on this trip?

The stars and spending time with Mel and Mom. I've missed them since I left for college and I'm looking forward to embarrassing Mel. And, of course, meeting the McGinnises.

2. What are you dreading?

I try not to go into any situation with dread, because that gives merit to that concern and makes it more likely to happen. That said, I would be okay not experiencing canoe tippage.

3. What is one thing everyone should know about you?

I'm sometimes slow to warm up to new people but that doesn't mean I don't like you.

4. What will it take to make this a successful trip for you?

Like Mrs. McGinnis, I'm hoping for insight into some things that are weighing on me.

See you soon,

Hunter

I bounce between his final answer and his comment about not giving merit to dread. I've read a number of books that say you get back whatever emotion you put into the world, so if you want to be successful, you have to project positivity. If you only share negativity with the world, that is what will come back to you. If Margo is as into self-help as Mom is, it would make sense that Hunter is also aware of this idea, but I've never heard a boy my age talk this way.

My eyes close and Theo's playlist—which I secretly love but don't tell him because what fun is that—washes over me as I try to imagine that smirk in real life. Is he as serious as he comes off in his email, or is there a playfulness that will take a few days to appear?

One other question lingers in my mind: Is he as cute as he seems in his pictures?

I find out three hours later when Mom comes to a stop at the end of a bumpy gravel road.

"Where are you?" she shouts at her phone. She and Margo have been on speakerphone for the past three miles and their excitement is contagious.

I lean forward between the front seats and scan the people lingering near the bright blue lodge. A tall woman with a dark brown ponytail and a phone pressed to her ear waves frantically. A miniature version of her stands nearby, and a tall boy with brown hair ducks into the lodge before I can see his face.

"I see you!" Mom shouts. She turns off the ignition, tumbles out of the car, and is racing to Mrs. Thompson before Theo and I even open our doors. They fling themselves at each other and jump in circles like schoolkids.

"I guess that's them," Theo says. His voice is flat, and he fiddles with the charger still attached to his phone.

"You okay?"

"Was it dumb to tell them I'm bi? What if he's weird about it and now we're spending the next five days in a tent together?"

Theo's usually so self-assured that these rare moments of doubt catch me off guard. "Would not telling them change anything?"

He shakes his head.

"Do you think he's cute?" I hold my breath. Please don't let us both like the same boy.

"Meh."

I exhale. "Then any issue would be on his part, and I didn't get the impression from his email that he's the judgmental type."

He raises an eyebrow. "You got that from giving merit to dread?"

"No, but he showed vulnerability about missing his family. That's not the sign of a douche."

He taps his fingers against his smile.

"What?"

"Twin Trust."

"You can't pull that out any time you want me to tell you something."

"My favorite sister's happiness is of the utmost importance. I'm just looking out for you."

"I'm your only sister."

"Therefore, my favorite. And the one I know best. Which is why I know you already like him."

"Stop it."

He whirls on me, his smile breaking into open-mouthed joy.

I push his jaw closed. "I'm not ready to like anyone. Not after last time."

Over the summer, I stupidly had a crush on Theo's friend Kit and when I finally got up the courage to make a move, he blew me off. It's been super awkward ever since.

"Things with Kit will come around."

"Do you know something I don't?"

Theo bites his lip, his tell that he's lying, but I don't have the energy to rehash old drama. Or push Twin Trust back on him.

"Please, just give it a rest."

He touches his temple. "Paused. For now."

"Let's go meet them."

We approach the Thompsons with less enthusiasm than Mom. Despite the getting to know you emails, introductions are always awkward, and I don't know how to start.

"Omigod, Naomi!" Melody squeezes her arms around me, the top of her head connecting with my jaw.

"Ow! Hi!" I hug her back and can't help but laugh.

"I'm so sorry!" She pulls back and her hazel eyes search mine. "Did I totally screw this up? I've been listening to your podcast and I've been so excited to meet you and I might be stanning a little and I totally just headbutted you."

My fingers graze my jaw. "Take a breath. I'm fine. And I'm excited to meet you too!" I smile at Mrs. Thompson. "All of you."

Theo extends his hand to Mrs. Thompson. "I'm Theo. The superstar is Naomi."

"I'm Margo, and this is clearly my mini-me, Melody."

"Mom, don't lie. You two bonded because you both gave your daughters names with the same first initial as yours," Theo says.

Mom and Margo look at each other and burst out laughing. "I can't say we ever noticed," Mom says.

He nods at the glass doors of the lodge. "Bathrooms inside?"

"Hunter's already in there," she says.

A flurry of nerves race through me at the mention of his name.

Theo winks at me as he opens the door and I bite back a response.

While Mom fills Mrs. Thompson in on the less boring aspects of our trip, I try not to be obvious about watching through the reflection of the glass doors for a sign of Hunter.

"I'm really excited we're in the same tent," Melody says. "I've always wanted a sister and while I've obviously had sleepovers and stuff like that, this is gonna be epic."

I tear my eyes away from the window and give her my full attention. "And I've always wanted a little sister. Theo's cool and all, but he is a boy." My rolled eyes earn me the giggle I was hoping for.

"Tell me about it." She keeps laughing, like we've got a shared secret, except now I'm thinking of her brother again.

Fifty years later—okay, it's only been two minutes—Theo holds the door for a boy a bit taller than him with dark glasses, shaggy brown hair, and a T-shirt that says Book Nerd. He nods at Theo, and everything slows as his gaze passes over our moms and his sister and lands on me. The corner of his mouth curls into that smirk, imprinting on my brain, and he says, "Hey," so softly it's like he mouthed it just for me.

My heart does a little loop-dee-loop. "Hey." I force myself to look away. His first impression of me cannot be a googly-eyed high schooler.

"Hunter, this is Naomi! Naomi, we listened to your podcast on the drive here!"

Heat flames my cheeks as Melody tugs on my arm and I meet his eyes again. My pulse skitters. I take a deep breath. "That—that's great." My voice shakes in a way it never does when I'm recording, and I don't miss Theo's amused smile.

Hunter steps forward, hand extended. His skin is exceptionally warm. Perhaps from the hand dryer in the bathroom? Points for washing his hands, but oh, hey, he's letting go and taking a step back.

"Nice to meet you." His voice is deeper than Theo's, but not like Morgan Freeman deep, and his eyes flick over me before he turns his attention to the moms.

"You, too," I say. "The getting-to-know-you questions were cool, but who emails, right?" A laugh that makes me sound like a crazy person bubbles out of my throat and I wish I could sink into the sidewalk.

"All my professors email regularly. It's pretty standard in college." His inflection is flat. His brow doesn't quirk adorably, and that smirk is nowhere to be seen.

Maybe I put too much into a cute smile.

"Oh, yeah, I mean, my teachers do, too." My voice trails off and disappointment pushes away the lightness I've felt since reading his email. Okay, so he's a pompous jerk. He may have fooled me by not being stuffed in that starched button-down in his pictures, but even in a T-shirt that looks so soft I want to rub against it—a T-shirt that shows off lean but toned arms and shoulders that look surprisingly solid—it shouldn't be hard to ignore him.

Mrs. Thompson claps her hands, making my family jump. Hunter and Melody don't react. She must do this a lot. "Speaking of the questions," she says.

"Thank you all for humoring us," Mom says.

Mrs. Thompson points at Theo. "We have good news for you."

Theo looks around like someone with a camera might pop out of the bushes. "Me?"

"You mentioned you're not a fan of setting up tents," Mrs. Thompson air-quotes *not a fan*. "And Nancy and I got to talking that tents might be a little more rustic than we wanted."

"You rented cabins?" Melody jumps up and down, still holding my arm.

A smile lights up Mrs. Thompson's face and she claps again. "Even better."

"We're staying in a hotel?" Theo asks.

"We've rented yurts!" Mom looks so pleased that I hate to ask the next question. But I'm not alone.

"What's a yurt?" Me, Theo, Hunter, and Melody say at the same time. The word sounds as foreign on their tongues as it does on mine.

"It's a large circular structure made of wooden slats and canvas," Mom says.

"So a fancy tent," Melody says.

"Yes," Mom says. "But they're already set up and are much more stable than tents. Especially ones we would set up." She and Mrs. Thompson share a smile and it strikes me that it's been a while since I've seen Mom this relaxed. Maybe it's being on vacation, but I think it has to do with being with a friend who really gets her.

"And these have actual beds, so we won't be sleeping on the ground," adds Mrs. Thompson.

"Now you're speaking my language," Theo says.

Hunter kicks at the pavement. "But I was looking forward to my tent collapsing in the middle of the night." Melody pushes his side and he gives her The Smirk— yes, capital T capital S— before breaking into a full smile.

My heart rebounds from his earlier comment. Maybe he didn't mean to come off so rude. But then his eyes meet mine and his smile shifts to a scowl.

My fingers itch to text Sage. She'll know what to say. But if I want to prove that I'm not a hack—that I really can do this advice thing—I need to figure it out for myself.

Because right now he's looking at me like I'm the last person on earth he wants to spend the next week with.

— 6 —
HUNTER

This can't be happening.

I got caught up in Mom's excitement while we waited for the McGinnises to arrive—she jumped around like the girls at my high school when they found out the K-pop band BTS dropped a new album—but when their car pulled into the parking lot, I fled to the bathrooms. Theo must have a gift because he made meeting next to the overly disinfected urinals not awkward, but the moment we stepped outside and I saw Naomi with Melody clinging to her arm like they were already best friends, everything froze.

It was like I was moving in slow motion.

Naomi is, to use Mom's word, captivating. Her laughter struck me the moment Theo opened the door and an energy I've never felt before pulled me closer. Her red curls brushed against her delicate pale skin, filling me with a yearning that left me feeling hollow. I managed to say hello before Melody jumped in about the podcast, and her response was a breathier version of what played in the car. She seemed embarrassed that we'd listened, which made no sense. Don't people record those because they want to be heard?

When we shook hands, a spark shot up my arm, straight to my chest, and I couldn't breathe. Couldn't see anything else but her smile and bright green eyes and those red curls that begged to be touched.

And now she thinks I hate her.

Because as soon as my brain caught up to my heart, I shot down her innocent attempt at conversation. The light left her eyes when the words left my mouth. My smile dropped along with my stomach and my scowly face, as Mel calls it, took over.

It's for the best.

And hopefully by the end of the week I'll believe it.

Melody tucks herself against Naomi's side, her eyes wide. "Are we still bunking together?" I think she's been more excited to spend time with Naomi than anything else about this trip, so I get why she wouldn't want that taken away, and I swallow the tinge of jealousy that Mel doesn't seem as excited to hang out with me.

"We talked about just getting two yurts and sleeping as families," Mom says. "But they didn't have many other reservations and gave us a good deal on the third."

"Yes!" Melody pumps her fist and looks at Naomi. "We are gonna have so much fun. Like epic. Huge."

Naomi laughs, the sound sending shivers down my back. Her gaze flicks to me and her smile drops, and I look away.

It has to be this way. I need to stay focused on my goals, not get tangled up in something emotional. Nothing good can come from getting distracted this early into college.

"Naomi, are you okay with a yurt?" Mom says. "In your email you said how much you like camping and I'd hate to ruin this for you."

Theo snorts as Naomi sputters a laugh. "Ruin?" she asks. "Are you kidding?" She waves her hand at the lake beyond the grassy field, a smile lighting her face. "We get to be in nature, but I don't have to put up a tent? That sounds like an upgrade to me." Her eyes find mine and this time I don't look away.

I wish I could explain in a look that this isn't personal. That so far, she checks all the things on my list— if I was interested in dating.

But I'm not. I can't be.

She breaks eye contact and smiles down at Melody. "That yurt isn't gonna know what hit it."

Melody grabs Naomi's hand and twirls herself in a circle.

"Hunt, I assume you're okay with this?" Mom asks.

All attention turns to me, and a prickling sensation creeps up the back of my neck. It's not that I'm not social, I just prefer to hang in the background until I get my bearings. We met the McGinnises three minutes ago and it's going to take a lot longer for me to feel balanced around Naomi.

"Not assembling a tent is A-okay with me." A-okay? When did I become a sitcom dad?

Melody stops her twirling, mouth spread wide in barely contained laughter as Mom slaps her hands together. Theo and Naomi jump, but clapping is like punctuation for Mom, and we're so used to it I barely even notice. "Now that that's settled, let's get unpacked," Mom says. "There's still time to get out on the lake this evening if we want."

"Or we could sit around a fire," Theo whispers next to me.

"Or go for a hike," Naomi replies. I didn't think she was close enough to hear him, but maybe they're dialed into each other the way you always hear about twins.

"A walk would be nice," Mrs. McGinnis says.

"I'm down for that," Mom says.

Mel rolls her eyes at me but there's no sense being embarrassed about Mom's never-ending attempt to use slang.

Theo pumps a fist in the air. "To the yurts!"

With some help from the guy working at the desk in the lodge, who points us down a dirt path along the lake, we find our campsite and park in a clearing in front of three giant canvas structures.

"Nancy and I will take the one in the middle," Mom says, and I can't help but glance at Naomi. There's no way Mom picked up on my attraction to her, and there's zero reason to even fantasize about sneaking into Naomi's yurt. And not just because my little sister will be sleeping next to her.

I shake my head at myself as Naomi says, "It's weird that there aren't many trees." She sees me shaking my head and it's like I told her I roast puppies in my free time. She turns to Theo, shaking off her sour expression. "It's weird right?"

He points at the sky. "The better to see the stars, my dear."

A blush tints her cheeks a shade of pink I'll never forget, and she rolls her eyes. "Duh."

Theo drapes an arm around her shoulder. "We can't both be the smart twin."

She shoves him away, but her smile is back. My chest tightens, from anxiety or nerves or regret, I don't know, but I know I don't like this feeling.

"We call this one." Theo points at the yurt closest to the lodge. "That okay with you, Hunter?"

"Y-yeah." I clear my throat, hoping to swallow back whatever emotions seem to be brewing. "Works for me."

We carry our bags inside after a bit of fumbling with the canvas door, and I immediately sneeze. Dust motes drift in the hazy sunlight coming through the pale yellow roof, settling on the criss-crossed wooden slats that make up the walls. Two sets of bunk beds line the walls, flanking a metal closet-type thing that looks like it came from a high school locker room. A table with four chairs sits to the right of the door and pair of under-stuffed chairs that have seen better days flank the left.

"Home, sweet, home," Theo says. "You want left or right?"

"Left is fine."

He drops his bags on the floor next to his bed and flops onto the bottom bunk as the door flops open and slams against the back of one of the dining chairs.

Melody stomps inside and points a finger at me. "Why are you being such a butt?"

Theo snorts from his bed and scrambles to the closet. The metal screeches as he opens the doors and ducks his head inside. "This thing is huge."

"How am I being a butt?"

"We can, like, fit all our stuff in here." Theo's voice echoes off the metal.

She nods, eyes wide, to Theo's back. "You know how."

Guilt twists my stomach. If she knew what I was actually thinking about Naomi she'd really lay into me. But this is how it has to be. "I apologize for my buttish ways. I didn't mean to make anyone feel bad." A thought strikes me. "Did she say something?"

Theo's head pops out of the closet at the word 'she.' "Intrigue. I like it." He slides a chair out from the table and sits. "Tell me more."

Melody's smile makes her seem older than her twelve years, and I'm gripped with a new worry that she'll crush on Theo. She claps her hands together the way Mom does and sits across from Theo. "It all started when we listened to Three Good Things."

Theo's eyes go wide and his mouth opens in a huge smile. "Did you like it? You know I'm the producer."

Her eyes go equally wide and she nods her head back and forth. "Obvi. I listened to the production notes."

"Production notes?" I ask.

"They're like the credits," she says without looking at me. "Or the acknowledgements in a book."

I roll my eyes but she's too focused on Theo to notice.

He taps his fingers on the table between them. "Keep talking."

"*I* started listening weeks ago." The way she emphasizes the I makes me feel even smaller. "I told Hunter how amazing Naomi is—the whole show," she quickly adds. "And we listened in the car on the way here." She waves a hand at me almost dismissively. "He's all anti relationships gotta focus on school blah blah—"

"How do you even know that?" I whisper.

"—but he was totally into it by the time we crossed into Utah."

"Which episode was it?" Theo asks.

"Three Good Things About Having a Sibling." Melody and I speak at the same time and I'm definitely blushing now.

That was the episode where Naomi got more personal about herself and her relationship with Theo. It's also when I felt the shift. When Mom repeated that Naomi was captivating. When I started questioning my self-imposed dating ban for a girl I'd never met.

But I didn't realize Melody picked up on all that, and now I've clearly outed myself.

"Or whatever."

"So why are you being a butt?"

"I told you. I didn't mean to be a butt."

Theo strokes his chin as he nods. "You did say that you're sometimes slow to warm up to people." He cocks his head. "But you didn't have that problem with me."

Frustration builds in my chest. I clench my fists to keep from lashing out and ruining this trip for everyone. "Can we not do this right now?"

"We're just teasing," Melody says.

"Well, please stop." I grab my phone from my bed and stalk outside, not caring that they're staring at me. Why is everyone so insistent that focusing on school is wrong? I have a goal and I'm doing everything I can to accomplish it. There will be time for relationships once I'm finished with college and working in New York.

The doors to the other two yurts are open and laughter spills out of the moms' door. Their happiness should make *me* happy, but it merely adds to my frustration. It's not that I don't want happiness in my life. My friends make me happy. Books make me happy. Spending time with my family, while sometimes exhausting, makes me happy.

I'm halfway past their yurt when Mom steps outside. "I'm going for a quick walk," I say.

"Did you get settled?" Mom asks.

I give a sideways salute before pointing over my shoulder at my yurt. "As much as I'm going to."

Mrs. McGinnis appears at the door with a pair of sneakers in her hand. "We'll come with you. I know Naomi wanted to go for a hike and I could definitely stretch my legs."

"Thanks, Mrs. McGinnis. But if it's not too much trouble, I'd like to go alone."

"First of all, none of this missus crap. It's Nancy, please."

I nod.

"Second, I understand needing a little time. You go do you."

Mom rests a hand on Nancy's shoulder. "We'll go in a few minutes." She winks at me. "Let him get a head start."

"Thanks." I escape before they start tag-team analyzing my need for alone time.

I follow the same dirt path we walked in on but head the opposite direction. Yurts give way to campers and motorhomes bigger than my dorm room, and a group of people relaxing in hammocks lift a hand in greeting as I pass. Naomi was right— it feels a little weird without many trees. I don't have a ton of camping experience, but I always imagined setting up a tent in the middle of a forest with nothing but the sounds of nature and a book to keep me company.

The path curves with the lake. Tents similar to what I thought we'd be sleeping in dot the ground near the shore, and farther ahead, the terrain rises toward the mountains. I stick to the trail, my thoughts bouncing from school to my future in New York as an editor, and the fear that it might not work out the way I want if I do what my heart's telling me.

To transfer to a school closer to home.

To move back into my old room and old life.

To be there for Melody.

The English and communication departments won't be as good as at UC Berkeley, but not much is on the west coast. As Mom inadvertently pointed out, I'd be giving up the rotating schedule of visiting lecturers, giving up the prestige that comes with a UC Berkeley degree, giving up my friends. But I'd be home with Mom and Mel. My little sister may act tough, but I've read between the lines of her texts. She's struggling with her friends and while I'm not one to toot my own horn—okay, I really am a sitcom dad—she misses me.

But if I cave now, how will I ever move to New York? The pressure to succeed will be different than it is now, but it will be amplified. And not just by the workload. My formerly super-involved dad who's now super-involved with his new family lives just outside the city where he grew up and I can't decide if it would be a good or bad thing to live so close to him. My gut says bad, but it also serves as motivation. I want to move to New York and succeed despite him.

And to spite him. To prove I can set a goal and stick to it.

Mel will be in high school by the time I graduate and won't need her big brother like she does now, but I'm afraid moving back will simply prolong the inevitable. Maybe it's better she learns to get through this now.

"Ughhhh!" I yell at the sky. A rustling in the tall grass along the trail startles me, much as I startled whatever was hunkering down there. I mumble an apology to the hidden creature and take in my surroundings. The campground is a speck of light against the darkening sky, hints of what's to come at nightfall already dotting the sky.

"Better head back," I say to no one.

When I reach the tents, my phone has a conniption in my back pocket. I pull it out and find several texts from Shawna.

Shawna: are you there yet?
Shawna: how is it? how is SHE?
Shawna: are you wishing I hijacked your undies?
Shawna: dude sorry, you know that's a joke
Shawna: hello?

There must be a WiFi booster at the lodge.

Me: We're here. It's cool. Staying in a yurt (??). My underwear has not been an issue, thankyouverymuch.

I start to put my phone away, then send another text.

Me: Did I come off as an ass when we first met?

Her reply comes several anxiety-filled minutes later.

Shawna: meh. not really. I just figured you're shy.

Me: so no dickish vibes?

Shawna: nah, but you do that with girls I suspect you might like

I look around like someone might be reading over my shoulder. Has my unwillingness to date somehow manifested into treating girls who I might be interested in like crap?

Me: For real?

Shawna: it's part of your charm. except it's not charming.

Mel was right. I was being a butt.

Me: Thanks. This is helpful.

Shawna: hold the phone (lol). you cannot ask this and not tell me why

Shawna: is it the girl? it's the girl isn't it

Shawna: your undies are totally playing a role. maybe not act one, but definitely by act three.

Me: omg stop

Me: I didn't mean to imply anything

Out here in the middle of nowhere, with no one to see, a blush warms my cheeks. I'm not so dense that I can't admit I'm attracted to Naomi, but nothing's going to happen. Especially nothing that involves my underwear.

Shawna: me thinks you protest too much

Me: She's cool and all, but you know my rule.

Shawna: mmhmmm. I also know you deserve to enjoy yourself

Me: Maybe so. But I can't get distracted.

Shawna: dude we're 18. It's okay to relax and have fun. You have plenty of time to worry about your future.

I wish I could be more like her and Darren and not let my concerns for the future dominate my thoughts. Figuring out what I want to do with the rest of my life was supposed to make things easier, but it's only opened another realm of worries. What if I don't take the right class, or I fail the test that will cost me a contract in the future, or I accept a job with a publisher that closes six months later and end up broke and homeless and have to live in Dad's basement?

And the biggest concern: what if transferring from Berkeley is the first step to ruining any chances for the life I want?

Me: maybe you're right.
Shawna: I know I am
Shawna: have fun
Me: I'll try

Shawna is right. I'm on vacation. If there's ever a time to relax and quit worrying about the future, it's now. I tuck my phone in my pocket and try to shake off the unease that seems to follow me every waking moment. I can do this.

I can have fun.

The sun has dipped lower in the sky by the time I return to our campsite. Everyone's sitting around the fire, and they look up in unison when I approach. My stomach flutters when I catch Naomi's eye, and full-on flips when she maintains eye contact. It's almost like she knows I vowed to stop being an ass.

The soft curve of her lips sends my pulse racing and right now, in this moment, I'd keep all my uncertainty about the future to know what she's thinking.

7

NAOMI

Hunter seems like a different person. The cranky, scowly boy from before has been replaced with a relaxed, friendly, dare I say hottie—and The Smirk is back. My pulse skitters in my chest and I'm grateful for the semi-darkness. My smile won't give away what I'm thinking and any redness in my cheeks can be blamed on the fire.

"Did you have a nice walk?" Mom asks Hunter.

He finally breaks whatever connection held his gaze to mine. "Yeah. Apparently, there's not much signal out there. My phone blew up when I got back to the campground."

"You're not supposed to be on your phone out here anyway," Mrs. Thompson says.

Theo shoves his phone under his leg and winks at Melody.

Hunter presses a hand to his chest. "I can't help it if my friends miss me."

Mom smiles. "Dinner's almost ready." The nearby grill sizzles with whatever meat they've brought and a half dozen potato-shaped tin foil logs ring the edge of the fire. Condiments, plates, and silverware are already set on the picnic table in front of the moms' yurt.

"Way to get out of helping," Melody says with a song in her voice. "You know what that means."

"Yes, I'll help clean up," he sing-songs back.

Theo and I have always had a close connection. It's the whole twin thing, plus the fact that we genuinely like each other, but most of my friends with siblings seem to spend more time bickering with each other than getting along. It's refreshing—and endearing—to see how close Hunter and Melody are.

Hunter has barely settled into his seat when his mom claps her hands together—making me jump, again—and announces dinner is ready. We assemble our plates and I pause in front of the table. Melody has claimed one corner, the moms are in the middle, and Hunter is on the other end. If I sit across from Hunter, I'll get to look at him, but what if he ignores me again? Or worse, is a total butt, to use Melody's word when she apologized for her brother's behavior earlier.

I take a step toward Melody when she points at the seat across from her. "Sit here!"

Perfect. Now it doesn't look like I chose not to sit with Hunter. I'm just appeasing his sister.

Nothing more.

We're halfway through our meal when Mom sets her silverware on her plate and clears her throat. "We'd like to go over a few ground rules for the campsite."

Theo and I exchange glances behind her back. What mischief are they thinking we'll get into? We didn't bring alcohol, there's nowhere to sneak off to, and aside from using our phones too much, there's literally nothing to do except hang out together.

"You've all camped before, so you know the importance of keeping animals out of our food supply," Mom says, and I relax. *These* type of rules. "Margo and I will keep the coolers in our yurt, but you're welcome to grab a snack or drink anytime you need one."

"But be sure to put any trash in the cans with lids," Mrs. Thompson says.

"Next, please stop with the Missus stuff," Mom says. "We're Nancy and Margo."

"Got it, Nancy," Theo says before Mom can clamp a hand over his mouth.

"Finally," Mrs. Thompson—Margo—says. "While Hunter offered to clean tonight—"

Melody gives Hunter a more exaggerated version of his smirk.

"—cleanup will be done in pairs by yurt. Tonight is Theo and Hunter. Margo and I will do breakfast, and Melody and Naomi will handle dinner tomorrow."

"What about lunch?" Theo's eyes widen. "Are you trying to say you're only feeding me twice a day?"

Mom pats his head. "Lunches will be on the water or while hiking, so we're all responsible for our own cleanup."

"There's a plastic bin near the water spigot," Margo says. "Theo, if you've never washed dishes without a sink, Hunter can show you how it's done."

Hunter stabs the last pieces of potato with his fork. "Please, I beg of you. Scrape as much food off your plate as you can so we don't end up with soapy dishwater stew."

Theo pretends to dry-heave and Melody giggles. "Washing dishes is my absolutest least favorite part of camping," she whispers as Hunter approaches.

He tousles her hair. "Did you ever think maybe that's why I always get stuck doing it the first night?" He air-quotes the word stuck, and I'm struck again at the way he seems to look out for her.

I lean across the table and nod at the campfire. "Let's grab the best seats by the fire."

She holds out her knuckles for a fist bump, and when I tap mine to hers, she opens her hand and makes an explosion sound. "I'm really glad you're here," she says. "I like hanging out with Hunter, and I miss him since he's been away at college." Her eyes follow him to the washing station before finding mine again. "But it's way more fun with another girl."

Her smile fills my heart with a kind of affection I normally only feel for Theo. "I'm really glad you're here, too." I feel a little guilty for worrying about how Melody would fit in with the rest of us, like she might somehow make this trip less fun. I'm beginning to think it'll be more fun because of her.

"Dibs on the yellow chair!" she shouts and sprints to the fire before I'm out of my seat.

I settle in next to her and my breath catches. The sky over the lake has turned an inky black and stars like I've never seen fill the sky. Back home, we can see the regular constellations, but here the entire Milky Way is front and center. Swirls of pink and orange reminiscent of the earlier sunset stretch high above our heads, entire universes awake and ready to put on a show. "It's like a planetarium on steroids," I whisper.

"We went to a planetarium for science class last year," Melody says. "This is way cooler."

Mom sits next to me and grabs my hand. "The view is exactly what I hoped it would be."

I turn my head. Her eyes shine in the low light. "Bucket list item officially crossed off?" I ask.

She nods, her eyes still on the heavens. "I was going to wait until the end of the week, but I can't imagine it getting any better than this."

"Happy early birthday, Mom."

We watch the stars, the only sounds the distant laughter from other campsites and the clink of silverware as the boys finish washing the dishes. When we're all seated around the fire, Mom leans forward, hands clasped in front of her.

"I want to thank all of you for not only coming on this trip, but for humoring me with the homework, as Theo so kindly called it." She makes eye contact with each of us before continuing. "Naomi and Theo probably suspected that the email wouldn't be the end of it, and they were right."

"Ugh, Mom. Really?" Theo groans.

"Margo and I thought we'd end our first day elaborating on one of the questions."

Theo raises his hand. "I vote what we're most looking forward to!"

"Same!" Melody says.

Hunter catches my eye and for a second it feels like he can tell what I'm thinking. That I was looking forward to meeting him.

Mom levels a look at Theo and he sits back in his chair. "Since we're still getting to know each other, we'd like everyone to talk a bit more about what it will take for this to be a successful trip."

"I have your original answers pulled up in case you've forgotten what you wrote," Margo says with a look at Theo.

He holds up his hands, his face a mask of innocence. "Why's everyone looking at me?"

"Dude, I think they're onto you," Melody says.

"Who wants to go first?" Mom asks.

Crickets chirp.

Tumbleweeds rustle along the dirt path.

It's so quiet we hear an owl hooting somewhere in Nevada.

Margo claps her hands together and Theo and I exchange a look. What is with the clapping? "I'll go first," she says. Her phone illuminates her face as she reads. "I said that the fact that our families are taking this trip together means it's already a success."

"That's cheating," Hunter says, his voice barely reaching me. "It's a non-answer."

"I'm going to elaborate," Margo says. Frustration laces her words, but as they pointed out, we don't know each other well enough to know if this is normal or something new.

"My kids already know how important my friendship with Nancy is." They smile at each other and it's adorable and beyond cheesy. "And while we talk almost every day, we haven't seen each other in person more than a couple times since that first conference in Austin."

"CounselCon," we say in unison, then burst out laughing.

"Okay, maybe we talk about that a lot," Mom says.

"My point is," Margo continues. "Bringing our families together feels like we're solidifying our friendship. Like you're a core part of my life and not just another online acquaintance. This is important to me."

Mom rushes from her seat and wraps her arms around Margo. "You know I feel the same way." Her voice is strained, like she's trying not to cry, which makes my eyes well with tears.

The four of us exchange awkward glances. Do we say something? Wait it out? The respect and adoration they so clearly feel for each other makes me wish Sage was here, but it is nice just having our families. I went into this trip expecting new friends, but maybe they'll be more like family by the end of this week.

Mom pulls away and returns to her seat. "I'll go next." She wipes tears from her eyes. "I've had some big decisions swirling through my brain for a while now and I'm hoping that by the end of this trip, I'll have a clearer vision for what lies ahead for me."

My mind flashes to a couple weeks ago. To Mom at the kitchen table, head in her hands, crying over a pile of papers. I snuck back upstairs before she saw me and I've been too afraid to ask her about it.

"What's going on, Mom?" Theo asks.

She looks at Margo, who nods encouragingly. "I'm considering a career change. It would require taking a few classes to get certified."

Is that why she'd been crying? Or is there still more she's not saying? I push back my concern and force a smile. "Mom, that's really exciting!"

"I'd essentially be starting over."

"You've done it before," Theo says, his voice thick with emotion, and I meet his eyes. We rarely talk about the months after Dad left, about the locked doors and tears and the void that swallowed our mom until she emerged from her room with shorter hair and a new determination to take on the world.

"Oh, Theo, you're going to make me cry again."

Hunter shifts in his seat. For someone who's as into books as he is, he's got to be used to expressions of emotion, but he looks like he'd rather be anyplace but here. Melody, on the other hand, seems enthralled. She's leaning forward with her elbow on her knees, chin in her hands, her eyes locked on Mom.

"What are you hoping—er, planning to do?" I ask.

"I'd like to be a life coach for women like me." She gestures at herself, then points at me and Theo. "Single moms trying to figure out their lives."

"If there's any way I can help, you know I'm here," says Margo.

Mom looks at me expectantly, but my head's spinning from her revelation. "Oh, I'm next? Okay." I pull up my notes app and find my answers. What seemed whimsical and optimistic at the time now just sounds flighty. "I said I'm looking forward to some time outside my regular life and a little inspiration for the next steps in my life."

"It sounds like Mom's not the only one pondering her future," Theo says.

Hunter's head snaps up at that, but his face is a mask of indifference.

"What next steps are you considering?" Margo asks. The intensity that has rippled through her since we met is replaced with a calm that begs me to confess my deepest thoughts.

Good thing I have a mom who has this same skill and I've learned to resist it. Because as nice as it would be to open up about the offer and everything it represents, I'm not ready to talk about it.

"Oh you know, senior year, college. That sort of thing." I risk a glance at Theo, who mouths "lies" at me. His twin-fu often leads him to the truth without me telling him a thing and—while he doesn't know about the offer I received from Auralacity, a regional production company, asking if I'd like to take Three Good Things, quote, to the next level—his ability to read my emotions needs to interpret that right now, I need him to let it go.

"Are you debating your major?" Margo asks.

This I can handle. I shake my head. "Communications is still one hundred percent my jam. Broadcasting is part of that, and there's a niche minor for podcasting, but I want to keep my options open for future careers as well."

Hunter nods—not really at me, more like in appreciation for the level of planning I've already done—but when he catches me looking at him, he quickly looks away.

Mom leans forward. "If there's anything I can help with, you know I'm here." She reviewed the contract as soon as I told her about the offer, and aside from encouraging me to write back with clarifying questions, she refuses to help me make the decision, claiming that I earned this on my own and it needs to be up to me.

"I do, Mom. Thanks."

"Theo, why don't you go next?" Mom says.

Theo's head snaps up, then he stands and his entire body slides into what I think of as performance mode. "Happily, Mother." He turns in a slow circle, making eye contact with each of us before continuing. "My answer, while brief, is part of a greater whole and it would be an offense to my art if I only read the final line. Hopefully you all picked up on the rhythm of my answers, but if not, I shall perform them—ahem, read them—for you now."

Melody bounces in her chair, wide eyes locked on him. Hunter seems just as transfixed, but Margo seems a little uncertain what's about to happen. I'm just excited Theo took the spotlight off me so quickly.

He clears his throat, takes a deep breath, then holds up a finger. "As a reminder, this answers all the questions. What we're looking forward to, what we're dreading," he raises a brow at me and I snort, remembering Hunter's answer about giving merit to the dread. "What we should know about each other, and as we've been discussing this evening, what will make this a successful trip."

We all nod, his captive audience, and he smiles.

He clears his throat again and reads from his phone, emphasizing every other syllable.

"Meeting my mom's long-distance friend and kids.

"Pitching a tent beneath the starry sky.

"I will embarrass myself for max bids.

"I have no secrets, you all know I'm bi."

He bows, bending at the waist and sweeping his arm toward the fire.

"Bravo!" Melody shouts, and he bows again as we clap. "But I have one question."

"Anything, ma petite."

She bites her lip, fighting a smile. "What will it take to make this a successful trip for you?"

I snort again, and Hunter looks my way. I give him a shrug like I'm not mortified I've now done that twice in front of him and sit on my hands so I don't press them to my cheeks, which are on fire.

Theo's mouth falls open and he gestures at himself with both hands. "Were you not listening?"

Melody rests her chin on her hands and bats her lashes. "I was. And I *love* that you don't have secrets, but you didn't really answer the question."

"Busted," Mom whispers.

Theo shoots her a side-eye before raising his eyes to the stars. "Okay, fine." He takes a deep breath and gives me a look that makes my heart stutter.

Oh, crap. What's he about to do?

"All I want is for my older and wiser sister to find the—ahem—inspiration she so desperately seeks."

"I'm not desperate," I snap.

"I don't mean that in a bad way," he says. "Your happiness is my happiness, and don't we all deserve to be happy?" He turns in another slow circle, still performing, and gives me a wink as he sits.

"Indeed we do!" Margo says. "Thank you, Theo. That was both unexpected and enlightening."

"Any time," he says.

"Kids, which one of you would like to go next?"

"Me!" Melody springs to her feet and mimics Theo's bow. "Mine's pretty easy." She ticks off her fingers. "Don't fall out of the canoe. Don't get attacked by a wild animal. Or any animal really." She points up. "See the stars." Then she looks at me. "And convince Naomi to let me be on her podcast."

I've been waiting for her to bring this up since reading her answers, mainly out of curiosity. I'm always looking for guests, so while Melody may think she needs to convince me, Theo and I already agreed it would be fun to have her on.

"I think that can be arranged," I say.

Her mouth falls open. "Seriously? Just like that?"

"On one condition," I say.

"Name it."

"You keep those wild animals away from me, too."

Hunter laughs softly, and something warm stirs in my belly. I want to keep making him laugh, to be the cause of that smile that seems to be reserved for his sister.

"Wait, I'm not done," Melody says. "Even though I can't— omigod, seriously I can be on your show?"

Theo and I nod, and Hunter blesses me with The Smirk.

And I melt in my chair.

Then quickly straighten. Fawning over a boy I met three hours ago most certainly qualifies as insta-love.

"Wow. Okay. So back to the question. There isn't really much to elaborate from what I wrote, but I'm really excited we're here and I know we're gonna have a blast." She plops in her chair and nods at Hunter. "All you, bro."

Our attention turns to him and he immediately tenses.

"Right. My answer was also brief, as you all know. I'm hoping this time away from classes and the regular world will help me gain insight into a few things that are weighing on me."

"Is everything okay?" Margo asks.

"Yeah. Yeah." He focuses on his hands, which are clasped in front of him. "This isn't—I mean, it doesn't matter." He runs a hand through his hair, and I feel a twinge of concern. He really doesn't like being in the spotlight.

"I get it," I say without thinking. "Not everything is appropriate for Campfire Confessionals."

He meets my eyes but it's impossible to tell what he's thinking.

"That should be a show!" Theo says.

"Kids, let Hunter finish," Mom says.

For being so in touch with how people think, she's completely missing that Hunter does not want to share with the class. Or maybe she's trying to force him out of his comfort zone. Either way, he looks miserable. All traces of his earlier smile are gone. His shoulders push forward, his hands clench in a fist, and his skin seems pale in the firelight.

"Sorry," he says. "Everything's okay—" he directs this toward his mom—"but I'm still working through this and would rather not get into it with everyone just yet." He shifts in his seat and drags a hand through his hair again. "I didn't mean to kill the kumbaya."

This time I snort for real, and his shoulders relax. Not all the way, but enough to make me feel like maybe my god-awful laugh hasn't completely ruined any chance I might have with him.

Not that I want that.

Since he's a jerk.

Who am I kidding? I'm only attracted to guys with a chip permanently lodged on their shoulder and his chip is so big he can't even sit up straight. And let's not forget the smile that makes me want to drag him into my yurt.

Insta-love be damned.

"I know it's still early," Mom says. "But I'm exhausted. Thank you all for sharing tonight. I know it's not always easy to talk about ourselves, but sometimes it can be helpful to get another opinion when you're working through something that seems impossible." Her gaze lands on me and all thoughts of Hunter's lips vanish.

Now I'm the one squirming in my seat.

"Sleep tight," I say with the biggest smile I can manage.

"I'll come with you," Margo says. "Melody, will you grab your toothbrush and come with me to the bathroom?"

Melody grips the arms of her chair and looks from me to Theo to Hunter, frantic. "This is so unfair. I'm not ready for bed. Just because I'm twelve doesn't mean I'm a baby. I can take care—"

Margo rests a hand on her shoulder. "I'm not sending you to bed. I wanted to say goodnight and thought we could walk together."

"Oh." She bounces out of her seat and points at me. "Don't go anywhere."

Hunter stands. "I'm gonna head to the bathroom, too."

Theo waves his hands around us. "The world is our urinal."

Hunter shakes his head but the corner of his mouth lifts. "I'll be back in a minute."

I don't mean to watch him walk away. Once he disappears into the darkness, I tilt my head back and the magnitude of the stars above us makes me gasp.

"You know you can't hide anything from me," Theo says.

My head snaps up. How? How does he know about the offer?

The fire makes his eyes look like they're dancing. "You li-i-i-i-i-i-ike him."

Oh, Hunter. This I can handle. "Yeah, well, he's a jerkface, so whatever."

"Two hours with a twelve-year-old and your insults have regressed."

"You're the one who just told him to pee outside."

"Is that why you were being weird with the questions?"

"Yeah, totally."

He raises a brow. "You know it's pointless to hide anything from me. I will figure it out."

I tap my finger to his nose. As much as I want to ask him about his plans after high school and get rid of this uneasiness that's become a constant buzz in the back of my mind, I'm afraid to hear his answer. What if I'm the only one who's terrified to be apart?

"Which should tell you that I'm not hiding anything. You've figured out all my secrets."

It's like putting a Band-Aid on a severed limb, but it'll have to do for now. Because the contract is due in less than a week and the moment I tell him about the offer, everything will change.

Partnering with Auralacity almost guarantees sponsorships, which is where the real money comes from. It's everything I dreamed of when I first had the idea for the podcast but part of me still worries that the sacrifice is too big.

And I don't know if I can do the show without him.

—⁓— **8** —⁓—

HUNTER

I hate to admit how relieved I am that we're not in tents. And it has nothing to do with Theo's apparent lack of anything resembling outdoors skills. Sleeping in an actual bed in a structure with a real door—even if it is made of canvas—far outweighs the nostalgic appeal of sleeping beneath the stars.

My phone's plugged in across the room next to my glasses. I'm burrowing into my sleeping bag when Theo speaks into the darkness.

"Hey, don't feel weird about earlier." There's a pause, and I'm not sure if he's waiting for me to reply or still has more to say.

I wait him out.

"My mom can be a little—let's just say there's a reason I don't have a filter. Naomi's got a little more self-control, but ever since the divorce, it's like a switch flipped in Mom." His voice hitches up an octave. "There shall be no secrets and no secrets there shall be. She's so used to us sharing everything that I think she forgets not everyone is comfortable opening up. Especially with strangers." He pauses again, but seems to be done this time.

"You're not really strangers," I say.

He laughs softly. "Well, we're not pen pals."

"True." I take a breath. I don't think he's expecting me to share now, because we *are* practically strangers. "Thanks for saying that. Like I said in my email, I'm not the type to tell everything I'm thinking. Not even with my mom." Especially not with Mom.

"So you're saying you're not an open book."

"I think she just caught me off guard."

"Well, get your guard up, because that won't be the last of it."

"Fantastic. Thanks for the heads up."

"Another heads up. I do not plan to carry my weight in the canoe."

"Roger that." Okay, seriously. Why can't normal things come out of my mouth? Or even cheeky, off-hand things like Theo. Envy isn't something I typically feel, but I wish I could care less about what people think and just say what's on my mind. Instead, I'm either a butt to the people I actually like, or I come off like a dad from the 80s.

Silence fills the yurt while I debate confessing to Theo. As an objective party, he could have useful advice, but years of keeping my thoughts to myself is hard to overcome. I open my mouth, close it, then roll to my side so I'm facing him in the dark.

"You awake?" I whisper.

His breathing deepens until he's snoring softly.

"Good night," I whisper.

~~~

The door of our yurt slams open, bolting me from a dream that our group of self-help aficionados would have a field day with. I was standing in my canoe with Theo paddling us in circles while I shouted that I'm transferring from Berkeley because I miss my mommy. It's a new twist on the recurring dream I've had since going to college, where I'm standing in the middle of Times Square, holding a stack of books I edited and shouting that I don't know what I'm doing. And that I miss my mommy.

The stupidest part is it's Mel who I miss. Or at least who I worry about.

Mel, who's now standing in our doorway.

"They're deciding canoes." Her tone implies I should understand why this is a matter of life and death.

Theo groans from under his covers.
~~~

"Why do we have to know this right now?" I ask.

"They're not sure if we need two or three canoes."

"Shouldn't breakfast come before decisions as important as the first canoe pairing?" Theo asks.

She moves across the room, her gaze skimming over *Into the Wild* facedown on the floor and sits on the edge of my bed. "Please tell them I can paddle just fine and do not need to ride in the middle in a booster seat."

"They won't actually make you use a booster seat," I say.

Theo sits up. His dark hair stands on end and his T-shirt's twisted around his body. "There's an option to ride in the middle?"

Mel shrugs. "If we only get two canoes, yeah."

"I vote for that option."

Mel huffs out a breath and glares at the ceiling. "Theo, don't make me say something I'm gonna regret."

"You are not allowed to be upset with me," he says, climbing out of bed and pulling on a sweatshirt. "I never claimed to be a lumberjack."

She giggles. "What does that have to do with anything?"

"Aren't lumberjacks, like, good at all things outdoorsy?"

"In theory," I say.

"Well, I am the opposite of that. Besides," he winks at Mel. "The odds of everyone staying dry greatly improve if I am not in charge."

"Ughhhhhhh." She drags out the moan until Theo and I are both laughing. "Fine, I will consent to riding in the middle for Theos' sake. But only for today." She points at him, and the smile falls from his face.

"Yes, ma'am."

I push her off the bed. "Scoot so we can get dressed."

After breakfast, we walk to the canoe livery at the edge of the lake to collect our pair of green canoes. Agreeing that Mel and Theo were riding in the middle didn't make things easier. Theo, Naomi, Mel, and I objected to riding as families and Mel objected to riding with the moms, which is how I ended up in a canoe with Naomi and Mel.

Sans booster seat.

If Naomi has an opinion about paddling with me, she doesn't let on. Mel was so excited to be with Naomi that I could probably go the whole morning without speaking.

The guy from the livery goes over basic paddling instructions before shoving us away from the dock and into the lake—which is really a huge reservoir surrounded by hard-packed earth and reddish mountains in the distance.

"Have you done this before?" Naomi asks over her shoulder. She pulls her paddle through the water, then lifts it over her head, switching her grip before plunging it into the water on the other side. The muscles in her shoulders flex as she moves, and while I'm no stranger to girls in tank tops, I never realized how sexy shoulders could be.

She twists to look at me, brows raised.

Because I haven't answered her.

A scowl darkens her face as she no doubt thinks I'm ignoring her, when in fact, I can't stop thinking about her. The way she so clearly cares about her mom and Theo, how patient she is with Mel and her abundance of energy, the way she moves through the world like she knows exactly where she belongs.

"Sorry." I shake my head to clear my thoughts. "I've canoed every summer at least once or twice. But if you'd rather steer, we can switch."

She looks surprised by the offer. Mel gives me a thumbs-up behind her back, and as much as I don't need my little sister's encouragement, I can't help but smile.

"I'm fine up here," Naomi says.

A yelp from the other canoe makes us turn. Waves ripple from the canoe as Theo attempts to stand in the middle. He's hunched over with his back to us, one hand gripping the crossbar. His legs wobble and the edge of the boat dips precariously close to the water.

"Theo! Don't you dare!" Naomi says.

"Hush, I'm concentrating!" He looks like he's holding his stomach, but he's laughing.

Nancy swats at Theo from the front of the canoe, while Mom seems frozen, her paddle in midair. She glances at me and mouths, "What is going on?"

"Theo, sit down before you tip us!" Nancy says.

"Naomi, what is he doing?" Mel whispers.

"He's trying to moon us. And unless you want to be scarred for life, I suggest you look away."

Mel bursts out laughing and joins the others begging him to stop. "Dude, no one needs to see that!"

He whirls around and almost topples over the other side. "I'm hurt!"

"Keep it in your pants!" Naomi shouts.

Defeated, Theo slumps to the floor of the canoe and drapes an arm over his eyes. "No one appreciates me."

"We'll appreciate you more if you don't moon us." My words slip out of my mouth too quickly. I worry he'll take it the wrong way, that it'll somehow come off like I'm being mean, but he peeks at me from under his arm and laughs.

"Kids, do you want to lead the way?" Mom points straight ahead with her paddle. The part of the lake where we launched the canoes is pretty wide, but it narrows into a river the farther south we go. The sandy shoreline is pretty desolate—mostly open space with a few trees here and there, like the people who dug out the reservoir were more focused on creating a massive body of water than something aesthetically pleasing. Other canoes dot the lake farther ahead, and a pair of metal fishing boats drift near the campsite.

Naomi digs her paddle into the water and pulls, and I mirror her movements. An odd satisfaction fills me as I work together with this girl who, before yesterday, didn't exist in my world. We glide through the water and the calmness of this place washes over me. Being in nature has always been like a balm when my brain gets overcrowded. I'd hardly consider myself a lumberjack, but I'd like to think I could manage without the comforts of civilization. At least for a week or two.

"Name three good things about riding in the middle," Naomi says, interrupting my thoughts.

Melody bangs her hands on the side of the canoe. The noise echoes of the water, shattering my moment of zen. "Ooh! Like your podcast!"

Naomi nods, making her ponytail dance across her neck. "The idea started way before the podcast. It's something my mom and I got into after the divorce, and it really helps to find the bright side of things."

"Okay," Mel says, and I imagine her scrunching her lips while she thinks. "I can pretend I'm the Queen of the Nile and you're both my slaves, forced to ferry me from one extravagant party to the next."

I swallow a laugh. "That's one."

She giggles. "I can moon people."

Naomi smacks her paddle against the water, sending a spray backward. A few drops hit Mel but most of the water hits me.

"Hey!" It comes out whinier than I intended, and I straighten as she turns around.

A blush colors her cheeks when she realizes what she did. "Sorry! That was an attempt to prevent anyone's pants from dropping." Her cheeks get even redder, and she touches a hand to her throat, which makes my throat go dry, because now I'm thinking about my underwear. Again.

"Okay, fine. I won't moon anyone," Mel says. "That's not really my jam anyways."

Naomi returns to paddling. "What's the third good thing?"

"I don't know, being here with you?" Mel says.

Jealousy squeezes my chest.

"I'm flattered, but we're already bunking together. Aren't you gonna get sick of me?"

"No way," Mel says. "You talk as much as I do. If it was just my family, Mom would spend all her time making us discuss our feelings and Hunter would spend all his time trying to get out of answering her questions."

"Hey!" I smack my paddle against the water, sending an arc of water so high over the canoe it's like I threw a bucket at them. They both squeal when the water hits their backs, and my mouth drops when Naomi's paddle slips out of her hands and into the lake.

"My paddle!"

"What the hell, Hunt?" Mel scowls at me.

"That was more excessive than I intended."

Naomi stretches over the edge of the canoe, but it's drifted beyond her fingertips. "A little help here?"

"Everything okay over there?" Mom calls from a hundred yards away.

"All good," I shout back.

I pull a stroke on the opposite side to steer us toward the wayward paddle, and Naomi's fingers outstretch as we slowly get closer. Once it's in her hand, she straightens, then cuts the paddle into the water, dousing me. Mel gets hit with the spray again and shouts into the sky.

"Omigod, stop it! Both of you!" She bangs her hands on the side of the canoe. "A bad thing about being in the middle is getting caught in the middle of your flirting!"

Naomi and I freeze. Is that what we're doing? My hope is that she'd forget what a butt I was yesterday and we could maybe work our way toward being friends, but I hadn't considered that she might be into me.

"Sorry," I mumble, wiping my glasses on my damp shirt.

"Sorry," Naomi says. Her shoulders slump, then she shakes off whatever she's thinking and goes back to paddling. "You were saying, Melody?"

"You think I remember after that?"

I burst out laughing. After a moment, they join me, and the tension in my neck loosens. I haven't completely screwed this up yet.

"You were saying how awesome it is that I'm here to save you from your scowly brother."

"I'm not scowly," I say. But my eyebrows crease as I say it, and my mouth has most definitely curved into a frown.

Mel turns to look at me and points at my face. "If you look up the definition of scowly, your face is totally what they show."

"Scowly isn't even a real word," I mumble.

Naomi looks over her shoulder, a smile playing on her lips. "You know I'm just giving you crap, right? Or do you need to email your professors to confirm that scowly isn't a word?" Her brow raises and I don't even care that she's making fun of me.

I force an exaggerated smile and she rolls her eyes before facing forward, but not before I see the smile that softens her face.

"Yeah, you're totally not flirting," Mel says.

Neither of us responds.

We fall into a rhythm that has us gliding along the shoreline, with Mel narrating as we go. Until now, I've never fully appreciated her ability to talk nonstop but it's helping to keep my thoughts at bay. Thoughts that have me questioning my no-dating policy for a girl who doesn't even live in the same state. But wouldn't that be ideal? A long-distance relationship would give me time to focus on school, with the benefit of, well, Naomi.

"Can I just say how stupid it is to sort people by sex organs?" Mel says.

"I'm sorry, what?" Naomi asks over her shoulder.

"Where did that come from?" I ask.

"For our cabins. Yurts," Mel says. "I know it's the construct society has decided makes sense, but it's completely antiquated."

"Someone's been learning new words."

She turns to scowl at me, and it's one hundred percent a look I've seen on my face. Maybe I am scowly.

"I'm just saying." Mel waves her hands at her sides like she can grab the words she's looking for from the air. "It doesn't make sense. Grouping people together by their genitalia, especially for sleeping arrangements, is dumb. Way back when it was probably a thing to prevent premarital sex, but people don't just like the opposite sex."

"I see what you're saying," Naomi says.

Mel trails her fingers in the water, watching the ripple until it's swallowed by my paddle. "Even with our group. Theo likes boys and girls, so it shouldn't matter who he's sharing a yurt with. And I," she pauses. "I haven't figured it out yet."

This is news to me, and I'm relieved that I don't have a reaction. If Melody likes girls or boys or both or none of the above, it doesn't change who she is or that she's my little sister. But it also emphasizes just how little I know about her life, and how desperately I want to be there for her while she figures these things out. "That's a really good point."

She lifts her head and smiles at me. "I know."

"To be fair," Naomi says as she paddles. "It is convenient that our families each have a brother and a sister. I think the moms were thinking more along those lines than trying to prevent premarital sex."

Mel whips around to give me her OMG Did You Hear That look—eyes wide, brows raised, lips pursed—and I give her my Shut Up She Didn't Mean That look—brows furrowed, lips mashed together—or my best attempt at anything to keep her from furthering this conversation.

Naomi doesn't turn around. She keeps paddling, staring straight ahead, but there's a stiffness in her shoulders and I swear her neck is redder than it was a moment ago. Maybe she realizes what she said and is embarrassed?

Or maybe all this talk about sex has her thinking about me and why oh why didn't I listen to Shawna about my underwear?

This has been the longest ten minutes in my life.

No one has spoken since I blathered about the moms trying to prevent premarital sex. In my head it sounded harmless enough, but as soon as the words left my mouth, it became achingly clear that of course the moms weren't trying to keep Theo from sleeping with the twelve-year-old, so I implied that we've all considered the fact that Hunter and I could have sex. Or might want to have sex. Or have considered having sex with each other.

Oh. My. God.

Maybe I should fling myself overboard and put myself out of my misery. But then the moms will freak out and what if Hunter jumps in to save me? That would be even more mortifying than this silence that will not end.

Or would it?

I'm eyeing the water when Theo bangs on the side of their canoe. "Pit stop, right ahead!" He points at a sandy area with outhouses and a small covered area with picnic tables.

Hunter steers us toward the shore, and I abandon thoughts of jumping in. We paddle in unison, gaining speed until the front of the canoe hits the sandy bottom and we jerk to a stop.

"Nice work, plebeians." Melody stretches her arms above her head. "Hunt, will you help me out?"

Before I can tell her to climb out the front to avoid getting wet, Hunter jumps over the side with a splash. The water's not deep—it barely brushes the bottom of his swim trunks—but he scoops Melody out of the canoe and carries her to dry land.

I'm watching the way the muscles in his arms and legs ripple as he sets her down when he turns and splashes back into the water.

Caught wide-eyed, I smile. "That was sweet."

He holds out a hand. "Do you need help?"

Am I perfectly capable of climbing out of this canoe? Yes. Do I believe women should be independent and not rely on men? Also yes. But those objections die on my lips. Instead, I slip my hand into his and let him support me as I step over the side of the canoe, trip on the edge, and slam into his chest. He stumbles backward and his free hand grabs at my side. My foot is still caught on the side of the canoe so before I can take a breath, we're underwater.

My heartbeat thunders in my ears, and there's a moment when everything goes still. His arm tightens around my waist, pulling me firmly against his body, and his fingers squeeze mine. Then my head pops above the surface and there's yelling.

Lots of yelling.

"Are you okay?"

"What happened?"

"That was epic!" That last one was Theo, of course. "Does that count as canoe tippage or is this damsel in distress gone wrong?"

I throw a handful of sand at Theo and push to my feet.

Hunter's still sitting on the bottom, the water up to his chest. His glasses sit askew on his face, and I reach to straighten them before catching myself.

"Um, sorry?"

He smiles up at me before chuckling. "I guess I wasn't as helpful as I hoped."

"Are you okay?" From this angle he looks like a little boy. Vulnerable and open to whatever comes his way, not the closed-off guy he's been since we've arrived.

"Just bruised my ego a bit."

"I really am sorry. I know falling in the water wasn't on your preapproved list of fun."

He seems to stumble over his words, like he's trying to decide what to say and keeps rejecting whatever's in his head. "It wasn't so bad."

My belly flips, and I let the feeling warm me from the inside, ignoring the voice in my head telling me that this is probably a really bad idea because despite the advice I spout on my podcast, my track record with guys is abysmal. It's been months since I've felt stirrings of any kind for anyone—not since I tried to kiss Theo's best friend at the Rose Garden in Portland. He was as graceful as you can be in that kind of awkward situation, but that split-second decision changed our friendship and now we barely talk to each other. Theo keeps telling me to give it time, that it'll eventually go back to the way it was, but I'm not so sure. And I'm not super eager to put myself out there for another guy.

Despite my hesitations, I hold out my hand to Hunter. For the second time in a few minutes, he places his hand in mine and the butterflies ramp up. His palm is solid, his grip steady, and I swear I can hear the drops of water falling from our arms into the lake. I help pull him to his feet and wow, this is the closest we've stood next to each other. He's the perfect amount taller than me—five or six inches—which means my eyes are level with his mouth. His lips. THAT SMIRK. We're both soaked and his hand is still in mine.

My tongue grazes my lower lip.

His eyes follow.

The tension between us builds and I'm sure he can hear my heart pounding through my tank top, but he doesn't seem to notice anything but me.

"Thanks," he says, his voice lower, rougher, than before. He takes a step back, dropping my hand, and the rest of the world comes back into focus.

I turn toward the shore and freeze. Everyone's watching us, a mixture of surprise (moms), amusement (Theo), and concern (Melody) on their faces.

"Do you two need a moment?" Theo waggles his brows and I kick water at him. Yeah, hanging out with a twelve-year-old apparently *does* lower my maturity level.

Hunter's hand brushes my lower back as he follows me out of the water. It's subtle enough that no one else seems to notice, but my skin flames beneath his touch.

The moms and Melody head for the outhouses, and Theo sidles up next to me. "Dude, something's going on with them."

"What do you mean?" Hunter asks.

Theo toes the sand. It's not like him to be careful with his words but he seems to be choosing them intentionally. "They were talking about their jobs and the whole thing with Mom maybe changing careers. Margo was giving her advice and it was all fine and dandy, then Mom kind of snapped at her."

My head jerks up.

Hunter stares at the outhouses like he can tell what they're thinking. "My mom can be a bit intense sometimes. Did they seem mad at each other?"

"Not mad. More like frustrated."

"They're practically best friends," I say. "They adore each other. I'm sure it's nothing." But Theo doesn't gossip just to gossip. Something they said concerned him enough to tell me.

"Mm-hmm," he says, clearly unconvinced.

"Do you think this has anything to do with that day?"

"When she was crying?"

"I thought she was looking for another job. But it could've been something else. Maybe money was a bigger issue than she's let on."

His brows furrow. "You think?"

The doors to the outhouse slam, ending our conversation. The moms walk toward us, smiles on their faces. If something's bothering them, they're not ready to share. Hopefully whatever's going on with Mom, she's able to talk about it with Margo.

After a short rest, we get back in the canoes. I show Melody how to climb in from the front so she doesn't need to rely on anyone for help—no matter how sweet it is how Hunter looks out for her—and I push us free from the sandy bottom with my paddle.

"Do you think you two can manage to stay in the canoe?" she asks.

"I'll throw you in right now," Hunter says. "It's not over your head. Yet." He laughs a deep, menacing laugh that sounds like a villain from a campy horror movie and Melody squeals.

"I take it back!"

Drops of water hit my leg and I glance over my shoulder. Hunter's hand is in the water, ready to splash her again. I'm sure there's a reason he didn't use his paddle—better control, maybe he had dirt on his hand—because him being courteous and trying not to splash me does not align with the jerkface I met yesterday.

On one of the earliest episodes of Three Good Things, we talked about how long you have to know someone before it's no longer considered insta-love. We came to the conclusion that it involves weeks, not days.

Which means whatever I think I'm feeling for Hunter isn't real.

The lake narrows until it looks more like a river and the moms lead us toward the middle. Whatever tension is going on between them seems to be gone for now. Or Theo is just working his magic. He's waving his hands as he talks, and Margo is doubled over laughing. Mom looks as relaxed as I've ever seen her and a stab of guilt twists in my stomach. I make a vow to be more proactively thoughtful, the way she is with us.

Then I push those thoughts aside and focus on the people in my canoe. Hunter clearly cares about Melody, which isn't hard to do. She's fun and clever and kind of makes me wish I had a little sister. "So, Melody," I say. "What would you be doing right now if you weren't here?"

"Oh, gawd," she says. "What time is it at home?"

"Almost noon," Hunter says.

"Counting the minutes until English is over."

"What?" Hunter gasps.

I peek over my shoulder. He's stopped paddling and the look of shock on his face makes me burst out laughing.

"You laugh," he says, looking at me. "But this—" He points at his sister. "This is an affront to my very being."

"You are so dramatic," Melody says. "'I'm sorry I don't worship at the throne of Gutenberg, but not everyone loves books like you do."

His mouth opens and closes. He wipes his glasses against the front of his shirt and in that second he looks exposed, defenseless.

My heart quivers and I avert my gaze.

"Mel, what can I do to change your mind?"

She sighs heavily behind me. "Can we not do this right now? Naomi was trying to make pleasant conversation and you've made it weird."

"It's not weird," I say at the same time he mumbles, "Sorry."

"Anyway," she says loudly. "Right now, I'd be wishing for English to be over because I have astronomy after that, and *that* is my jam."

"You're into space?" I ask.

"I think so." She sounds uncertain, like she's afraid I'll judge her for revealing this detail about herself. "We're only a month into it, but it's so fascinating. Everything out there is so much bigger than us. Like, no matter what stupid crap happens down here, the universe keeps on spinning, you know?" She tacks on the last words with hesitation, like she needs the qualifier because she doesn't want us to know she actually cares about this.

Which pisses me off. Something's clearly going on with her and she's either afraid to talk about it in front of Hunter or she's afraid to talk about it period.

"Is everything okay?" Hunter asks.

Melody trails a hand along the side of the canoe. "Oh, yeah. Totally."

They're quiet for a beat, two, three, so I rush to fill the silence.

"You would love my friend Neb. He's the most geeked-out space boy I know. He was even named after a part of the universe."

"A nebula?" Melody asks.

"Like the Marvel character?" Hunter asks.

"Interstellar gas, dude."

I'm secretly pleased that Melody knows more about this than he does.

"Yes, after the space dust thing, not the Marvel chick," I say. "Are your friends into astronomy, too?" I guess the answer before she replies.

"Not really. My two best friends don't have it this year, and we don't really talk about that kind of stuff anyways."

Her confirmation makes something deflate inside me. I can't be the only one who hears the sadness in her voice. "What do the three of you like to do? I bet you're a force to be reckoned with." That sentence is one hundred percent something I've heard come out of Mom's mouth, but I roll with it.

There's a scraping sound on the bottom of the canoe. I turn and she's rubbing her foot against the metal seam beneath her seat. She smiles, but it doesn't reach her eyes. "Oh, you know, we like to make videos for social media and look at fashion accounts."

Hunter watches Melody but doesn't say anything more. If he cares about her as much as he seems to, this has to be killing him.

"There's this park with soccer fields and a playground that a lot of kids hang out at." She holds up a hand, palm out. "Not that we play on the playground."

"No judgment here," I say. "I've never met a swing I didn't like."

Hunter laughs at this, and I'm torn between wanting to keep Melody talking and imagining him on a swing, his feet pointed at the sky, leaving whatever's bothering him on the ground below. I choose to focus on the more immediate need.

"Is everything okay with them?" I don't expect her to answer honestly, not right now. But I've opened the door for later.

"Oh, yeah. Totally." Her voice is a little too loud, her cheerfulness forced. "They're super jealous I'm on this trip."

I smile for real. "Mine are too."

"Um," Hunter interrupts. "Are they stuck?"

Not far ahead of us, the moms and Theo have stopped moving even though the canoe is surrounded by water. "They must have hit a sandbar," I say.

"Do you need help?" Hunter shouts.

The three of them lean forward then back, forward then back. The canoe scoots a few inches and Margo lets out a frustrated scream.

"We wanted to get to the river," Mom shouts.

"Stay back!" Theo says, waving his arms at us. "Save yourselves!"

Hunter and I stop paddling, but our momentum and the gentle current carry us closer.

"I don't think we should stop," Melody says. "They're perfectly capable of getting out of there."

"I'm not so sure," I say. The three of them seem to be arguing amongst themselves, and Theo keeps shaking his head. Margo's face is flushed, and she looks like she's about to completely lose it. "Does your mom not handle problems well?"

"She doesn't like not being in control," Hunter says. "So being stuck in a canoe in what looks like mud is pretty much torture for her."

"Fine!" Theo shouts. He fumbles with something on the bottom of the canoe, then without preamble, flops into the water. He stands in the knee-deep water, hands on his hips, but in a matter of seconds, the water is up to his thighs. "I'm sinking!" he squeals.

"Keep moving," Hunter says. We're close enough now that he doesn't need to yell, which means we're in danger of getting stuck ourselves.

Theo clings to the side of the canoe and both moms shriek as it tips to the side.

"Let's back up," I say.

Hunter doesn't react right away, so I push my paddle through the water in the opposite direction, but without him to counterbalance my efforts, we spin in a circle.

"Hunt, come on." Melody's voice comes out a whine as she pleads with her brother.

Hunter finally reacts, but it's too late. There's a scratching sound as the canoe hits the bottom. We stop slowly, without the sudden jerk like when we stopped to use the bathrooms, and then we're stuck.

"Awesome," Hunter says under his breath.

Theo's still struggling with their canoe. The water's barely up to his knees but the bottom is so mushy it keeps sucking him down. He's moved to the front and is attempting to yank it free, each step causing him to sink deeper into the mud.

"Little help?" I call to Theo.

If looks could shrivel a person on the spot, I would be dead. "I am already so far beyond my comfort zone that I have nothing left for your well-being." He gives the canoe another tug before grabbing onto the point at the front. "I told you to save yourselves."

"He did warn us," Melody says.

"Not helping." Hunter pulls his shirt over his head and peers over the side.

My mouth goes dry. It's not that he's ripped or chiseled or however it is they describe overly muscly men, but he's a boy I have a crush on and he's now half naked. "Wh-what are you doing?"

He meets my eyes and for a moment we're just two teenagers chatting about whatever. Then The Smirk appears. "I thought I'd make another attempt with the damsel in distress thing."

Yeah. Well. I'm gone.

"Except this time you have four damsels and a Theo," Melody says.

"I'll focus on the two of you for now. Wish me luck." He winks—either at her or me or both of us, but it sends my pulse racing—hands his glasses to Melody, and climbs out.

"Luck!" we both say.

His attempt to get his footing is not graceful, and his hair is every which-way from getting splashed, but it's still got me breathing faster. So much for being independent and not wanting a guy to come to my rescue.

Theo pumps his fist in the air. "Compadre!"

Hunter gives him a wobbly smile and moves to the front of the canoe. To where I am. His hands rest on the rounded metal point, less than a foot from my bare knees, and he peers down at me. Without his glasses I get that same kick in the gut as before, and it's all I can do to act normal.

"My hero?" I don't mean it to come out a question, but it lightens whatever's building between us and we both laugh.

"This mud is disgusting," he says. "You can't stand still or it sucks you in."

Melody's suddenly right behind me, her arms resting on my shoulders, her head next to mine. "Thankyouthankyouthankyou."

I barely manage to hold in a yelp as the canoe pitches sideways. Melody stumbles into me and I lurch forward, grabbing the sides as Hunter's eyes widen. He's still holding the front but now he's on a different rescue mission—trying to keep us from tipping.

"Sit down!" His arms and shoulders, and wow, even his chest, flex as he steadies the canoe. "Come on, Mel. That's canoeing one-oh-one."

She's still leaning on my back and sighs into my ear. "I was just saying thank you."

"It's like you *want* us to tip," he says.

She finally sits down. "No. Absolutely not."

Hunter reaches farther into the canoe, his hands dangerously close to my knees, and grips the edge. With each tug, we jerk forward, and he falls backward. It's beyond awkward being this close to him while he's struggling. There's obviously an attraction, at least on my end, and me staring at him while he flounders probably isn't helping.

"Would it be easier if we got out?" I ask. "I feel stupid watching you do this by yourself."

He shakes his head. "There's no sense in all of us getting covered in mud. And I doubt Mel will willingly subject herself to that."

"You're a smart man, Hunt."

I look over his head at the other canoe. The moms are once again floating, their paddles trailing in the water. "Theo got them out."

Hunter wipes water from his face and looks over his shoulder.

"Let me show you the trick," Theo shouts. He half flops, half dives toward us.

"I never thought I'd see the day my indoor-cat of a brother knows a trick about a canoe." Is Hunter the type of guy to accept help or will he go all macho and insist he can do it himself? My gut says there's not a macho bone in his body, but my gut has been wrong before.

Theo slogs through the water, stumbling with each step. "You gotta keep moving." He's panting like he just swam a hundred-yard butterfly instead of a twenty-yard dog paddle. Just before he reaches us, he jumps, arms and legs spread wide, and lands hard on his belly. Water splashes over the canoe, around the canoe, into the canoe.

"Theo!" I shout, my Mom Voice turned all the way up. Melody squeals behind me while Hunter, who's already completely soaked, just laughs.

Theo surfaces, all smiles. "The trick," he repeats, "is to keep your feet moving." His hands are still under the water and his smile turns devious.

"Do not," I say.

He lifts his hands, revealing globs of mud and seaweed and whatever sludge lives on the bottom of the lake.

"Theo you're my favorite person on this trip and I promise to take your side on anything you say if you just pleasepleaseplease don't throw that at me." Melody takes a deep breath.

It's breathtaking how quickly her loyalties have shifted. Although everyone who meets Theo eventually loves him.

"I would never," he says.

"Mm-hmm." I one hundred percent guarantee that was his plan.

His brow quirks. "Is that a dare?"

"I hate to interrupt, but can we, you know, work on getting the canoe free?" Hunter asks.

"Right, right." Theo smacks his hands together like Margo, sending mud flying, then smears the rest under his eyes. "It's getting Lord of the Flies out here." He holds out a muddy hand to Hunter, who shakes his head.

"I'm good."

I wipe mud off my arms, then dip my hands in the water. "Next time do the mud first, then the splash."

Theo taps a finger to his temple. "Hunter, you stay there and I'll push from the back."

"Is this part of your trick?" I ask.

"Shut it," he mumbles.

After a few grunts and a very loud curse from Theo, the canoe regains its buoyancy. Without thinking, I touch Hunter's hand, which is still gripping the point of the canoe. "Thank you. Seriously."

A flush pinkens his cheeks and he drops his gaze to our hands. Which are somehow still touching. I quickly pull back and his lips tighten. "Sorry this was such a cluster."

"You've met my brother. That pretty much defines the majority of my existence."

"You'll miss me someday!" Theo says it casually, like it's no big deal that sooner rather than later we'll be on our own, living separate lives, and I won't get to see him every day.

Guilt washes over me. Not telling him about the offer feels like the ultimate betrayal. What if he's glad to be apart from me when he learns the truth?

Then he splashes me from behind, snapping me out of my head. Hunter jumps, stumbles over his legs, and lands on his back.

"Wow," Melody says. "My brother is so not smooth."

When Hunter surfaces, his face is even redder and the pink creeps down his chest. "I'm gonna get back in the canoe now." He holds the side of the canoe, rocking us from side to side, and flops into the back with a groan. I get a final glimpse of his chest as he pulls his shirt back on, then quickly look away.

The moms have paddled closer, and Theo somehow manages to climb in without flipping them. "Ready to head back?" Mom asks.

"Yes," we all answer.

"This has been great and all," Melody says. "But you all have destroyed my fantasy of being ferried around like the Queen of the Nile."

"More like a passenger on the Titanic," Hunter says.

It's quiet as we paddle back, and I wish we could rewind to earlier with the splashing and flirting and him not feeling self-conscious. Even Melody seems to have run out of things to say, and by the time the docks come into sight, I'm worried the mud ruined all the progress we've made this afternoon.

10
HUNTER

"I can't get a shower fast enough," I say.

Naomi makes a weird noise. Our eyes lock for a second, but I look away. My display of pure un-athleticism surely doused whatever interest she may have in me. Dried mud cakes my legs, pulling at the little hairs, and I smell like the bottom of a cesspool. Theo's still got mud streaks on his face, but he wears it like a badge of honor.

Maybe the difference is our self-confidence. Or rather, the fact that he has confidence and I do not.

I grab the moms' cooler from the dock and head toward the yurts.

My phone buzzes with new texts when I grab my shower stuff.

Darren: I need to hear more about this yurt

Darren: Specifically if they're as rustic as they sound and can they take one's virginity

I laugh through my nose. Darren's as adept with the world of literacy as I am, but he's even less outdoorsy than Theo. He'd be happy never setting foot off a paved sidewalk. But as for the virgin crap—

Me: Sex is very much not happening

I toss my phone on my bed and step outside. Theo's sitting near the firepit, but no one else is around. "I'm heading to the showers."

Ten minutes under the warm water has me feeling more like myself. It's stupid to worry about what Naomi does or does not think about me because despite what Shawna and Darren say, she doesn't fit into my plan. My focus needs to stay on my future and figuring out if I'm going to transfer home.

My resolve weakens when I leave the bathroom at the same time as Naomi. Her red curls, still wet from her shower, brush her face and my chest tightens with a need to know what her shampoo smells like.

She turns to face me, and a smile brightens her face. "Fancy meeting you here." Her gaze drops to my T-shirt and her eyes widen. "Do you go to Berkeley?"

My fingers graze the logo screaming across my chest. "Yeah?"

She cocks her head at the question mark at the end of what should have been a statement. "It wasn't a trick question."

I force a laugh. Two seconds with this girl and my grasp on the English language escapes me. "Yes, I'm majoring in Media Studies, minoring in English. I want to be an editor at one of the big publishers in New York. Find books that kids want to read and help authors make a name for themselves. Then push those books out into the world."

She shifts her weight from one foot to the other. Her gaze bounces from my shirt to the ground between us and she bites the corner of her lip. "You really have it all figured out."

At this moment, I feel like I have nothing figured out. Leaving a campus that still feels like a foreign land won't be hard—after four years in high school I often felt like an outsider there, too—but saying goodbye to my friends will be harder. I've finally found people who don't make me feel like a freak for loving words and what if I don't find my people at a new school?

"Or maybe not?" Her gentle tone eases me out of my spiral.

"No. Yeah." I drag a hand through my wet hair and her gaze follows my movements. "I know what I want to do. It's the *how* part that I'm still not sure about."

She bites her lip again and I'm realizing she does that when she's thinking. "Are you not happy at Berkeley?" Her eyes widen a bit, like it's impossible to imagine such a thing.

"Berkeley is awesome. Everything you hear is true. The professors are incredible, and I've already found my people." But it's not home and I'm worried about my sister.

"That's important. The people part." She toes her flip-flop against the pavement and speaks to the ground. "Berkeley's been my dream since I started thinking about college." Her eyes flick to mine to gauge my reaction, then quickly drop again.

A million scenarios flash through my mind. Naomi smiling at me while we study. Walking through campus holding hands. Her getting upset because I don't have time for her, because I'm too focused on classes. Fighting, then ignoring texts until she's a memory I avoid when I see her red hair in the cafeteria. I clear my throat. "Communications, right?" Too late I remember the way she reacted to the conversation the night before and hold up a hand. "You don't have to get into it if you don't want."

Her lips tighten before she lets out a breath. "It's okay. Communications makes sense for me, and I might minor in sociology or something people-related. That all makes sense to me."

I could nod and let her be vague or I could draw her out like I do when editing my friends' papers. Make them get to the heart of what they're trying to say. "So what's not making sense?"

Her nostrils flare and her eyes widen, then she takes a step back. "I'm not—I don't know."

I don't believe her but I don't press her further. "You've got time to figure it out. Have you sent in your application?"

"They're due soon." Her normally pink cheeks pale and I fight the urge to know everything she's thinking. Especially whatever's got her so scared.

I take a step toward her and bump our elbows together. "Like I said, you've got time. You'll figure it out."

She peers up at me and something in my chest twists. This close she smells like vanilla and honey. Her pupils dilate and she catches the corner of her lip between her teeth. While I've never slept with a girl, I have kissed a few and everything about this moment tells me I should kiss her.

Instead, I take a step toward the campsite. "Ready to head back?"

She blinks several times before nodding. "Yeah."

We're quiet on the short walk, but it's not uncomfortable. My mind drifts to the image of us walking together on campus. Having someone in my life—someone I can confide in, who I can trust—is appealing, but my career has to be my focus right now. I've already spent too much time worrying about Mel. Adding a girlfriend won't leave enough brain-space for school and I won't make the same mistake Mom did and risk not graduating because I've fallen in love.

Naomi, of course, is oblivious to my internal struggle. She peers through the trees to the blue sky above us, a look of contentment softening her features.

The moms are working on dinner when we get back. Plastic bags with marinated chicken and chopped veggies sit on the picnic table and Nancy's lighting the fire in the grill.

"Oh good," Mom says. "Hunter, can you take over while I shower?"

"Let me put my stuff away." There's a moment when Naomi and I both hesitate, which is silly because we'll see each other in five minutes.

Theo's sprawled on the plywood floor.

"What are you doing?"

He looks up. "My earlier heroics were exhausting, but I'm not such a heathen that I'd lay on my bed before showering."

"Fair enough." I grab my hoodie from the end of my bed but pause before heading back outside. "Was there any more…" I wave my hand like I can grasp the words I'm searching for from the air. "How were the moms the rest of the trip?"

He pushes into a sitting position and rests his chin on his hand. "Mostly fine. Your mom kept bringing it up, like how to change careers and what certifications she needs, but Mom would shut her down." He strokes his chin, more serious than I've seen him. "I can't tell if she just didn't want to talk about it in front of me or what."

"Lucky for us, they've got all week to work it out." I don't mean for it to sound sarcastic, but I don't have a reputation for being a butt for no reason.

"I'm glad my mom has your mom," Theo says. "She has friends at home but no one she seems to trust the same way." He looks me straight in the eye and I'm startled by his intensity. "Finding your people is important."

I laugh, but it falls flat. "Did you hear Naomi and me talking? We were just saying that."

He taps his head, the shit-eating grin I've grown used to back on his face. "Twin-fu."

"I have to take over dinner. You've got twenty minutes to shower."

"Perfect." He lays back on the floor, but stops me as I'm stepping outside. "We are lucky," he says.

I pause in the doorway, head cocked.

"Not everyone has families as supportive as ours. Who put up with whatever ridiculous crap we throw their way and not just tolerate us, but support us." Serious Theo's staring at the ceiling. "I consider that very lucky."

Maybe he's not as confident as he acts. Or maybe he's confident because he's got an amazing family backing him up.

Just like I do.

"You're right. Thanks for reminding me." I jog down the steps, a new determination to tell Mom what I'm thinking coursing through me. Theo's right. We both have parents—or at least mothers—who will stand by us no matter what. Even if I announced I no longer wanted to be an editor but was instead going to pursue a career in rodeo clowning. Mel wouldn't let me hear the end of it, but they'd stand by me every step of the way.

I take a breath. Transferring doesn't have to be a bad thing. If I lead with what I'll gain instead of what I'd be giving up, it might be over faster than I expect.

Mom smiles when she sees me.

I take a deep breath. No time like the present.

But she waves a pair of tongs at me. "You can handle the chicken? We still need to shower."

Nancy's transferring the veggies to a tinfoil pouch, their bathroom stuff resting next to her on the picnic table.

"Yeah, sure." I take the tongs from her and a worry line creases her forehead.

"You okay?" She smooths my forehead, where I no doubt have an identical line. Her hands smell like teriyaki.

I duck away from her touch and force a laugh. "Quit rubbing raw chicken on me!"

"Be back soon!" They practically skip down the path like a couple schoolgirls. Theo's right. I've never seen her this relaxed with anyone except Mel and me. It's like a side of her I haven't seen since the divorce has suddenly reemerged. Maybe this version of her will only see the benefits to me leaving Berkeley.

I'm rubbing lemon-scented hand sanitizer on my forehead when Naomi approaches.

"I don't think you're supposed to cook with that."

"Clearly you've never cooked with the Thompsons."

She blinks, stopping in her tracks.

I hold her gaze for several beats before the corner of my mouth lifts.

"I'm sorry, was that a joke?" She moves to the picnic table, steps on the bench, and sits on the table surface. We're still not eye level, but it's closer than when she's standing. Her blue T-shirt accentuates her piercing green eyes and she studies me like she's trying to figure me out. The silence isn't as uncomfortable as I would expect, but I break eye contact when I transfer the raw chicken to the grill.

There's a spark to her personality that's impossible to ignore. Her gaze isn't judgmental, just curious, and the longer she watches me, the more I want to know everything that's going on inside that head of hers.

I'm nestling the last piece on the grill when I break the silence. "Am I not allowed to make jokes?"

She leans forward so her elbows are on her knees. "Quite the opposite. I invite jokes. I just didn't think—" She cuts herself off and I look up. "Can I ask you a question?"

Her expression is open, curious, and I'm simultaneously dying to tell her anything and afraid to share even the smallest detail. Because once I let her in, I don't think I'll ever get her out.

I wedge the tin foil packet of veggies on the edge of the grill and nod. "Sure?"

She picks at an invisible thread on her jeans. "Why were you so rude to me when we got here?"

Her directness surprises me, and I quickly realize it shouldn't. Everything I've learned about her indicates that she's not one to shy away from difficult conversations, even if right now she looks like she'd rather be anyplace but here.

And I don't have an answer for her. At least not one I'm willing to share.

"I'm sorry. I don't have an excuse." Aside from the fact that your voice captivated me and seeing you in person was like a shot to my heart. "I was still pissed I had to miss a guest lecturer at school. And I was tired from the drive."

She nods but doesn't seem convinced.

I wouldn't be convinced either. "Would it help if I told you Mel ripped me a new one for being a butt?"

She snorts, and a smile breaks the tension on her face. "She told me."

"I shouldn't have taken it out on you. I'm sorry," I say again.

She seems to roll my words around in her head and an urgency grips me. Right now, I want nothing more than for this girl to accept my apology and move past my Cranky Pants Hunterness, as Mel so lovingly calls my mood swings.

"It wasn't the greatest way to start the trip, but I get it. That drive sucked." She picks at her knee again, a smirk playing on her lips. "And you didn't have Theo trying to moon other cars."

I burst out laughing, the sound echoing off the trees. "Is that a common thing with him?"

"More common than I'd like."

As if summoned, Theo skips down the path from the bathroom, hair dripping wet, and plops in a chair near the fire. "Did anyone bring a firestarter?"

"You mean like a match?" I ask.

He rolls his eyes. "No, one of those highly combustible logs that do all the work for you." He looks at Naomi. "Since we didn't bring our lumberjack."

They exchange a laugh to a joke I don't understand, and the uneasiness I felt when we first arrived, when I was a dick to Naomi, resurfaces. But I swallow it back. Naomi's honesty helped clear whatever awkwardness was lingering between us and I don't want to take a step backward.

"I saw a bunch of logs and twigs on the backside of my yurt," Naomi says. "I'll help you bring them over." As she climbs off the picnic table, she gives me a subtle once-over that's not subtle enough. Her cheeks redden, and she leads her brother to the wood pile.

They get the fire going as I work on dinner, and by the time the moms come back from their showers, Mel's emerged from her yurt and we're ready to eat. Light conversation surrounds me, with Mel and Theo doing the heavy lifting. My earlier concern that she would crush on the older boy has subsided. She still seems fascinated with him, but he's a fascinating person. I envy how he owns who he is without excuses or apology, and his ability to entertain anyone within earshot is a gift. Mel seems to be studying him—from his vocal inflections and hand gestures to the way his eyes light up when he's about to drop the punchline—and I mentally prepare myself for her to start emulating him.

I also can't stop worrying about what Mel said in the canoe that concerned Naomi. Mel and I have never kept secrets from each other, but I can't ignore that ever since I got home, she's avoided talking to me. But she's the most important person in my world, so all I can do is keep trying—whether she likes it or not.

The sun dips lower in the sky, pinks and purples streaking across the horizon in a preview of the show to come. When Mom first mentioned camping at a dark park, I had to look up what it was. Unbeknownst to me, visiting places with minimal light is a thing, and it sounded cool. Then I discovered that to be far enough from manmade light, you have to travel to the middle of nowhere. The closest one to our house is Joshua Tree National Park, but Mom and Nancy wanted to be near water, which ruled out any of the desert states. So Utah it is. We're only an hour outside Salt Lake City, but the lights from the city don't reach this far.

Mom claps her hands, snapping me to attention. Theo and Naomi exchange a look, but my ability to decipher their twin-speak is nonexistent.

"Tomorrow we're going to Antelope Island!" Mom claps again, but this seems to be from excitement rather than trying to get our attention. "It takes a little over an hour to get there, so we'll leave right after breakfast and bring our lunch."

"I hope your arms aren't too tired," Nancy says. "Because we'll be on the water again."

"I don't want to be in the middle!" Melody whines.

Nancy shakes her head. "They only have kayaks. No canoes. And the kayaks don't hold three people, so you'll definitely be paddling."

Naomi rubs her hands together. "Ooh, I've always wanted to try that."

Mom continues, "They offer single and double kayaks, but we thought it'd be easier if we do doubles since none of us are exactly kayak masters."

Theo sighs dramatically. "I did not sign up for physical exertion."

Naomi leans out of her chair and smacks his leg. "Quit being a baby. It sounds fun."

Their chatter washes over me. I lean my head back to look at the stars, at the swirls of galaxies far above us. The unending pinpricks of light melt together, so bright the individual constellations become a blur. My chest suddenly feels tight. My problems sometimes feel like they'll completely overwhelm me, but out here, with the universe seeming so close that I could reach out and touch it, my decisions don't seem as unsurmountable.

Maybe this trip will be better than I expected. Naomi's been a surprise—albeit unwelcome to my life plan—but being out of my regular routine and away from school makes the decision a bit easier. As if the stars, so clear in the sky, provide clarity down here on Earth as well.

Mom catches my eye and mouths, "You okay?"

For the first time in ages, I think I am.

11

NAOMI

Hunter's totally zoned out staring at the sky. Not that I can blame him. When I looked up dark parks it sounded pretty cool, but like most things on the internet, the pictures didn't do it justice. I've seen the Milky Way before, but it's like if every candy bar in existence had a universe named after it and then got together and hung out over Utah. It's probably like this everywhere in the world, we just can't see it because of the city lights.

The beauty above me makes me feel small, but not insignificant. Just very aware of my tiny role on this planet. Figuring out what I'm supposed to do while I'm here feels even more important—bigger somehow—than it did back home. Like if I make the wrong decision, it'll send a ripple across the world that I can't undo.

Maybe that's what Theo's worried about. That whatever he's planning will somehow change things. Or maybe he's afraid to go after what he wants because I've tied him to the podcast.

"Do you mind doing the silverware?" Melody asks. We're just about done washing dishes and she's been washing while I dry. "I hate feeling around on the bottom of the bin with the dirty water and food bits floating around." She gags, and I reach for the sponge, welcoming the distraction from my thoughts.

I stick my hand into the water and a slimy chunk of what I hope is a vegetable gets stuck under my fingernail. "Now I get why Hunter asked everyone to scrape their plates yesterday."

"They invented dishwashers for a reason," she says.

We finish the dishes and join everyone by the fire. "I can't get over how gorgeous the stars are," I say.

Everyone murmurs in agreement, but no one speaks. I lean back in my chair and stare at the sky, but as massively impressive as it is, after a few minutes of gazing deep into the abyss, my fingers get twitchy. My phone's tucked in the pocket of my hoodie, and while I've tried not to be on it when everyone's hanging out, they seem to be deep in food coma.

I pull out my phone and text Sage.

Me: Neb would lose his mind here

She answers almost immediately.

Sage: I miss you!

Sage: he's really jealous of your trip

Sage: he's already talking about doing something like that after graduation

My heart pounds on her behalf. It's still fall, and while it's obvious to anyone who sees them that they're crazy for each other, they've only been dating a few months. Planning for next summer is about as commitment heavy as high school gets.

Me: I miss you too

Me: summer trip is a big deal

Sage: you could say that

Sage: speaking of big deals, how's Mr. I Can't Be Bothered with High Schoolers?

I haven't texted Sage since yesterday, so she has no idea that Hunter has turned out to be a decent guy. And that he goes to my dream school.

Me: there have been developments

Sage: did you kiss!?!?!?!!

I burst out laughing. Theo quirks a brow at me from across the fire, then Hunter's gaze finds mine and suddenly I'm imagining what it would be like to kiss him. If Sage was sitting across from me, she'd see right through my BS. But we're hundreds of miles away, so my secret is safe. For now.

> Me: NO. But I called him out for being a jerk
> and he apologized
> Sage: good for you. so now what?
> Me: I guess we're friends?
> Me: Because insta-love isn't a thing
> Sage: yeah yeah

I risk a glance at Hunter. Can he sense that we're talking about him? That I can't stop thinking about him? He seems lost in his thoughts, his face more relaxed than I've seen him. It's different from when he took his glasses off and seemed defenseless—right now he seems content.

The fire pops, shooting embers into the sky. The smoke curls upward until it mingles with the display far above us, and I'm struck again with this feeling of being small yet significant.

My show might be new, but it's touched people and has grown more quickly than I expected. Getting the offer from Auralacity to not only produce my show but to promote it as well proves that. They wouldn't offer to collaborate with just anyone and I know this is a huge opportunity.

If it's what I want.

And if it weren't for two little details in the contract saying Auralacity only features podcasts from the Pacific Northwest and that they would pair me with an experienced producer, I would already have agreed. Normally I'd have emailed them back right away to ask them to clarify, but I'm worried they'll change their minds if they think I'm being difficult. Accepting the offer would mean changing my dreams, and possibly Theo's as well—even though he doesn't know it yet—and I want to make one hundred percent sure I'm okay with this new plan. The trade-off for letting Theo down and cutting him out of the podcast is that the money would help at home. But taking a full course-load at a challenging school while putting together a podcast might be more than I can handle.

> Sage: are you hoping for something more?

I have to reread our last texts to remember she's talking about Hunter. Because she doesn't know about the offer either.

Me: it's stupid, right?

Sage: not if you like him.

Do I like him? I peek at him from the corner of my eye and catch him looking at me. My heart stutters. He's probably judging me for breaking the no phone rule.

But he lifts his phone from under his leg and tips it toward me, like a toast. Then he busts out The Smirk and my heart trips over itself again.

Me: all signs point to yes

Sage: if I remember the wise advice you gave me with Neb, give the guy a chance

Me: those don't sound like my words

Sage: okay I don't remember exactly what you said. But the point is, you're both there and you like him and it sounds like you have a lot of free time

She follows her text with a bunch of winking emojis and I hold in a laugh.

Me: oh, get this. He goes to Berkeley

Sage: WHUT

Me: I know. But I don't even know if he's interested

Me: It feels stupid to be thinking that far ahead

And if I accept the offer, I won't be able to go to Berkeley.

Sage: what would you say on your show if someone asked this advice?

My eyes roll skyward, and I'm struck again at the magnitude of the stars. They stretch as far as I can see and feel so close that I could reach out and touch them.

Me: you play dirty

Sage: 3 good things about having a brilliant best friend

Me: lol. I'd tell the person to keep an open mind. To give it a chance. That ruling out a chance

at happiness because of details like living in
ANOTHER STATE, while sounding practical, won't
make the heart happy. So they should let things
happen and not worry about the future.

"You writing a novel over there?" Theo asks.

"Yes."

Hunter laughs under his breath and my pulse goes haywire. This is bad. I can't deal with this uncertainty for the rest of the trip. I'm not ready to totally put myself out there, but maybe Theo can run reconnaissance. He lives for this kind of stuff.

Me: it might be time for Operation Middle School

Sage: I think I missed a step

Me: 3 good things about having a twin. I'm
sending Theo in

Sage: I'm glad you convinced yourself

Me: I need to be sure after last time

Making a move on Kit, while not the stupidest thing I've ever done, has had the longest lasting impact. Theo's assurance that things will eventually go back to normal doesn't help. And while Hunter does live hundreds of miles away, making an awkward rejection less risky because I won't have to see him every day in school, the moms are probably gonna want more family trips like this one. So I won't see him randomly in school, but we'll have to spend entire weeks together.

And then there's Berkeley. If I go. My girl-power female-pride rawr-ness immediately shuts down all thoughts about turning down the offer and going to Berkeley just because Hunter will be there. I refuse to chase a boy across state lines. When I decide, it needs to be because it's the right decision for my future.

Sage: I get that. So feel him out
(hahahaahahahahhhaha) and go from there

I snort, drawing everyone's attention.

"Would you like to share with the class?" Theo asks, brows raised.

"Absolutely not."

```
Me: Gotta go. thank you for your advice
Sage: I think you advised yourself
Me: well thanks for listening.
Sage: just promise to tell me what happens
Me: deal
```

I tuck my phone into my hoodie pocket and run through possible scenarios to figure out if Hunter is interested. Talking to him is the most obvious, but also the riskiest. Especially if I let my hormones take over and do something stupid like try to kiss him. Enlisting Theo could backfire because the boy can't keep a secret to save his life. He'd go in with the best intentions but would break under the slightest provocation—and something tells me Hunter would start asking questions that Theo would find too boring to bother deflecting. Which leaves Melody. She's smart and observant and could tell me a lot of what I'd like to know about Hunter, but she'd also see right through my questions.

My gaze drifts to the sky, but it holds no answers either. Maybe a change of scenery.

"I'll be back in a minute," I tell no one in particular.

Melody leans forward in her seat but hesitates before standing. "Do you want me to go with you?"

I smile. "Nah, I'll just be a minute. But save my seat, 'kay?"

As I make my way to the bathroom, my thoughts jump between the Hunter dilemma and the bigger, more important decision about my future. I'm self-aware enough to know that the fallout from Kit has me second-guessing myself, like I'm no longer capable of trusting my own instincts, and while Sage's point to follow the advice I would give on my show is valid, it doesn't make it any easier. I want something to happen with Hunter, even if it doesn't last past this week. I want my show to be successful. I've also always imagined myself going away to school, even if it would mean being apart from my brother for the first time in my life.

Because that's a factor in all this too. Theo can't deflect about what he wants to do forever, so I'll just have to turn on my podcast charm and force him to talk about it.

If I break this down into what I can control, Hunter is at the top of the list. I don't need to make a decision about school this week—although I need to soon—but Hunter is here now.

As I walk back to the campsite, I make a deal with myself. I'll amp up the flirting and see where it goes. If he's a jerk, I'll move on. Simple enough. But saying and doing are two different things. My resolve weakens as I round the bend to our firepit, then I freeze at the edge of the path.

Theo's in my chair, telling Melody a story that has her cracking up. He quirks his brow at me without pausing, like he knew what I wanted from him without me asking.

Now the only empty seat is next to Hunter. Who's looking at me.

No time like the present?

I push my shoulders back like that's going to give me courage and sink into the chair with one foot tucked under me so I'm angled toward him. Take a deep breath. And go for it.

"So what do you do for fun when you're not in class?" Okay, I never claimed I was *good* at flirting.

If he's surprised by the question, he doesn't show it. "I've got a heavy course-load because I'm planning to graduate in three years. So nothing too crazy." He pauses and I wait him out. "Go out for pizza, movies, that kind of thing. What about you?"

"My podcast takes a lot of my free time, but otherwise I mostly hang out with my best friend Sage. Although I don't see her quite as much now that she's got a boyfriend." He frowns, and I rush to defend her. "Not in a bad way. Neb's awesome. Not like her ex. They're awesome together and I'm super happy for her." Omigod shut up.

His frown turns into a baby smirk and maybe my rambling isn't as bad as I think. "You don't have a boyfriend?"

Okay, hello! This is the direction we need to go. I drag a finger along the armrest of my camp chair and shake my head. "Not right now." My heart thuds so loudly I'm sure he can hear it. The question I should ask in response is obvious but terrifying.

Either answer will change the rest of this trip because if he has a girlfriend, I'll be pining for him in misery, but if he doesn't, there'll be a giant *Will they or won't they?* hovering over us.

"What about you?"

The corner of his mouth quirks. "No boyfriend for me."

I'm such an ass. I assumed he was straight, even though I know better than to assume. Clearly I read too much into the casual touches and little looks he's been giving me. What I thought was flirting in the canoe must have been just friendly playfulness. Heat burns my cheeks and I open my mouth to apologize.

But he beats me to it. "I'm sorry, I shouldn't have said that." His eyes flick to the fire, then to my hand, which is gripping the side of my chair. "That was a bad joke."

Relief floods through me, followed immediately by irritation. Did he just make a gay joke? I look around to make sure Theo didn't hear and realize we're alone. When did everyone sneak off?

"I was playing off your words," Hunter says. "My friends and I do that. Curse of studying English, I suppose. I really didn't mean to say anything offensive." His words tumble out of him in a rush and my temper cools.

"I guess I did give you an open-ended question." My voice comes weaker than I intended and I lean back in my chair, putting distance between us. This proves why insta-love is a fantasy. You can't possibly know enough about a person when you first meet to develop actual feelings. By getting to know them first, any bigoted or racist tendencies will come out before you've committed.

"I don't have a girlfriend. I—I don't date."

Suddenly all his awkwardness makes sense. I lower my voice. "Are you aro?"

He shakes his head. "For as much as I love words, I really suck at communicating." He levels his gaze at me. "I like girls. I just, I'm really focused on school and have basically sworn off dating."

Relief rushes through me again, followed by disappointment, and I have a moment of mental whiplash. "Oh." This isn't as bad as when Kit gripped my shoulders and gently pushed me away, but I'm glad for the foot of space between our chairs.

He leans forward, elbows on his knees, and stares at the ground. "I'm really sorry. I feel like every time I talk to you, I screw things up somehow."

A flutter of hope stirs inside me. If he's worried about screwing things up, maybe he does like me, despite his no-dating rule. A spark goes off in my brain and I shift into Podcast Chick mode. "I get the whole not wanting to date thing. Graduating in three years is an impressive goal and I'm sure all the drama that comes with mingling with the opposite sex would be a distraction."

He laughs softly and turns his head to look at me. "I'm not opposed to mingling with the opposite sex." His inflection puts air quotes around my words. "One of my best friends at school is a girl."

I'm not sure we know each other well enough for my next question—in fact, I know we don't—but the darkness gives me the same confidence I feel in the studio when my guests call in. Even though I can see his face, I bulldoze forward. "Did someone burn you in the past?"

His gaze drops back to the ground. "No. I dated a few girls in high school. Nothing serious. I just really want to concentrate on school." He sounds like he's convincing himself more than me.

Something else has got to be going on. I mentally tick through a catalog of explanations, and they all come back to one thing: He's afraid. "When did your parents split up?"

His head whips toward me. "What?"

Bingo. I don't spend my weekends reading self-help books for nothing. I take a breath, keeping my face impassive. "I'm just wondering if maybe that's why you're against dating. I mean, aside from the school thing."

A breeze stirs the fire, sending embers dancing toward the heavens. He works his jaw but doesn't answer. He doesn't say anything.

My stomach tightens.

I pushed too far.

The embers dissolve into the stars, adding color to the already magnificent display.

And he still doesn't say anything.

"I'm sorry. You didn't ask me to analyze you and just because I do that on my show doesn't mean you need me busting into your head and telling you what I think."

He faces me again and I'm startled by the way his eyes shine in the firelight. "It's okay." His voice sounds like he swallowed gravel from the path. "It's not something I talk about. The divorce and…" He gestures at himself, at his heart.

"Your mom doesn't make you talk about it?"

He shakes his head.

"Man, that's all we talked about. For years. I think my mom was freaked that their divorce would cause some kind of permanent emotional damage." I realize too late that that's probably what Hunter's dealing with, so I switch gears to keep him from dwelling on it. "I started reading her therapy books around that time. They helped me understand that my parents' failed relationship was not a reflection on me or my future ability to have relationships." I take a chance and poke his elbow.

He glances where I touched him. "I hear what you're saying. And I'm not denying it makes sense. I just…" he trails off. He leans back in his chair and focuses on the sky. "They make you feel so small."

It takes me a moment to realize he means the stars.

"I like that they make me feel like I'm part of something bigger than myself."

"You're good at this." The compliment lingers between us, tangling in the smoke from the fire and wrapping around me.

I only allow myself a moment to savor it before deflecting. "At making people feel uncomfortable when they least expect it?"

He laughs through his nose. "At making people think."

I hear Sage's voice saying 'you know what else I'm good at,' but honestly, it's been so long since I've kissed a boy that it's quite possible I've forgotten how to do it. "I need to work on my timing though."

His hand trails along the edge of his armrest as if in invitation, but his gaze is still on the stars. Does he want me to touch him again? Is he even thinking about me like that? "Your timing for what?"

My heart pounds in my ears. I've forgotten what I said. "What?"

The Smirk is back. Then he reaches across the space between us and grazes my arm with his knuckles. The pressure is light, casual. Two layers of clothes keep our skin from touching but my body can't tell the difference. His hand continues down my arm until he touches my hand, just for a second, and everything inside me lights up. Heat sparks from the point where his pinkie touches the back of my hand and shooting straight to my belly. "I think your timing is perfect."

12
HUNTER

The next morning, I'm replaying that line in my head as I brush my teeth. *I think your timing is perfect?* What the hell does that even mean? It was an internal battle of epic proportions, fighting back the reflex that I can't be bothered with dating against the very clear fact that I'm interested in Naomi. Purposefully touching her—not disguising it as a casual bump or helping her out of the canoe—shifted things between us. At least it did for me. And now that I broke that barrier, I can't stop worrying that I'm going to plot twist myself into repeating my parents' mistakes.

If Naomi was confused by my randomness, she didn't let on. We chatted a little longer, mostly about our families, before the moms hollered for us to get some sleep since we're leaving early today.

The sun is still thinking about waking up and the fluorescent light in the bathroom buzzes overhead. The door flings open and a rumpled Theo shuffles in.

"This is vacation. Why are we up this early?"

I spit into the sink and wipe my mouth with the back of my hand. "I think the moms are working from the same playbook." The sports analogy feels awkward on my tongue. Where do these dad comments keep coming from?

Theo shakes his head as he starts brushing his teeth.

"Anyway, it's over an hour away, so we can sleep in the car."

Theo holds up his free hand for a high five. "My man!" Toothpaste dribbles out of his mouth, but he just laughs.

"See you back there." I slap his hand and pause before pushing the door open. My heart beats a steady rhythm at the thought of running into Naomi on the path. It was mildly awkward when we said goodnight, but in that blissfully exciting way when neither really wants to say goodbye. I shake my head. We'll be spending all day together. Seeing her right now shouldn't matter.

But it does.

A squirrel darts across the path as I step outside, the only movement in the quiet campground. The early morning air still holds the chill from overnight and hints of the sunrise dilute the stars. It's strange to think that they're above us all the time. Logically I know this, but it's easy to forget something that isn't right in your face.

Naomi's setting out bagels when I return to the campsite and gives me a sleepy smile. Her hair is tied up on top of her head and her oversized sweatshirt makes her look both adorable and a little sexy, if that's even possible. I'm filled with an urge to pull her into my arms, bury my face in those curls that surely still smell like vanilla and honey, and hold her close.

"Morning." My voice croaks but no one seems to care.

"Grab some breakfast," Mom says from near the car, pointing in the direction of the picnic table. She shoves a pile of towels into the backseat. "And please make sure your sister is up."

Nostalgia wraps around me the way I was just thinking of holding Naomi. When I still lived at home, waking Mel up was part of my morning routine. Some days I'd fling the door open and jump on the bed, and others I'd crouch on the floor and tickle her nose with a stuffed animal until she woke up. I didn't realize I missed that tiny part of my day until just now. I take a few steps toward the girls' yurt, then pause. "Is it cool if I go in there?"

Naomi opens a jar of peanut butter and dips a knife in. "What? Yeah, sure." She waves me toward the yurt, her attention on her bagel.

A table lamp casts shadows across the bare floor. Unlike my yurt, which somehow has clothes covering every square inch, theirs is tidy. Or at least contained. Naomi's jeans from last night are draped over the back of a chair, and I push away the creeper urge to touch them.

Focus, dude.

A Melody-shaped lump fills one of the upper bunks. Her dark hair peeks out of the top of her sleeping bag, and the lump rises and falls as she breathes.

The other bed—my heart races. The sleeping bag is flung open and a pair of pajama pants with yellow ducks rests on the pillow. This little detail strikes me in a way I don't expect. Like I'm seeing an intimate part of Naomi. Then the strap of a pink bra catches my eye and my body warms.

Relax. Girls wear bras. This is a completely normal thing and nothing to get excited about. Except it's Naomi's. And it's not a white cotton bra, it's got lace and maybe silk—it's impossible to tell in the low light and there's no way I'm picking up her bra to investigate—and my thoughts jump straight to imagining how it feels. How it would feel with her wearing it. With me taking it off.

"Hunt?" A voice as creaky as my own comes from the sleeping bag lump.

How long have I been standing in the middle of the room staring at a bra? "Hey, time to get up."

The top of her head pokes out, just enough for me to see her eyes. "Why do we have to get up so early on vacation?"

I cross my arms and do my best Mom impersonation. "Because we will have fun on this vacation if it kills us." Mom didn't actually say that, but it makes Mel smile.

"What's for breakfast?"

"Bagels. There's peanut butter and cream cheese, and probably strawberry jelly." My brain has latched onto the detail that Naomi likes peanut butter on hers.

"Okay, I'm getting up." But she doesn't move.

I take one big step toward her, my foot thumping on the ground, and hold my arms out to the side like a weightlifter. My voice lowers. "Don't make me carry you outta here!" I take another step and she squeals.

"No, no! I'm coming!"

The floor shakes with each step, but I keep stomping toward her. She sits up before I reach the bed and I jump so my feet are on the bottom bunk and I'm gripping the railing that keeps her from rolling out in her sleep.

She slaps at my hands—not hard enough to make me lose my grip, just enough to keep up the game—and dissolves into giggles. "I'm up! I'm up!"

I shake the railing back and forth and the entire bed groans.

Her eyes go wide. She stops laughing long enough to peer over the edge of the bed, and I use that opportunity to tickle her side. She laughs again and smacks my hand harder. "Okay, okay."

I hop off the bed and take a couple steps back just as Naomi comes inside.

"Everything okay in here?" Her eyes dart between us, then scan the room, landing on something behind me. Her cheeks flame and she hurries to her bed.

I turn enough to see her shove her bra inside her bag and hope my face isn't as red as hers.

"Hunt thinks he's hilarious," Mel says.

I stretch a hand toward her, and she squeals again. "Correction. I *am* hilarious."

Naomi pauses in the middle of the room. "Everyone's eating and the moms are getting antsy." She smiles. "Can I just say, I love how tight they are but they're so extra together. Shouldn't they be opposites, like yin and yang, so one balances the intensity in the other?"

I can't help but smile. Her brain fascinates me. "We'll be there in a sec."

She looks around the room, an odd expression on her face.

"Can you, um, excuse me for a minute? I'll make sure Mel gets her butt to breakfast."

I'm an idiot. Now I know my cheeks are red. "Sorry, yeah. This is your yurt after all."

"That's such a weird word," Mel says. "Yurt, yurt, yurt."

"It's like the more you say it, the less it sounds like a real word," says Naomi.

Mel giggles. "Sounds like an abbreviation for yogurt."

"Quit stalling," I say. My arms cross over my chest and I narrow my eyes until she finally climbs down the ladder at the end of the bunk.

"Ooh, is there yogurt?" Mel asks.

"I'll find out," I say. "Hurry up."

The door slams when I step outside, and I rub a hand over my face. Take a deep breath and exhale slowly. Because as much as I want to be content being friends with Naomi, I can't deny that I like her. In an *I want to drag her into my yurt*—that really is a weird word—*and kiss her senseless and maybe feel her bra* kind of way.

An hour later, we pile into Mom's SUV and I'm still thinking about Naomi. Mainly because she's sitting in the seat next to me, her bare legs crossed, one foot bouncing to whatever she's listening to on her headphones. Theo and Mel are in the back row sleeping, while the moms reminisce about the last conference they attended.

It's too early to text Darren, but I do anyway.

Me: on my way to see bison

My phone buzzes a few minutes later.

Darren: thought you were camping

Me: going to Antelope Island. To float where the buffalo roam

Darren: I'm no geographer, but I think bison are land creatures

Me: they drink water. Gotta come out sometime

Darren: more canoeing?

Me: kayaks today

Darren: you flip yet?

Darren's aware of my general lack of anything resembling athletic prowess, so it's a fair question.

Me: not technically a flip but I fell in

My gaze drifts to Naomi. That moment when we fell, when her body pressed against mine—there was definitely something there. I'm not sure who squeezed whose hand first, but there was squeezing.

Darren: kayaks are easier to flip dude

I groan out loud and Naomi raises a brow at me.

"My friend Darren's saying kayaks flip more easily than canoes."

Naomi pulls out an earbud. It tangles with her hair but she either doesn't notice or doesn't care.

My fingers twitch, wanting to tug it free, but I keep them to myself. Nothing good can come from these feelings for her, even if Darren insists he was joking about the no-dating pact.

"Kayaks are smaller so they're more responsive. So yeah, they flip easier, but they're easier to control, too."

The corner of my mouth lifts. "I thought you said you've never kayaked?"

"I haven't. But I excel at looking things up online." She nods at her phone, which has a picture of a lake on it. "For instance, did you know this lake is salt water?"

I lean closer to look at the picture. Hints of honey and vanilla do weird things to my brain. "And the question as to why it's called the Great Salt Lake is answered."

She swipes up on the image, revealing stunning pictures of bison grazing near salt flats. "Do you think we'll actually see any animals?"

"I hope so." As long as they're far away. And don't charge at us. "Do bison swim?"

A snort sounds in the back of her throat. "Can't say I ever thought about it." She holds up her phone and asks, "Do bison swim?" Instead of the mechanical voice answering her, small text appears on her screen. "American bison have varying swimming behaviors and abilities," she reads.

"That's helpful."

"Let's assume they do and not get too close. Deal?" Before I can react, she holds out her hand and we're shaking on it, like avoiding a two-thousand-pound creature with horns is something that needs to be agreed upon. Her skin is soft and warm and sends a jolt through my stomach and into my boring cotton underwear. We release our hands, and she goes back to scrolling on her phone, seeming unaffected from touching me.

Darren: I'm just teasing man. you'll totally rock the kayak

Me: rocking's what made us fall last time

Darren: us???????

I watch Naomi in my peripheral vision.

Me: not us-us. But yeah, the podcast girl

Darren: are there bikinis involved? Please say there's bikinis involved

Me: dude

Darren: I'm living vicariously

Me: yes, there's a bikini

I don't mention that there's also a tank top and purple shorts, albeit very short purple shorts, and that I haven't actually seen her in just her bikini. But she mentioned the salt water so maybe she's thinking about swimming. And not falling in swimming— actual swimming.

By the time we arrive at Antelope Park, I've shifted in my seat so my back is to Naomi, and not just because the view out the window is like something out of a sci-fi movie. Thinking about her in a bikini has led to other, less family-friendly thoughts and no one needs to see my hard-on this early in the morning.

The narrow strip of land we're driving across barely seems wide enough for a car, let alone a two-lane road, the still water on either side of us reflecting the early morning sky. Mountains jut into the sky directly in front of us, snow covering the tops even though it'll be in the 70s later today. The area is so desolate it's hard to believe we left a city ten minutes ago.

Maybe we made a wrong turn? The moms are so involved in their conversation it wouldn't be surprising if they accidentally brought us to an animal preserve or abandoned farm. The road curves with the bend in the bay and we stop next to a van with a trailer loaded with kayaks that's parked near the water.

"Does a windowless van seem sketchy to anyone else?" Naomi says.

"No one rents on the island, but we made arrangements with this company to meet us out here," Mom says.

We wait in the car while the moms sort out the rentals, and my body's back to normal by the time they return.

"We rented double kayaks, so figure out who's riding with who," Nancy says.

"I call Naomi!" Mel shouts from the backseat.

"I call Nancy!" Mom shouts just as loud, and we all laugh.

"Looks like you're stuck with me," Theo says. "I can't promise I'll paddle the whole time, but I do promise not to flip us on purpose."

"Works for me."

Twenty minutes later, a driver slash kayak expert walks us through how to paddle, which is basically the same as with canoeing except the paddle has a blade on each end, then loads us in the kayaks and we push off. The sun is still making its way across the sky, casting long shadows on the land surrounding the lake. A cluster of bison graze in the distance—a very far distance, thankfully—and white clouds dot the sky. The water is flat as glass, a mirror image of the clouds reflected in its surface. Each dip of my paddle sends tiny ripples shimmering outward from the kayak.

"This is really gorgeous," Theo says from the front of the kayak. "Makes having to exercise not so bad."

The other kayaks are nearby, but not close enough to easily talk. Naomi paddles with strong, confident strokes while Mel stares at the bison. The moms lead the way, already deep in conversation.

Utah requires everyone under eighteen to wear a life jacket, but those are now wedged around our feet. Because kayaks are smaller than canoes, our supplies are divided among the three kayaks. A soft cooler filled with snacks and water bottles is strapped on the back. If we do flip, more than just my pride is getting wet.

The lake doesn't have much of a current, so Theo's lazy strokes are plenty to keep us pointing in the same direction as the others. The serenity around us calms my senses and I'm grateful for the silence.

The moms lead us farther along the shore until we pass another group of bison and a small herd of deer. "There must be fresh water on the interior of the island," I say, not really expecting a response.

"The island has a bunch of springs," Theo says. "And bison only drink water once a day."

I'm glad he can't see me, because I'm sure my mouth hanging open would offend him.

He turns around to give me a head nod. "My sister isn't the only one who knows how to look things up online."

Now's my chance to ask about Naomi. But where do I start? I'm in college. I shouldn't have to resort to asking the brother of the girl I like about her.

"So tell me, what does Monday morning normally look like for you?" Theo asks, and my chance to ask about Naomi is swept away like the water beneath my paddle.

"It's what, around nine?" My schedule flips through my head. "Finishing up Bio 101."

"I thought you were an English major?"

"It's my minor, but you still have to take pre-reqs like science and math and history. Most people get those out of the way the first couple years, so you don't really get into the classes that have to do with your major until junior year. Sophomore year if you're lucky." The college deities blessed me with an advisor who got me into a three-hundred-level editing class, and I'm the only freshman.

"So you can buy yourself time if you don't know your major." There's a wistfulness to his voice that I haven't noticed before, and it strikes me that any time the conversation turns serious, Theo either changes the subject or falls silent. But right now, it seems like he wants to talk.

"Are you planning to go to college?"

He shrugs. "I don't know. It's what everyone does, right?" He rests his paddle across the kayak and watches the shoreline as we glide by. "If I don't go to college, what else am I supposed to do?"

Last year, when everyone was applying to colleges, my best friend asked the same question. Now he's somewhere in North Dakota learning to fly planes with the Air Force. Or learning the things he needs to learn before he can learn to fly planes. "Do you mean like the military?"

Theo twists around as far as he can in the small space and waves a hand at himself. "Do I look like I'm cut out for the military?"

"My friend Taylor didn't think he was either, but he's liking the Air Force so far."

A light seems to go off inside Theo. His body, his gaze, everything sinks a little lower, as if the kayak might open up so he can sink into the water. I know the feeling well, but it's jarring to see in this guy who, since the moment I met him, always seems to be on. "I can't join the military."

"Hey, no. I didn't mean to say you should." I rest my paddle across my lap and the water around us stills. "There are a lot of different things you can do. Just because I can't think of anything right now doesn't mean you don't have options." For me, college was always my path.

"I've been thinking about it for a year and I still don't have an answer." He turns back around and dips a paddle in the water, trailing it alongside the kayak. "I'll just go to college and hope I figure out what I want to do by the time I finish my pre-reqs."

"You don't have to have it all figured out right now." Suddenly the year difference in our ages feels like much more. I'm only eighteen, but I feel like my window of time to 'figure things out' has slammed shut and if I make the wrong decision, I'll pay for it for the rest of my life.

"I didn't mean to get so heavy," Theo says. "But all this quiet makes it impossible not to think."

"I know what you mean."

"So what are you trying to figure out?"

"Your sister." Omigod, I didn't mean to say that out loud.

Theo barks out a laugh, a sharp noise that echoes off the water. "She does have a way of getting under your skin."

I'm grateful he doesn't turn around because I'm beyond embarrassed. Straight-up mortified. Their twin-ESP thing is probably already firing off and she'll know what I'm thinking in a matter of minutes.

Would that really be so bad?

"I didn't mean to say that." But maybe a little honesty isn't all bad. I'm not ready to get into the whole do-I-or-don't-I-transfer thing, and Theo could actually help with the Naomi situation.

"I won't say anything if you don't want me to, but I can be quite the matchmaker."

"I don't even—I don't date."

"Who said anything about dating?"

My grip on my paddle tightens and I pull it through the water. "This feels inappropriate. We're talking about your sister."

"Relax, dude. I said I'm a matchmaker, not a pimp."

His bluntness elicits a laugh from me.

"I'll just say that if you've thought about moving beyond just friends, you wouldn't be alone."

It takes me a moment to pick through his meaning, then a slow smile spreads across my face.

"Cut yourself some slack," Theo says. "You've got that sexy geek thing going for you." He pretends to lift a pair of eyeglasses, and I touch mine. "Girls dig that. Especially girls I'm related to."

His words act like a balm. It's like he injected his confidence into them and now they're telling me that allowing myself to like Naomi, to consider trying something with her, is not only feasible, it's a good idea.

"Good to know."

He laughs softly and picks up his paddle. "We should probably catch up to them."

The other kayaks are so far ahead I can barely tell who's in which kayak. We paddle steadily until we're within shouting distance. Mel points at the shore where there's a sandy beach, a covered picnic area, and an outhouse. It seems early for a bathroom break but being outnumbered by women has taught me to never question the frequency with which they need to go to the bathroom. Plus, as Theo pointed out, the world is our urinal so it's a little easier for us.

A group of college-aged kids stands in a circle on the shore, koozie-wrapped drinks in hand. Their kayaks rest in the rough grass farther inland, paddles strewn every which way. They seem my age but the guys apparently got the genes that broadened their shoulders and chests so they look like men, and the girls fill out their bikinis in ways that I thought only existed in movies. They laugh and bump fists and do all the normal things you do with friends, but watching it from the outside, it feels like they're part of something I'll never understand.

The sliver of confidence I felt being slightly older than Theo and Naomi evaporates. I can't compete with these guys.

"Now we're talking," Theo says.

"I guess the girls are cute," I say.

"They're like the After picture in a gym ad."

"I guess if you're into that sort of thing."

"I'm into pretty people. And those are pretty people." He pulls a hard stroke and the kayak spins. I've been overaccommodating for his lack of paddling and his sudden assistance catches me off guard. I straighten us out and we speed toward the shore.

A cluster of bison graze several hundred yards beyond the rest area, clearly unconcerned with the humans encroaching on their space. One lifts its mammoth head when the moms' kayak touches the shore, then goes back to chewing. Mel and Naomi glide onto the shore next.

"Paddle hard!" I say, steering us toward the open beach to the right of the girls. But Theo paddles on the right, sending us into their kayak. A hollow thunk announces the collision for everyone on the beach, and Naomi's yelp causes several of them to laugh.

"Hunt! What are you doing?" Mel yells, making them laugh even harder.

"These things have a mind of their own," Theo says. He jumps out of the kayak, landing in water up to his waist, and pulls us the rest of the way to shore. But he doesn't stop there. He keeps pulling until the entire boat is on dry land. It's the most energy I've seen him expel since we've met.

I grab the sides of the kayak and step onto the hard-packed sand. "You're quite agile for a guy who hates exercise."

He nods in the direction of the college kids. "Having an audience makes all the difference in the world." Several of the girls watch us over their drinks, but the guys pointedly ignore us.

"You wanna help us too?" Naomi asks.

Theo gives a deep bow, which sends Mel into a fit of giggles, then drags them onto shore next to us. "Now if you'll excuse me, I must make the acquaintance of a particularly beautiful blonde just over yonder." He wipes his hands on his wet shorts and saunters right up to them. They laugh at something he says, and before I can unstrap the cooler, a blonde in a lime green bikini touches his arm.

"Welcome to the full Theo show," Naomi says, holding out her hand for the cooler. Our hands brush in the transfer and the college kids no longer matter. Let them drink and laugh and make fun of me for crashing into another kayak. I don't care.

Naomi rests the strap of the cooler on her shoulder and rubs the spot where our hands touched. "You thirsty?"

My eyes go wide. "Excuse me?"

She taps the cooler, then her mouth falls open. "Oh wow, sorry. Yeah, wasn't thinking that way. Please just ignore me."

As if that were possible.

Laughter from the group draws our attention, and Mel grabs my arm. "I'm going over with Theo."

The moms are still near the bathrooms, so I step in. "I don't think that's a good idea. They're drinking." *And you've been acting differently since we arrived, and I no longer know what to expect from you.*

She rolls her eyes, something she used to only do to Mom. "Well, *I'm* not going to drink. I'm just gonna say hi." She prances off without another word and Naomi and I are left alone.

"Should we claim a picnic table?" she asks. A few empty tables sit scattered between the outhouse and what is quickly becoming a party.

Theo tousles Mel's head and his approval of her somehow acts as validation for the rest of the group. They high-five and fist bump and share smiles all around. How do some people instinctively know how to step into a group of strangers and immediately get along? It hurts that my sister is better at it than I am—something she got from the father she barely remembers. He's never met a crowd he can't wrap around his finger.

"Um, sure." I head for middle ground, not too close to the outhouses and out of earshot from the party, but I can't stop watching them. One of the guys slings an arm around Mel's shoulders, dwarfing her small frame against his obscenely muscled one, and I freeze.

Naomi rests a hand on my back and nudges me forward. "Theo's not gonna let anything happen to her. He may seem like a flake, but his protective brother genes are strong."

I try to focus on her touch and not the pulses of anger and nerves battling inside me. "Mom'll freak if she sees that." Mel's smiling up at the guy like he's an Adonis dropped in her lap. It's not like I want to physically drag Mel away from them, but nothing good will come from her hanging out with drunk college kids.

The guy in question drops his arm just as the outhouse door slams. *So he does have survival instincts.* He must sense my glare because we lock eyes as the moms walk toward us. My protective brother gene, as Naomi called it, fires on all cylinders and I swear flames shoot out of my head. But instead of mouthing an apology, the guy smirks.

He actually smirks.

Then he shifts his focus next to me. To Naomi. Strokes a hand over his bare chest. "Hey, darlin'!" he calls. "Why don't you ditch that loser and come find a real man?"

— **13** —

NAOMI

There are moments in life when the next words you speak can make or break an entire situation. Say the right thing and the day and your life sail along the way you hoped, but fumble the execution and everything is ruined. Or worse, say nothing, and everyone involved dies a slow, agonizing death, wishing you'd said anything, anything at all.

I rest a hand on Hunter's arm. He startles at the contact but doesn't shift his gaze from the dude-bros. "Yeah, I'm good," I shout back. "But thanks."

Not my best comeback, but Hunter's shoulders relax and he exhales. My hand's still on his forearm and before I can stop it, my finger traces the muscle running from his elbow to his wrist.

His eyes meet mine and my hand falls to the table.

"Mel's too smart for them," I say.

"And Theo?" he asks.

"Theo's in his element." Several more beats pass, and I grab my phone to stop myself from reaching for him. I scroll through my notifications and my heart stops at a new email from Auralacity.

"Re: Contract"

Hunter's staring at the lake and doesn't notice that I'm not breathing.

My fingers shake as I tap on the message.

Dear Ms. McGinnis,

We hope you've had enough time to review the contract and have made a decision. We're working on our schedule for the next quarter and need your signed contract by end of the day Thursday. I apologize for the shortened time frame but trust that's enough time.

Go in good sound,

Tyson

The edges of my vision go dark and for a second I think I might actually pass out. This is real. And if I'm not careful I'm going to screw it up. Mom's always getting on me about replying to emails, and this proves she's probably right. Because while I've thought of little else since getting the first email from Auralacity, signing the contract will be the biggest decision I've ever made and the longer I dwell on it, the bigger it feels.

And now they need a decision in two days.

"What was all that about?" I jump as Margo swings her legs over the bench on the other side of the table, a quizzical expression on her face. "And why is my twelve-year-old daughter surrounded by a group of…" She peers over her sunglasses as the group starts jumping in a circle. "Half-naked swimsuit models?"

I force a laugh, my brain still on the email, and tuck my phone in my pocket. Hunter doesn't seem to notice my change in mood. He's still glaring at the guys, his fist clenching and unclenching on the table.

"Melody, sweetie, come eat," Margo calls.

The wall of half-naked swimsuit models—she wasn't wrong in that description—parts and Melody skips toward us.

"Bye, guys!" She waves over her shoulder, then stops and faces them again, hands on her hips. "Theo! Come on!" Confidence oozes from her. Most kids would be intimidated around a group like that, but it doesn't faze her.

Theo quickly follows, his huge grin telling me he got at least one phone number. What he does with them I'll never understand, but the excitement for him is the chase.

He links his arm through hers and the two of them laugh as they walk toward us.

Part of me wants to talk to Mom, but she looks so relaxed I don't want to add to her stress. "And who are your new friends?" I ask Melody, shaking off the email. Theo's hyper-sensitive to my emotions and I still haven't figured out how to tell him about the offer. And what it could mean. A couple girls are still watching Theo, and the dude-bro who catcalled me catches me looking and winks. My eyes roll and I shift my body so I can't see them.

"They go to Arizona State," Theo says.

"That explains the tans," Mom says.

"And they're cheerleaders!" Melody crisscrosses her arms over her chest then punches them in the sky. "Even the guys!"

"That explains the six-packs," Margo says, and both moms giggle.

Theo fake gags. "Omigod, no ogling guys young enough to be your son! Or at least no sharing your thoughts about them."

Mom reaches behind her to swat Theo's arm while Hunter casually glances over at the group. It's impossible to tell what he's thinking, but his shoulders don't tense up, so maybe cheerleaders are less threatening than however he'd mentally categorized them. Cheerleaders can still be obnoxious dicks, as the one dude-bro already proved, but you can't be all bad when you're overflowing with team spirit.

"We're not ogling," Mom says.

Margo giggles again. "We're simply admiring the scenery."

"And the wild animals." Mom snorts, and Hunter smirks at me.

"Yes, that's where I get it from."

"Your taste in men?" Mom asks.

"No! God! I don't even want to think about that." Hunter's smile fades and something tenuous between us starts to slip. "Those guys are definitely not my type." Big muscles might be nice to look at, and probably feel amazing, but that's not what does it for me. "Who wants to be with someone who spends that much time worrying about their appearance?"

Theo raises his hand. Melody puts hers partway in the air, watching Theo for his reaction, as the moms raise theirs.

"You all are hopeless," I say.

Hunter unzips the cooler, sets water bottles and granola bars on the center of the table, and watches Melody for a moment. If he's concerned, it doesn't seem like he's going to say anything right now. Mom pulls out a bag of apples and a jar of nuts, and everyone digs in while my mind swirls. Partnering with Auralacity could mean I'd see actual income while still in college. I didn't start a podcast to make money, but if I can make a career out of this, it'd be stupid to turn them down.

Even if it does mean saying goodbye to Berkeley.

What better place to clear my head than here?

I finally look beyond the college kids to the scenery around us. The ground near the shoreline is flat, but beyond the clearing where we're sitting it quickly rises to snow-covered mountains. Birds glide on a breeze high above us, their calls piercing the relative silence, and a herd of bison graze on a plateau in the distance. I thought I'd be freaked out to be this close to animals the size of my car, but they seem more interested in eating lunch than what we're doing. The sun is almost directly over us and it's warm enough that I'm considering ditching my tank top, but this increased awareness of Hunter has me overthinking everything. One part of me wants to flirt, to show a little skin to see what happens, but the other part worries it'll just look desperate.

I try to telepathically ask Theo what to do. When he meets my gaze, he waggles his brows and his lips twitch in a subtle gesture toward Hunter. He can't possibly know what I'm asking but I can hear his answer in my head. *"Take off your shirt!"*

Margo shifts on the bench so she's straddling it. She said in her email answers that she's highly motivated and can come off as intense, and that was not an exaggeration. Energy seems to ripple off her as she scans the horizon and she looks ready for the next adventure.

"What's up, Mom?" Hunter asks.

She drums her fingers on the table. "I know we tell you you're supposed to wait half an hour after eating before swimming, but I need to be in that water now."

"The half hour thing is a myth," Theo says. "Besides the extra salination will help us float." Our mouths drop in unison, and he presses a hand to his chest. "What? I know things."

"Then let's go," Margo says, then pauses before looking at Melody and Hunter. "If you feel a cramp, stay where you can touch the bottom."

"Yes, Mom," they both reply.

Margo stands, and without another word, shimmies out of her shorts, tosses her T-shirt on the bench, and heads for the water. Melody and Mom hurry after her, discarding clothes as they go.

Theo yanks his shirt over his head and races for the water. "Last one in is a salty egg!" He passes the rest of them and leaps into the water, stretching out his body so he has maximum contact, therefore creating the maximum splash.

And now Hunter and I are alone.

When everyone else was sitting at the table, the distance between us felt normal. But now that it's just the two of us it suddenly feels intimate. My heartbeat picks up at his closeness. Our thighs are barely a hand's-width apart and our arms rest near each other on the table.

Melody squeals but neither of us turn away. It's not that we're looking at each other, but we're not *not* looking at each other. He seems focused on the small gap between our elbows while I'm entranced by the way his fingers trace the grooves of the picnic table. Back and forth, back and forth. If I let myself, I can almost imagine what that would feel like on my arm or cheek or throat. I take a quick breath, grateful for the distraction from my thoughts, and exhale quietly through my nose.

"What were you and Mel talking about?" he asks.

The question startles me out of the moment, and my head snaps up. "I don't think it's my place to say."

"Should I be concerned?" His voice is soft, like he's afraid to hear the answer but can't bear not knowing.

"I don't know yet. But keep doing the big brother thing." Our eyes meet and it strikes me that we're both struggling with sibling issues. "Melody clearly adores you so just let her know you're there for her."

"What if that's not enough?"

I don't know how to answer, and the silence drags out. After several minutes, we speak at the same time.

"Do you feel like swimming?"

"Do you want to join them?"

"Sorry." Again in unison.

"Yes," I say.

His pinkie twitches, and I'm filled with the urge to reach for his hand, to pull him closer on the bench while the others are distracted in the water.

The others.

Someone's surely watching us.

I glance at the water and sure enough, Theo gives me a thumbs-up while floating on his back. "What are you waiting for?" he shouts.

If my brother can slide a double meaning into a statement, he will. So I know he's not just telling me to get in the water, he's pushing me to make the first move. But I tried that before and I'm not ready to face that kind of rejection again. Especially since we have three more days of vacation.

Hunter looks at me, head cocked. A hint of a smile plays on his lips and wow, I really need to know what it feels like to kiss him. But not here.

"Let's go." I push to my feet, letting my side brush against him as I climb over the bench, and am faced with another dilemma: there is no good way to take off my clothes without it feeling like a striptease. I can't ask him to turn around because he's going to see me in my bathing suit in two seconds anyway, but I cannot gracefully pull my shirt over my head without risking my top riding up.

In one motion, Hunter stands and pulls his shirt over his head, the same way he did the day before while canoeing, and sets his glasses and shirt on the table. We're less than a foot apart and when he smiles at me, I'm dumbstruck. My pulse is practically pounding out of my chest. His hair sticks out a bit on one side and he looks defenseless without his glasses. My gaze skims over his chest and my mouth goes dry. My tongue wets my bottom lip, which draws his attention, and he inhales a shaky breath.

"I-I guess I should take off my clothes, huh?"

His eyes widen for a beat and the sun feels extra hot on my neck. "Yeah." His voice comes out a whisper, rougher than it was a moment ago.

My mind flashes to us waking up in a dorm room, limbs tangled together, this same expression on his face as he leans closer to kiss me.

I clear my throat, shaking the image from my head. Take a step back. If I take the offer, that fantasy will never come true.

My shorts slide down my legs easily and join his shirt on the table. He has the politeness to turn away when I reach for the hem of my shirt. Even though he's not watching, there's still the group of guys near the water that would probably love a free show, so I lift my shirt slowly, careful to keep my bikini top in place.

Hunter inhales sharply.

Okay, maybe he is watching.

I press one hand over my boobs and yank my shirt with the other, checking to make sure everything stayed in place. My fingertips smooth the edge of the material when Hunter turns to face me. To his credit, his eyes never dip to my chest, but he looks uncomfortable. Like really, really uncomfortable. I toss my shirt on the table and hope my shaky smile disguises the nerves that are suddenly racing through me.

"Ready?"

If I knew him better, I'd link my arm through his and drag him toward the lake, but we're in this weird in-between stage and the tension between us makes me keep my arms to myself.

He blinks a couple times before nodding.

The lake is a couple hundred feet away, but it feels like we're crossing the Great Plains. Theo gives me a pointed look, followed by an open-mouthed smile, and fortunately Hunter doesn't notice because he's staring at the ground, looking miserable.

"You okay?" I ask.

His head pops up. "What? Yeah."

"It's just…" I'm a toucher. My instincts tell me to reach out to him, but I get the feeling he might leap out of his skin if I do. "You seem tense."

"Oh." He runs a hand through his hair as he lets out a breath, and a little of the tension seems to ease out of him. "Good thing we're staying in a yurt."

"What?"

He tilts his head. "My mind was someplace else."

He wasn't fighting the urge to ogle me. He was thinking of something else entirely. My mouth ticks into a frown but before he can see, I rush ahead of him and spread my arms out wide. "How can you think of anything else when you're in a place this gorgeous?"

This time I catch his gaze flick over me, a quick up and down, before he meets my eyes. I spin in a circle, stopping to face the water. Melody's underwater near Theo with her feet sticking in the air and the moms are floating on their backs, their hands fluttering like little motors, pushing them away from us.

I continue to the water's edge without looking back and vow to enjoy the rest of the day without worrying about the offer or tormenting myself over that stone wall of a boy. He's impossible to read, and just when I think I understand him, he busts out a dad joke. When my toes hit the water, I adjust my ponytail so my hair's piled on top of my head and keep wading in. Just as my knees get wet, Hunter splashes into the water, runs past me, and dives into the shallow water.

He surfaces with a shake of his head next to Theo. They do a dude-bro high five before turning back to me. "Are you coming?" Hunter asks.

He has two personalities. That's the only explanation.

Hunter's crouched so only his head and shoulders are above the water. I take a step closer, and The Smirk hits me with full force. Combined with his wet hair, which is plastered to his forehead in a swoop that most guys can't accomplish even on a good hair day, he's switched from a nervous boy to someone who could rival the cheerleaders.

When the water reaches my hips, I sink lower until my knees hit the sandy bottom. The water's like nothing I've ever experienced, even in the ocean. The article I read about this lake said the salt levels are ridiculously high, which explains why it feels like I have to fight to keep my arms at my sides.

"Let yourself float," Theo says. His head's laid back in the water, his eyes closed against the bright sun. He opens one eye to look at me. "Your hair will be okay."

My hand touches my hair automatically. A few curls hang near my throat but it'll survive a little salt water. I lean back, ready to catch myself on the bottom, but it's almost like I'm wearing a life jacket. My body bobs once, twice, then levels out on the surface.

Hunter follows suit, but like a typical boy, he just lets himself fall into the water. Once he's floating, he finds my eyes and gives me another smile.

Someone should really teach him how to control that thing.

The world goes quiet when my ears dip below the surface. The blue sky stretches forever and the feeling I described to Hunter comes back. Where I feel tiny and insignificant, but part of something so much bigger than myself.

Drops of water land on my face and I close my eyes. The silly boys will not ruin this moment for me. Then I'm full-on splashed. My legs flail as I find the ground and I come face-to-face with Melody.

"Hey," she says. Her smile tells me she's the culprit, not Theo or Hunter, who are still floating nearby.

"Have you ever done anything like this?" I ask. I'm realizing how little I know about their family. Do they go on trips, or is this the first time she's been beyond their town? Margo obviously travels since that's how she and Mom met, but that doesn't mean she brings her kids along.

Melody trails her fingers in the water. Ripples shimmer on the surface, breaking up the reflection of the sky. "Not like this. We did a week-long camping trip last summer, but Mom rented a motorhome." Her fingers trace a pattern over and over, then she lowers herself to her shoulders. "I was excited to stay in a tent."

"It's fun, but there are downsides too. You're more likely to get wet if it rains, and bugs get in, and you can hear animals rustling around outside."

Her eyes grow wide. "I don't do wild animals. I put that in my questions for a reason."

I laugh. "I'm right there with you." I hold out my fist and she bumps it, but skips the explosion flourish at the end. "Here's to not getting attacked."

Her gaze drifts back to the bison in the distance. "They're gonna stay there, right?"

From behind Melody, Hunter flips to his stomach and inches toward us. He holds a finger to his lips, so I quickly look back at her.

"They don't drink salt water, so we should be good."

Hunter glides through the water, his shoulders flexing as he pushes himself toward us.

"Good, 'cause this is pretty and everything but I'd rather watch nature from a deck. I don't need anything that lives outside coming near me."

Hunter's head lowers until he's fully submerged. I fight a smile, but Melody's still watching the bison. A tiny part of me feels guilty for not warning her, but I also really like the feeling of being in on something with Hunter. Even if it's just a playful prank.

Before I can respond, a blood-curdling scream rips from Melody's mouth. She thrashes at the water, then her entire body flips sideways and she goes under. Hunter bursts above the surface, her ankle in his hand. The phrase prouder than a peacock pops into my head, and I burst out laughing.

"You're going to drown her."

"Nah, she's fine."

Melody swings her arms at him, her momentum lifting her head out of the water. She takes a deep breath and reaches for her ankle. "Hunter omigod let go of me!" Then with a splash, she sinks under again.

He releases her leg, and in seconds she lunges out of the water at him. He catches her against his chest, and with another smirk at me, falls backward, taking her into the water with him. Another screech ricochets through the air.

"I'm glad you never attack me like that," Theo says from behind me, startling me. Hunter and Melody continue to wrestle in the water, splashing both of us.

"Only because we've always been the same size. But I've considered it."

He pushes out his lower lip in a pout as they both emerge panting.

"You know I love you," I say.

Hunter's head cocks to the side, and Melody takes advantage of his distraction to splash him again. He lunges for her, grabbing her around the waist.

"Throw me!" she says, and in a flash, he crouches low before launching her into the air. She lands several feet away with a huge splash, and he swims toward her, singing.

"Melody, Melody, sing me a Melody."

Her smile nearly swallows her face. "Omigod stahhhhp." She swats at his shoulder but clearly loves the attention. He swims circles around her, singing the line over and over until she splashes him again.

Theo moves closer to my side. "Twin Trust moment."

My eyes widen. "What's up?"

"He totally likes you," he whispers.

I splash him in the face. "He does not. And would you stop abusing the Twin Trust?"

"The handbook clearly states that use of Twin Trust is at the users' discretion."

"Twin Trust is meant for serious things, like whatever's going on with Mom." My breath catches. This is the perfect chance to bring up our future. "Or what we're doing after graduation."

He pumps his fists and whispers, "Insta-love, insta-love," blatantly ignoring my attempt at a serious conversation.

I mask my disappointment with a smile, while my heart clenches at the thought of Hunter having actual feelings for me. "No one insta-loves anyone." I give Theo my Mom Look, the one that usually accompanies my Mom Voice. "How can you possibly know that?"

"He told me." He laughs to himself. "I don't think he meant to. He kind of blurted it out, but yeah."

"How does one blurt out that they like someone else?"

"I don't know. Dude seems pretty wound up." He bumps his knee against my leg. "Maybe you can help him with that."

"Omigod, Theo." I push his face until he's underwater and move away from him.

And closer to Hunter and Melody.

Affection stirs deep inside me. It's only been a couple days since we met, but I care for them. Want them to be happy. And despite what Theo says, it's not insta-love. It's because Mom and Margo are so close, which is like an auto-approval of the rest of the family. Either way, I don't want this connection to end with this trip.

Now I just need to figure out how to make that happen.

—ᗯᗯ— 14 —ᗯᗯ—

HUNTER

The car stops, jerking me from a dream. We were back in the water at Antelope Island, but instead of wrestling with Mel in the water, Naomi was the one in my arms.

The same Naomi who's now looking at me with a mix of amusement and apprehension on her face. "Have a nice nap?"

You have no idea. "Yeah." I lean forward, grateful for the towel in my lap because otherwise she'd be less amused and more horrified.

Mel and Theo are both passed out in the backseat, and the front seats are empty.

"Where are we?"

"Just outside the campground. The moms are grabbing a treat for tonight."

"In-treating," I say, and immediately regret it. Why why why with the dad jokes? Even Dad doesn't tell jokes this bad.

Her brows raise. "That was bad."

"I know. I'm sorry. I don't know where they come from."

"It's endearing." Her gaze drops to her lap, the smile going with it. "My dad was big on jokes like that. He said it was a requirement to get through the day with twins."

The shift in emotions catches me off guard. "He's not anymore?"

"We don't really hear from him much. Mom got full custody and we see him on random holidays and all that, but it's not the same, you know?"

I nod. I know exactly what she means. And ever since she brought up that their divorce might be why I'm anti-relationship, I can't help but wonder if she's right. That it's more than not wanting to repeat their mistakes. If being dedicated to school and my future are just an excuse, when really I'm afraid of putting myself out there for another person since I've seen firsthand what it's done to Mom and Dad.

Naomi sighs. "Now when we're together it's like he's trying to cram in all the things he's missed and we never get to that level of just hanging out and being silly."

I toss the towel on the floor, the need for it gone. "It was kind of the same with us. He was gone for work a lot the last couple years and I was twelve when he left for good. Mel barely remembers a time when it wasn't just the three of us."

"Hello, formative years." Her smile is gentle, like she's not sure if she should tease, but I appreciate her attempt to lighten the mood.

I glance in the backseat. With her eyes closed, Mel looks like the little sister who waved goodbye when they dropped me off at Berkeley and I'm gripped by a determination to help her with whatever's going on.

"Yeah. It wasn't the best. But we got through it. Mom needed help with Mel, and I became the man of the house. Mom worries she forced me to grow up too fast, that I forgot how to have fun, but I don't think that's true." My heart pounds at the admission. I've never said this to Darren or Shawna, and certainly not to my friends back home. But Naomi doesn't judge me, she listens. Her head nods as I talk and her eyes implore me to continue. "I'm beginning to understand why you're so good with your guests."

She straightens, a smile lifting the corner of her mouth. "Is that a compliment?"

My head drops into my hand and I push my hair back. Why was I such a dick to her? She's the most genuine, caring person I've met in a really long time. "It's true."

"Well, you're not as bad as I thought you were either."

Theo laughs from the backseat, followed by Mel. "I told you that you were being a butt!" she says.

My cheeks heat and I hold out my hands. "Okay, okay. I'm sorry."

"We much prefer this side of you," Theo says. Naomi gives him a sharp look and my pulse kicks up. We?

Just then, the trunk flings open, ending the conversation. "We've got cake!" Mom shouts into the back of the SUV.

Mel claps. "But why?"

"For my mom's birthday," Naomi says. "It's not for another couple weeks, but they want to celebrate tonight."

The moms climb into the front seats and as we pull onto the road, I settle against my seat. Interesting things can happen at a party, even if it's just the six of us sitting around the fire like the previous nights. The darkness encourages sharing secrets, and the festive atmosphere lowers inhibitions. People think it's just alcohol that does that, but a shared proximity, especially over several days, can create a level of trust that you don't get seeing someone in class once a day.

And I think I'm ready to see where that proximity leads.

Back at the campsite, after we've showered and finished dinner and the stars emerge for their nightly show, Mom lights two candles on a small cake and begins singing.

"Happy birthday to you." Her voice is strong and confident. Not at all embarrassed to be singing by herself.

We join in for the rest. Theo and Naomi yell Mom while the rest of us say Nancy, so her name comes out a mangled Mom-cy. Naomi's singing voice is huskier than I expected, and the vibrations in her throat grip my chest.

Mom hands out slices of cake and Theo moans. "Who needs sex when you've got double chocolate?"

I choke on my cake, and I'm not the only one. His comment sends Mom into a coughing fit, while Mel bursts out laughing. Nancy gasps and throws a napkin at him. But Naomi just rolls her eyes before shrugging at me as if to say, "you see what I mean?"

Mom takes a drink and then raises her cup to him. "Theo, I agree."

This time Mel and I groan. "No!" I wave my hands in front of my face. "This conversation stops now."

Theo settles back into his chair and smiles at the bite of cake on his fork. "Don't listen to them," he says. "You're living your best life."

Naomi points her fork at Nancy. "You did this."

"Yeah, by having sex," Theo whispers. Then he faces Naomi. "Three Good Things about having cake instead of sex."

"You're serious." She stiffens and I swear she says something to him in twin-speak, because he shrugs.

"I'll go first," he says. "Cake stays on your hips longer than someone's hands."

Nancy shakes her head. "I'm sorry," she whispers to Mom.

"I love this," she whispers back.

"You realize this is not how Three Good Things works," Naomi says.

Theo leans toward her and gives her a shit-eating grin. "The rules are fluid, and you know it."

"Fine," she says. "If cake doesn't text you the next day, you don't care because you can make more cake."

"Valid point," Mom says.

"And number three," Theo says. "Cake tastes good when you swa—"

"Theo!" Everyone except Mel yells at him to stop.

He jumps in his seat, nearly dropping his cake in his lap. "What? Cake tastes good when you—"

"Theo, I beg you," Naomi says.

"Swallow it with milk," he says. The grin on his face suggests he's loving this.

"I told you," Naomi mouths at me. "No boundaries."

I should be uncomfortable with the way the conversation has turned. Theo gives the impression that he's experienced sexually, but I can't tell with Naomi. If this continues, my only contribution will be stories about a clan of warrior cats and how they defeated a rival gang. But I don't care. Naomi and Theo—and their mom—don't seem to have a judgmental bone in their bodies.

Naomi's still watching me, waiting for a reaction, so I smile.

That must be the right thing to do because she lowers her gaze, then looks up at me through her lashes.

This is flirting, right?

After another round of cake, the moms gather our plates and say goodnight.

"Already?" Mel asks. "I don't have to go to bed yet, right?"

"We're not going to sleep," Mom says. "We're heading inside for adult time so you all can chillax without us."

Mel groans. "Mom, no one says that anymore."

"But keep it PG-13." Nancy points at Theo.

He bows in his seat. "I will be the perfect gentleman," he says, with extra emphasis on the I. He winks at me and I'm not quite sure what to make of it.

My head falls back against my chair and once again the stars amaze me. In school we studied astronomy and saw pictures of the Milky Way and the galaxies beyond it, but seeing it in person, when the stars seem close enough to reach out and touch, is unreal.

"It's crazy, right?" Naomi asks.

I lift my head to look at her, and she juts her chin at the sky.

"Like I knew that was up there, but I had no idea it was so big," she says.

"That's what she said," Theo whispers.

"Don't you have a cake to swallow?"

He props his feet on one of the empty chairs. "Nope, I'm good."

She looks back at me and something in her expression makes my stomach tighten. "Would you..." she stops. Takes a breath. Darts a glance at Theo, who nods, then back at me. "Would you want to go for a walk?"

Everything inside me bolts to attention. Yes, I would like that very much. But is there a discrete way for us to leave Mel and Theo? Or does it even matter? Theo's suddenly interested in his phone, and Naomi's chewing on her lip like she's unsure she should have asked. I've never likened myself to the hero from a novel, but the courage Rusty shows in *Into the Wild* when he ventures into the woods to join Shadowclan and becomes Firepaw fills me with an uncontrollable urge to sweep Naomi into my arms and carry her away where we can be alone.

Instead, my brain spits out the word "Now?"

She blinks several times. Looks around the fire. "I guess not?"

I push out of my chair and smile down at her. Start to hold out my hand, tuck it in my pocket, then yank it out again. "That came out wrong." My hand extends toward her on its own. "Yes, let's go for a walk."

Her teeth release her lip, and for a moment my gaze locks where her tongue grazes over her flesh. My heart thuds in my chest as she places her hand in mine and I pull her to her feet. And she doesn't let go. With a quirk of her brows at Theo she says, "not a word," and leads me away from the fire.

"Stay with Theo," I say over my shoulder to Mel.

She gives a little salute before turning her attention back to her tablet.

A few steps later and we're alone.

"Where do you want to go?" I ask.

Naomi's hand is warm in mine and her thumb drags back and forth, making my nerve endings go haywire. "You said it was pretty at the other end of the campsite, right?"

I point at the sky. "I think it's pretty everywhere. But I'm not sure how far we should go from the campground in the dark."

She tugs my arm against her side as we walk. "I don't think there are any bison around here."

I sense her smile without looking at her. The excitement and longing inside me feels both foreign and familiar, and I want to push those feelings even further. "Perhaps not, but there could be other wild animals."

"Is that really what you're afraid of?"

Damn, she's perceptive. "You really cut right to it, don't you?"

"Sorry. I just call it like I see it, and there's obviously something bigger going on with you."

"You're not wrong."

We near the row of tents beyond the yurts, far enough from our campsite that no one can see us, but still not far enough. We walk until we reach the edge of the lake, where a lone bench sits close to the water. If someone were to paint the way the stars fill the sky, it would look like an exaggeration. They dip so close to the ground that their reflection in the water makes it feel like the galaxy might envelop us if we step too close to the shore.

"Want to sit?" I ask.

"Sure."

She lets go of my hand as we settle on the bench, but once we're seated, she grabs it again. And rests our entwined hands on her thigh. "I'll tell you mine if you tell me yours."

I laugh softly. "Only if you want to."

She takes a deep breath and her grip on my hand tightens. She's staring at the stars, which gives me a moment to watch her. Her hair is loose around her face and the light from above makes her skin look otherworldly. And her lips—yeah, her lips are parted slightly as she chooses her words, but all I can think of is how they would feel against mine. She turns, catching me staring. Our faces are mere inches apart.

It would be so easy to lean closer.

She inhales, her breath shaky. "I told you Berkeley is my dream school." She waits for me to nod before continuing, which I do, but I'm already uneasy about where this is going. "It's all I've wanted since I started thinking about college. The program is phenomenal, and the campus is beautiful, and it's right in the middle of the best parts of California." She bumps her shoulder against mine. "But I don't need to tell you that."

"No. Yeah, it's awesome."

"Right? Well, now I'm not sure if it's going to happen."

Her words hang between us and the ethereal vision of us on campus together fades to nothing. Several emotions battle for attention. Disappointment that we won't be at the same school, concern that she has to give up her dream, and a tiny bit of relief that she won't affect my decision to transfer. "Why not?"

She faces me, an uneasy smile on her lips. "This company from Seattle, Auralacity, reached out to me about my podcast. They want to get me on a bigger platform, help me reach a bigger audience. Basically, monetize Three Good Things and make me a star. But they only work with podcasts based in the Pacific Northwest, and if I go to California I'll be outside their territory."

Images of Naomi walking on campus shift to her behind a microphone with a pair of giant headphones clamped on her head, her red curls wild around them. Her smiling and laughing and playing it up for the camera, because don't all successful podcasts also record video? Then her on a red carpet with cameras flashing, people shouting her name, a faceless guy on her arm. Okay, that might be a leap, but her personality is made for that kind of success.

She squeezes my hand. "You're literally the only person I've told about this besides my mom. Can you please say something?"

"Wow, yes. Sorry. That's amazing. And you would be amazing. I mean, you are amazing." I drag my hand over my face. "That's an incredible offer."

"So you think I'm amazing?"

My thoughts freeze. I really did just blurt that, didn't I? "I mean, you know you're awesome."

"I think the word you used—three times—is amazing."

We smile at each other, and for a second I'm pulled out of the moment, up into the stars so I'm looking down at the two of us on the bench. There's barely space between us and the intimacy of what we're sharing puts all kinds of wild ideas in my head, all of them ending with us kissing.

The corner of my mouth lifts. Then my hand follows, touching a strand of her hair. "Yes, I think you're amazing.

And I get why that's such a difficult decision." I drop my hand. "Changing your dreams, even if it's for a good reason, is hard."

It seems like she wants to say more, so I let the silence stretch out.

After several minutes, she sighs. "It would be amazing. And I'd still go to school, so it's not like I'd be giving up on that. But it wouldn't be the same."

A thought strikes me. "Wait." Her brows furrow and my heart pounds at what I've just realized. "Going to school in another state doesn't make you a resident there. You still claim your parents'—or your mom's—house as your home address."

Her mouth falls open. "Are you sure?"

I nod, excitement building. This means she could still go to Berkeley, even if I'm not there. "My friend Shawna is from Michigan and that's how it works for her." I squeeze her hand. "Maybe Aural—what's their name?"

"Auralacity."

"Maybe they'll agree for you to record in California since they'll still be produced in Oregon."

She exhales slowly. The relief I expected shifts from worry to something close to panic.

Something else is going on. "Is it about Theo?"

Her head dips and after another pause, she shrugs. "He's more important than he lets on. He helps edit the shows so I... so they—" She stops.

There's clearly more going on than she wants to share. Which I get. The fact that she's telling me her secret means I have to share mine, and saying it out loud will make it real.

She looks up at the stars and her hair falls away from her face. My gaze travels along her smooth jaw and down her throat. The moonlight makes her pale skin glow, but the sadness in her eyes when she looks at me tamps down my earlier thoughts of anything physical happening between us. Right now she needs a friend, nothing more.

"You don't have to tell me," I say.

She swipes under her eyes with her free hand and tilts her head so her hair is covering her face. Takes an uneven breath. Exhales. "What if I'm no good without him?"

Clarity strikes me quickly. Theo edits and produces her shows. He knows her better than anyone. No one can ever replace the trust they have in each other. "Do we need to revisit three minutes ago when I said you're amazing?"

She sniffs, then gives me a smile. "Maybe."

"Have you talked to him about this?"

Her head shakes quickly. "Not about the offer. Or even what happens after high school."

My earlier conversation with Theo plays through my mind. "Not at all?"

She looks me in the eye. "Is it terrible if I say I have no idea what he wants to do? We have this whole Twin Trust thing where we're supposed to tell each other everything. We've never had secrets. It's even above the bro code. But he gets super weird whenever anything hinting at the future comes up. Like, we took the SATs and all that, but he doesn't seem to want to talk about it and I hate that I don't know what he's thinking."

"If you want my advice, and maybe you don't. But if you do, I think you should start by talking to Theo."

"We talk about everything. I don't know why this feels off limits."

"Maybe because it'll be the first time you'll be apart." Mel dances through my mind. She's already changed in the couple months I've been gone and I hate that we aren't as close as we used to be.

Naomi presses her shoulder against mine and holds it there for a moment. "I thought I was the advice person here."

I lean into her. "I'm kind of going through that now. With Mel. It's not the same as you and Theo since we're not twins but—"

"You don't need to justify how much you love your sister."

"I know."

"No, really. You obviously adore each other. It's sweet."

It shouldn't embarrass me to admit I care about my sister, but my cheeks warm. "Anyway, if you're feeling this way, Theo probably is too."

She rests her elbows on her knees and looks out over the water. A breeze sends ripples over the surface, lifting her hair. "So," she says, turning to face me. "What's your secret?"

My mouth falls open and sweat beads on my forehead.

"Don't back out on me now," she says.

I take a breath, but my chest constricts. My fingers flex and straighten. "It's somewhat similar to yours."

"You got an offer for your podcast, too?" I give her my are-you-kidding look and she swallows her smile. "Sorry, go on."

"You're aware how amazing Berkeley is."

She whispers, "There's that word again."

I press my elbows into my thighs and silently ask the stars to take me away from here. "You know what? Forget it."

She grabs my arm. "I'm sorry. Really. Sometimes I have no filter. But you can trust me." Her eyes implore for me to continue, and I let out a sigh. Her thumb swipes over my bicep before she releases her grip and a different emotion settles in my chest, something bordering on hope.

Sharing this with Naomi will make it easier to tell Mom. And deep down I've already made up my mind so I may as well get used to saying it out loud. "I'm thinking about transferring to a school closer to home. Like in our town."

"And leave Berkeley?"

I nod.

"You must have a good reason to leave someplace so amazing." Her face doesn't crack, but a hint of a smile lifts my lips despite my best efforts not to.

"Mom hasn't outright said it, but things haven't been great since I left for school. Mel used to tell me everything. I can tell she's having a hard time, but since we left for this trip, it's like she no longer trusts me." My hand settles on my arm. "I'm worried about her."

Naomi's quiet for a moment. "And you're willing to give up Berkeley for her?"

I don't need to explain how important my sister's happiness is to me. Naomi gets it. And that's comforting. "Yeah, I am."

"Wow."

"Bakersfield, where we live, has a state university so transferring should be easy enough." But transferring isn't the hard part. It's possibly saying goodbye to the track I'm on and everything that comes with it.

"It sounds like you've already made up your mind."

"I think I have." I rest my head in my hands with my face turned toward her. "But what if it's the wrong decision?"

She mirrors my position and bites her lip. "One thing I've learned is if you're gonna make a decision, own it. This is a lot bigger than whether or not to chop your hair—"

"I vote no on that," I whisper.

"Noted. But you're doing it for good reasons. You need to ask yourself, if things don't go exactly the way you want, will you regret transferring?"

There's a lot to regret about leaving my dream school but being there for my sister outweighs any of that. "I don't think I will."

"Well, there you go."

A long, slow sigh escapes me. "Thank you."

"I didn't do anything."

"You helped me realize that making my family a priority doesn't mean I'm giving up on my dreams. Most people leave for college and never think twice about what they left behind, but it's all I can think about."

She studies me like she wants to say more. Her eyes search mine and another breeze lifts a strand of her hair. My fingers twitch with the need to touch her, but I don't want to do anything stupid that might break this spell that's been cast over us.

"Thanks for letting me see this side of you," she says. The hair dances against her cheek and this time I indulge my twitchy fingers. Her eyes close when my fingertip brushes her jaw. Then her lips part. Just enough for me to believe she's thinking the same thing I am.

I lean closer, already anticipating how her lips will feel against mine, when a shriek echoes over the water and we jump apart.

"What was that?" I say.

"That sounded like Theo."

15

NAOMI

"You recognize his scream?" Hunter asks.

With a shrug, I jump up from the bench. "We better go see what's happening." I don't want to admit Theo's a bit of a screamer. Some things should stay in the family.

I also don't want to admit how badly I wanted Hunter to kiss me just now. With my eyes closed I couldn't be certain he was leaning in, but I swear I felt his breath on my face just before my brother ruined the moment.

We jog along the path and full-on run when another scream sounds, much closer this time. When we reach the campsite, Theo and Melody are clinging to each other on top of the picnic table. The fire still blazes, the chairs sit where we left them, and aside from the two of them jumping around, everything looks the same as when we left.

The moms come running from behind us. "What happened?" Mom asks.

"I SAID I DON'T DO WILD ANIMALS!" Melody shouts.

Hunter rushes to the picnic table and reaches for her, but she doesn't move from Theo's side. Hurt flickers across his face, but he shakes it away with a jerk of his head.

"Where is there a wild animal?" I ask. Nothing seems out of place, but the people in the lodge did warn us that critters could come say hello.

Theo shines the flashlight from his phone toward his yurt.

"It went that way."

"What did?" Hunter asks.

We all look to where Theo pointed but the light doesn't shine far enough.

"The bandit of the night!" Theo gestures around his eyes like a mask, then shudders. "We were minding our own business when it crawled under my chair and tried to steal our snacks!"

Mom reaches for his hand. "I'm glad you survived."

"You mock," he says. "But you didn't see the determination in his eyes. He's not done with us."

Melody whimpers and Margo gestures for her to get down. "I doubt it'll be back with all of us here. Raccoons are more scared of people than we are of them."

"I don't believe that," Melody says.

Theo shakes his head. "I'm telling you. That beast will keep trying until it gets what it's after."

I peer up at him. "So you're just gonna stay there?"

"Obviously not." His lower lip pushes out and he bats his eyes at me. "Will someone make sure it's gone?"

Hunter turns on his phone flashlight. "Since you said it went toward our yurt, I'll check."

"You should bring backup," Melody says.

Hunter scans our faces. Both moms avert their eyes, and it's clear Theo and Melody aren't moving.

I sigh. "Fine, I'll help." I give them my best eye roll. "You all are ridiculous."

"You're my hero," Theo says.

Hunter leads me up the path to his yurt, and my brain jumps from raccoon duty to the almost-kiss barely five minutes ago. Is he thinking about it too?

He lowers into a squat and shines light at the crawlspace beneath the deck surrounding the yurt. "If it's still around it most likely went under here."

"You don't think there's a nest or something, do you? Do raccoons live in nests? Or is it a den? I admit my knowledge of animals' sleeping habits is lacking."

Even in the dark I can sense The Smirk.

I sway toward him. Let my hand rest on his shoulder. "I didn't say it back there because I didn't want you to have to deal with this alone, but I'm not super stoked about coming face to face with a raccoon."

"You and me both," he says under his breath.

He sweeps the light the length of the yurt.

"Yurt really is a weird word," I say.

He laughs and looks up at me. "Three Good Things about staying in a yurt."

My insides quiver. Like full-on swoon. "One. Solid doors that keep out raccoons."

"Agreed. Two. Semi-comfortable beds." His gaze jumps back to the crawlspace, as if his thoughts took the same turn mine did.

Maybe I should have suggested a detour before the raccoon hunt. I lean closer to peer over his shoulder, and he turns his head slightly as my hair brushes his cheek. "Three. You don't—"

A hiss cuts me off mid-sentence and I shriek. There's scratching and rustling and Hunter jumps back, knocking us both to the ground.

"Omigod, let's go!" He scrambles to his feet, pulling me up by my elbow, then grabs my hand and I stumble after him. We run toward the fire, hands clasped tightly. The thought that his reaction was mildly heroic flits through my mind. Yes, he knocked me over, but he didn't leave me at the mercy of the raccoon.

Everyone's sitting around the fire when we return. Theo's eyes jump to our hands and a satisfied grin spreads across his face. I scowl at him, and he shakes his head.

"I take it from your scream that you found the raccoon?" Margo asks.

"I'm not sure if it was the raccoon, but there's something under our yurt," Hunter says.

I snort. "Yurt."

"So who's taking me tonight?" Theo asks.

"Everyone's sleeping in their assigned spaces." Mom rolls her eyes, then they narrow as they land on my hand in Hunter's, and she gives me an extra-pointed look.

I untangle my fingers from Hunter's and tuck my hands in my back pockets.

"We should be fine near the fire," Margo says.

Theo points in the direction of the raccoon. "We were literally next to the fire when it ambushed us."

"Is all the food put away?" Mom asks. "Because as sparkling as your personality is, dear Theo, that's what it was after."

He crosses his arms in a huff. "Whatever. All I'm saying is I'm not going anywhere alone. All of you are my buddies now."

Hunter's hand bumps my hip and my stomach flips. Was that a super subtle way of asking me to be his anti-raccoon buddy? I glance at his hand and will it to make contact again, but he shoves it into the pocket of his hoodie.

We settle around the fire, and as the conversation bounces from raccoons to the latest self-help books, I get lost in the stars. It's too dark to see the mountains on the other side of the lake, their presence only noticeable by their jagged outline against the galaxies. The bright pinpoints of light sweep across the sky above us like a canvas, swirling together like, well, kind of like milk.

"It's so crazy how it actually looks milky," I say to no one. As soon as the words leave my mouth, I expect someone to mock me, and when Hunter clears his throat, the earlier butterflies shrivel up and die.

"Whoever named it the Milky Way was not the most creative," he says.

Melody scoffs. "Someone in my class actually thought it was named after the candy bar. Can you believe that?" Her normally cheerful tone has an unfamiliar bite.

Everyone stills. Her words hang in the air until Theo clears his throat.

"Actually, I asked the same thing in front of my entire class." All playfulness is gone from his voice and for a second, he reverts to the self-conscious boy he was in sixth grade.

Melody presses her lips together, then says, "Oh." She crosses and uncrosses her arms, finally settling her hands in her lap. "That had to have been the absolute worst."

"It wasn't my best moment." From the way Theo told the story afterward, he played it off like a joke, but having the class laugh at him instead of with him was something he swore would never happen again. "Having kids laugh at you is never fun."

Melody's eyes go wide, then her gaze drops to her lap. "The kids in my school can be so mean." She presses her lips together again. Our conversation about school comes back to me and I make a mental note to ask her about it later.

"That's middle school for you," Theo says. "I'd like to tell you that high school gets better, and it does a little, but the teasing never goes away."

"Until college," Hunter says. "Although they still make fun of you for asking idiotic questions."

"This conversation is uplifting," I say.

Margo claps her hands together, startling me and making Theo jump. How Hunter and Melody don't react to that, I don't know. "Listen," she says. "You can't go through life worrying about what other people think about you. Yes, it's important to consider how your words affect others, but you're all good kids and I can't believe any of you would intentionally say anything hurtful to someone else."

Melody's head dips forward until her hair covers her face.

Hunter leans toward Melody. "Is everything okay?"

She doesn't lift her head. "Not now, Hunt."

"But later?"

"Sure, whatever."

Hunter deflates inside himself. This has to be crushing him.

The conversation drifts again, and my eyelids grow heavy. Spending so much time outside has wiped me out. The voices grow softer and the pops of the fire lull me into a warm cocoon.

I'm woken with a gentle hand on my arm. "Naomi, everyone's gone to bed." Hunter's crouched next to me so our faces are on the same level. Sure enough, the rest of the chairs are empty and the fire is nothing but a pile of smoking ashes. I turn back to him and my breath catches. He's focused on my lips.

"Th-thanks for not leaving me to the raccoons."

"I would never." His voice is barely a whisper. His fingers curl around the armrest of my chair, right at the edge of my sweatshirt. "Thanks for listening to me earlier. Saying it out loud, it seems really obvious what I should do."

"Move back home?"

"I think so."

I don't want his decision to influence mine. Until three days ago he wasn't a factor in anything, so he shouldn't have an impact on my future. If what he said about keeping my residency in Oregon is true and I don't have to choose between Auralacity and Berkeley, I should stop worrying and sign the contract.

But an unease I don't want to name niggles in the back of my thoughts. And I can't ignore the twinge in my heart at him leaving Berkeley. I'd barely had time to imagine us walking the campus together before it was no longer a possibility.

His finger grazes my arm. "You okay?" With the fire out, it's almost completely dark and the stars reflect in his glasses, concealing his eyes.

I nod. "Just thinking about my own decision. It's hard to give up on the future you always imagined for yourself."

"But you're not giving up. You're shifting courses." He says it so earnestly that it makes me smile.

"Our situations really are very similar."

His face grows serious and I can't tell what he's thinking. I'm reminded, again, that we've only known each other for three days, and for that first day I thought I hated him. Well, hated with a side of heavy-duty crushing.

Heat rushes to my cheeks. My fingers find his and we stare at each other beneath the stars, and time seems to pause in this little corner of the universe. My heart pounds in my chest, and when his gaze drops to my lips, a flurry of butterflies unleash in my belly. I lean closer and he rises to meet me when something scratches the concrete firepit.

We both freeze. "What was that?" I ask.

"Something's by the fire," he whispers.

Sure enough, two pairs of eyes glow in the starlight. And they're staring right at us.

"I think that's our cue." I grab my water bottle from under my chair and slowly stand. Hunter follows me to his feet, and we tiptoe backward, our focus never leaving whatever fire demon is watching us.

When we reach the steps to my yurt, he tugs on my sleeve to stop me. "I'll go with you to the bathroom. Meet back out here in two minutes?"

My emotions are all over the place—excited to not have to say goodnight just yet and terrified of being hunted by the fire demon—so I just nod.

Melody's already asleep, so I grab my bathroom stuff and head back out. Hunter's a perfect gentleman as we hurry down the path to the bathroom, and a perfect gentleman when he says goodnight back at our yurts. And I'm left tossing and turning half the night, not sure how to get him to kiss me. At some point I text Sage for advice, knowing full well her phone's on Do Not Disturb and I won't hear from her until the morning.

When morning does arrive, I'm exhausted. My arms ache from back-to-back days of paddling, and my nerves are shot from things not happening with Hunter. Maybe I need to get over my vow to not make the first move.

A text from Sage is waiting for me.

Sage: drag him into the woods

Me: I was just considering that but my arms are too tired

Sage: aren't they giving you a day off?

A day off would be perfect. Not only will my arms get a much-needed break, but by not being trapped in a "personal watercraft," as the instructor kept calling it, I could spend some serious quality time with Hunter.

Me: you are brilliant
Sage: it's not often I get to give YOU advice
Sage: so things are going well with him?
Me: much better. He wasn't lying when he said he's slow to warm up to people
Sage: but he's warm now? ;) ;) ;)
Me: that's what I'm hoping to find out

"Do we have to go in another boat today?" Melody's voice croaks from across the room. "My arms don't work anymore."

"I was just thinking the same thing."

Me: I've already got one on my side. Wish me luck.
Sage: Luck!
Sage: Oh! And your episode is live. Theo's magic worked

Relief hits me hard. Deep down I know I should trust the technology but there's something really satisfying about clicking Publish.

Me: thank you!!

I reach for my hoodie on the floor and pull it on before getting out of bed. Since the moms were expecting to travel to another lake today, my best chance to convince them to skip it is catching them before they load the car.

Mist hovers over the lake in the distance and the air has a chill I've never felt at home. A brisk dry coldness that cuts right through to your bones. A thin wisp of smoke rises from the firepit, and the scent of coffee lingers. They're up, but they must be in the bathrooms.

I hurry down the trail, giving a polite smile to the couple my grandparents' age who look decked out for an all-day hike. It's been weird not seeing many people since we've been here, but Mom did mention it's the off season.

Voices stop me before I enter the bathroom. Mom and Margo are here, and they don't sound happy.

"Can you stop pushing for five minutes?" Mom says, her tone right at the edge of what Theo and I have learned means take cover or else.

"I'm just calling it as I see it," Margo says, her voice equally tight.

"Well, can you not see it for five minutes while I finish getting ready?"

A sharp crack echoes through the window as something hard slams. Margo storms out of the bathroom and startles when she sees me standing in the path.

"Everything okay?" I could pretend I didn't hear them fighting, but I wouldn't have a popular advice podcast if I avoided the sticky questions.

"We were just talking."

"Yeah, I think everyone in a hundred-foot radius knows that."

Her normally stoic demeanor seems to falter, just for a second. "I'll see you back at the campsite." She moves past me as I step toward the bathroom.

Inside, Mom's leaning over the counter, her forehead pressed against the mirror.

"Everything okay?" I ask again.

She lets out a sigh to rival all sighs and tosses a brush on the counter. That must be the source of the slamming. "Do you ever wonder what the point is to all this? The hustle and late nights and wanting something even if you don't know if you'll succeed." It no longer feels like she's actually asking me, but I answer anyway.

"I'm seventeen. That's pretty much my constant state of being."

She lifts her head and gives me a weak smile. Her eyes are red like she's on the verge of crying—or was already crying—and I hurry to her side. I press a hand to her back and rub in small circles, the same way she's done to me a million times when she's trying to make me feel better.

"Is this about the career change?"

She nods.

"Whatever it is, it can't be so bad that we can't sort it out." I say the words she's said to me as often as she's rubbed my back.

She sniffs. "When did you get so grown-up?"

I glance at my wrist, where I've never worn a watch. "Sometime last week."

This time she smiles for real. "I'm really proud of you. You know what you want and you're going after it. And you don't let anything as ridiculous as self-doubt stop you."

If only she knew. "Can I ask a stupid question?" I mouth along with the answer I know is coming.

"There's no such thing as a stupid question." She levels her gaze at me. "What's going on?"

"Is it true that I keep my residency at home even if I go to college out of state?"

The corner of her mouth lifts. "According to the tuition for out-of-state students, yes."

"So I'd be okay even though the offer from Auralacity says they only work with podcasters in the Pacific Northwest? Because if I go to Berkeley, I'll be in California."

"It's a technical loophole we'll have to discuss, but I'm sure it can be worked out." She moves closer and pulls me into her arms. "Oh, sweetie. Did you think you had to choose?"

Embarrassment heats my cheeks and I nod against her shoulder. The safety of her embrace comforts like nothing else. It represents home and the love I've known my entire life, one Theo and I have never questioned. Will that change if he and I go to different schools?

And how will I do my show without him?

Panic flutters in my chest, but I shake it away. The conversation I overheard when I approached the bathroom comes back to me. "What happened with Margo?"

She glances at the door where Margo left. "I'm second-guessing myself and Margo won't let me. But how can I possibly go back to school at the same time that you and Theo are starting college? We'll be paying off student loans until your children are retired."

This proves that accepting the offer will help with bills at home. "Mom, I know it's your nature to put us first, and we appreciate that. Wouldn't have it any other way." I give her a cheesy smile to prove my point. "But we're practically adults and you need to do what makes you happy. Besides, I thought you said it's only a one-year program."

"It is."

"Okay, so that's one issue solved."

Her brow quirks. "Just like that?"

"Yes. Now the bigger issue."

As she watches me, the sadness in her eyes fades.

"Can we please skip canoeing today? I can't lift my arms."

She bursts out laughing and pulls me into a hug while my noodley arms dangle at my sides. "You got it."

She's all smiles as we walk back to the campsite, but that smile grows tense when she sees Margo. "What do you say we give the kids a day off?" Mom asks. If you didn't know her, she sounds like her normal cheerful self but there's a strain in her voice that shows how uncertain she is.

Margo looks up from the package of cream cheese. Her head cocks. "And skip canoeing?"

I jump in. "Yes. Please." I twist my body so my arms swing back and forth. "My arms beg you."

Margo rubs her shoulder. "I could use a day of rest myself." She gives Mom a hesitant look and I'm tempted to throw them in their yurt until they work this out. "Are you okay with this?"

"We have been going pretty much nonstop since we arrived. Might be nice to sit by the lake and read."

They share a tentative smile. That's good enough for now. "I'll let Melody know."

She's still in bed when I go inside, so I cross the room, climb the ladder without a sound, and leap onto her bed. Her elbow catches me in the side, and I let out a huff of air as she squeals and laughs and undoes all the awkwardness from outside.

"Your wish has been granted!" I laugh into her pillow. Strands of her hair tickle my nose.

"No more boats?"

"Not for today anyway. The moms took zero convincing. I don't think they wanted to admit that they're tired, too."

"Then I'm going back to sleep."

I push myself into a sitting position and am swinging my legs off the edge of the bed when she stops me with a hand on my arm.

"Wait." She averts her gaze, the happiness from seconds ago sliding off her face. "Can I talk to you for a second?"

"Sure." I press my back against the wall alongside the bed, then tuck my knees to my chest and rest my chin on them.

"You know how earlier I said my friends and I aren't really into the same sort of things?"

She hadn't gone so far as to say that, but that's what I'd picked up on. "Yeah. You like astronomy and science and they..." Her earlier description of them watching and making videos rolls through my mind. "Don't."

She nods slowly, like it's taking all her energy to move her head. "I don't know what to do. We've been friends since forever but ever since we got to middle school it's like they're different people."

"How so?"

"Like they're super into clothes and makeup and boys, which yeah, that's all cool, but they used to care about school too. Now it's like it's embarrassing to admit you actually study." She settles farther into the blankets and peers at me with watery eyes. There's a hesitation, like she wants to say more.

I lean on an elbow so I'm almost lying down and look up at the ceiling. Sunlight brightens the canvas dome at the center of the room, highlighting the dust floating in the air. Several moments pass, but she doesn't continue. "Is there more than that?"

She burrows down farther until the blankets cover her face. "Sometimes they can be mean. To other kids. Nothing crazy vicious," she quickly adds. "Mostly comments in the hall and at lunch, and they've made up rumors about people."

Insta-rage flames my cheeks. "Are they bullying you?" My protectiveness isn't new—Sage has brought out this reaction in me countless times, especially when she was dating her horrible ex—but I'm surprised it's this strong for a girl I barely know. Maybe it's the connection I feel to her entire family prompting this pulse of anger tearing through me.

"No!" She shakes her head under the blanket, then more softly says, "no."

I tug the blanket lower until I see her eyes. "You can tell me what's going on."

"It's awful."

"I promise I won't judge you. You listened to my show, right?"

Her lower lip trembles as she nods.

"I want to help you figure out whatever's happening. I know we haven't known each other long, but I don't like seeing you upset."

Her eyes search mine and as I hold her gaze, tears catch in her lashes. "I don't want you to hate me."

My stomach churns. Nothing good ever comes from that statement. I force my face to stay neutral before allowing a small smile. "I forgave your brother for being a butt, didn't I?"

Her lips twitch, but I don't get the full smile I was hoping for.

"I promise I won't hate you. The fact that you feel bad means you're not an awful person." The little voice in my head—the one that sounds a lot like Theo when we're recording a show—warns me not to give her a pass too quickly. Middle schoolers can be horrible and as much as I'd like to believe the sweet kid I'm sitting next to could never hurt another person, she's fighting back tears at the thought of telling me what she did.

She sniffles, then takes a deep breath.

"When I said they can be mean to other kids, it's not just them. It's me, too." She pauses, waiting for my reaction.

I nod for her to continue.

"It started with little things. Like, if someone was wearing a shirt that Nelly—she's my best friend—that Nelly didn't like, she'd say something when we'd walk by them in the hall. She'd ask if they got it at Goodwill, or if it was their mom's reject or something like that. The person would look really upset and she'd just laugh. And then look at us all pissed off if we didn't laugh, too. So we did.

"That wasn't so bad, even though I felt a little guilty for going along with it, but then Jessica—that's our other friend. Well, was our friend—" Her face drops when she says this. "Jessica liked Bronson, but so did Nelly, and it would have been okay if Jessica had just said no when he asked her to go to the movies, but she was selfish and didn't think about how it would make Nelly feel and when Nelly found out that they held hands she kind of lost her mind."

"Wow." Melody seems way too young for this level of drama. When I was twelve, I was aware of boys and clothes were starting to be important, but it never would have come between me and my friends.

Melody nods. "I know, right? Jessica should have just said no. She knew Nelly liked him and was working on a plan to get him to ask her to the fall dance."

"That's not—"

"So then Nelly started spreading rumors about Jessica, saying she was kissing other boys behind Bronson's back. I knew it wasn't true but..."

My stomach twists into a knot. "Did you help spread the rumors?"

Her fingers knead the top of her sleeping bag. A tear slides down her cheek, catching between her clenched lips. "I had to. Nelly was super pissed and said I wasn't a real friend if I didn't stick up for her."

I reach for her shoulder. "There's a big difference between sticking up for your friend and lying about someone else."

She squishes her eyes closed. "I knew you'd hate me."

"Hey, no." I shake her shoulder gently. "Now, I only know what you've told me about Nelly and Jessica so it's hard for me to know the full story. But you obviously feel bad about what happened, and I've always believed that your gut doesn't lie." It's something Mom first said when I was around Melody's age, back when my biggest drama was which after-school club to join. "What does your gut say?"

"It hurts."

"And why do you think that is?"

She watches me for several beats. "Because I wasn't fair to Jessica. She was my friend too and I know she didn't kiss anyone." Tears continue to roll down her face and she wipes them away with the edge of her sleeve. "It's too late to change it."

"Hey." I push her hair off her forehead and smooth it behind her ear. "It's never too late to make something right. It might feel like that right now, and it might take some work for Jessica to listen to you, but I swear it's possible." This isn't the first time I've given this advice, and I hope she doesn't recognize these words from my podcast.

"That's what you said to the guy who ambushed his friend at the model UN and got him get kicked out." Her voice sounds far away, like she's talking from the other side of the room and not right next to me.

I bite my lip. So much for hoping she wouldn't remember. "Yeah, but advice is universal. That's why I have the show. So that what I tell one person will hopefully help a lot of other people." I touch her cheek. "Like you."

"Do you ever talk to the people afterward?"

"The people on my show?" She nods, and I shake my head. "Why?"

"I'm just wondering if they tell you if the advice worked. Like, did that guy make up with his friend? Or did he tell him to go to hell and they never spoke again?"

This is the very question I try my hardest not to ask myself. When I'm lying in bed at night, feeling like a fraud, I assure myself over and over that I'm doing good. That Three Good Things will change lives—that it *is* changing lives—and I'm not just talking into an empty void, adding useless chatter to an already overcrowded channel.

Clearly Auralacity doesn't think so, but what if they change their minds after I've already signed the contract?

"I haven't followed up with any of them again," I say. "But that's a really great idea."

Her face brightens ever so slightly. "Like a recap show! You could play parts of the original show and then give an update on where they are now."

My tongue feels thick in my throat. I could swallow my words, but she's trusting me, so I owe it to her to do the same. "But what if I haven't actually helped anyone?"

She pushes onto her elbows and looks me in the eye. "Are you kidding? Mom's been doing this forever but the way you explain things makes way more sense to me. Like I can see how I'd use your advice in my actual life."

"Really?"

"Totally."

I bump my knee against her hip. "Does this mean you're going to try to make things right with Jessica?"

"I think I have to. But—" Her lips clench together. "What about Nelly?"

I take a deep breath. "It's never easy to walk away from someone that you've known forever, especially if you consider them your best friend."

Her eyes go wide. "Is that what you think I need to do?"

"I would never tell you to end a friendship with someone." Sage and her ex, Pax, run through my head. He manipulated her for so long that she could no longer make decisions for herself, yet I never spoke up. If there's anything I regret from that time, it's that. But I can avoid making that mistake now. "If you don't like the kind of person you are when you're with her, maybe it would be okay to put some distance between you. I get that it might be hard, and if she figures out what you're doing she might try to retaliate—"

Melody's eyes grow increasingly wider as I talk.

I hold up my hands. "Or maybe she won't do anything. But she might not react well, so it's probably smart to gradually back away from her."

She stares over my shoulder. The tears that had dried when she focused on my problems return. "What if she spreads rumors about me, too?"

I hate that she's in this situation. That no amount of advice from me or her mom or Hunter will make this easier for her. "All you can do is hold your head high until another rumor starts. And try to correct anyone stupid enough to believe her."

She takes a shuddering breath and when she exhales, she seems to shrink even smaller. "I'll try."

Maybe I really am helping people. "You know you can always call or text me when it gets hard." Because it's going to get hard. If what she says about Nelly is true, that girl could make Melody's life a living hell. At least for right now.

"Let's go get breakfast."

I stop her with a hand on her arm. "Just one thing."

"What?"

"You really need to talk to Hunter about this. He's worried about you."

She rolls her eyes. "He's too busy with college and his career."

"That's not true. You're the most important thing in the world to him."

"How can you know that?"

I graze her cheek with my thumb. "He told me."

"Oh."

"So will you talk to him?"

She pauses, and the torment Hunter must feel courses through me. Finally she looks up, but her expression is hard to read. "I'll think about it."

— **16** —

HUNTER

Mel and Naomi kept giggling and glancing at each other all through breakfast, and now that we're out on the trail I hiked the first night, I'm determined to find out why. The moms hung back at the campsite, and Naomi and Theo are a hundred feet ahead of us on the trail. Far enough away that they can't hear us, but close enough that I can see the muscles in Naomi's legs when she walks.

"You really like her, huh?" Mel's question snaps my attention back to her, and I can't ignore the heat warming my neck.

"What do you mean?"

"It's okay. I really like her, too."

"Is that what all the giggling was about at breakfast?" My tone is teasing, but her smile fades.

"Oh, we were just talking about something at school. Girl stuff. You wouldn't get it."

I'd like to argue that I'm an enlightened male who can grasp whatever issues the two of them were discussing, but while Shawna gives me the benefit of the doubt, I'm not sure my little sister will. "Try me."

Her gaze drops. "Can't we just enjoy the hike?"

I clamp my lips together, holding my breath for a moment. "Mel, I know something's going on. I feel like you've been avoiding me since we got here."

She's quiet for several moments. "It's not a big deal. Naomi gave me advice, so I'll be fine."

I don't believe her, but I don't want to push her away. "You're making me feel like Yellowfang." Throwing out the character from *Into the Wild* who's considered a spy and a traitor might be a little much, but I've got to try something.

She shakes her head, but the corner of her mouth lifts in a smile. "You're so dramatic."

"I just want to help."

"I don't think you're Yellowfang. You'll always be my Graypaw." She bumps my arm and a mix of love and relief fill my chest.

"And you're my Firepaw."

"So you like Naomi?" she asks again.

Despite my frustration, I let her change the topic. "Yeah, I mean, she and Theo are cool. I was worried she'd be really into herself with the podcast and all, but she's cool."

"You said cool twice."

"She's really cool."

She gives me a sly smile. "You do like her."

I'm not getting into this conversation. But then Naomi's laughter carries back to us, and I can't stop my gaze from returning to her.

"Are you gonna kiss her?"

"What's the point?"

Mel stops in her tracks. "Excuse me?"

"What?"

Mel presses her hands to her chest and looks like I've wounded her. "Isn't the point of kissing, you know, the kissing?"

I move past her. "I'm not talking to you about this."

"I'm not a baby."

I stop suddenly and turn to face her. "Are you already kissing boys?"

"Or girls," she says. "No. But that doesn't mean I'm an idiot."

Guilt hits me in the chest. She's the most important person in the world to me and I've somehow made her feel like I think she's stupid. "I'm sorry. That's not what I meant." I drape an arm over her shoulder and nudge her to keep walking. "You know you're my favorite person."

A smile lifts the corner of her mouth. She looks up at me and tears shine in her eyes. "I miss you. I get that school's important and you're gonna be this big-deal editor in New York someday, but I miss hanging out with you."

The pressure in my chest grows heavier. I want to reassure her that things might be changing, but I don't want to get her hopes up until I talk to Mom. Instead, I hug her closer. "I miss you, too."

"What do you think Dad's doing right now?"

My foot catches on a rock and I nearly take us both down. "Where did that come from?"

She shrugs, and I let my arm fall to my side. "We're talking about missing family. And I don't know if I actually miss him because you have to have some kind of relationship with someone to miss them, but when I said New York, it made me think of him."

Because even though Dad doesn't live in New York City, where the heart of the publishing industry lies, he's close enough that I couldn't avoid seeing him if—when—I move there. I try to imagine him with his new wife in their stately house with white pillars holding up the roof, but the image stops with him drinking coffee and reading the paper. Has he switched to reading on a tablet like most of my professors? Or has he "stuck to his guns," like he used to say, and avoided the technological advances that have made our lives easier?

"He's probably at work," I say.

"Don't you wonder what his life is like?"

My jaw clenches. "I try not to."

"But he's our dad."

"And he's made it clear where we fall on his list of priorities." I reach for her arm and pull her against my side. "Even though I'm at school and not at home, and even after I get a job and move away, you will always be important to me."

Her lower lip wobbles. "Do you promise?"

I crisscross my heart with my finger.

"Then do me a favor?"

"Anything." I prepare myself for daily video chats or homework help or coming home more often to visit. Whatever it takes to keep her happy, I'll do it.

"Kiss Naomi." She sprints ahead of me, her laughter carrying over her shoulder while I'm left standing in the dusty path. When she reaches Naomi and Theo, she turns back and waves for me to hurry up.

So I do.

Theo's telling a story about when they went to see the solar eclipse last summer, which was right before I left for college. I was trying to spend as much time as I could with Mel, so the two of us drove as far north as Mom would let us—which, it turned out, wasn't nearly far enough—and watched from a mall parking lot. Then we grabbed lunch and drove home. It wasn't as exciting as I hoped, but Mel couldn't stop talking about it, and that was all that mattered.

When the terrain grows steeper, we form a single-file line and through Mel's wizardry, I end up behind Naomi. It doesn't take long for us to get ahead of Theo and Mel—probably because Mel's taking her sweet time, pointing out every plant and rock along the way. I should be grateful for the assist, but now that I've admitted that I like Naomi, I'm not sure what to do next. It's not like I can drag her behind a rocky outcropping. And even if I did, I'm still not entirely sure she wants that.

Naomi stops at the edge of a ridge and looks back the way we came. Sunlight reflects off the lake near our campsite and puffy white clouds break up the blue sky. Theo and Mel are still climbing so it's probably a good idea to let them catch up. Naomi shields her eyes from the sun. "Can I ask you a question?" The spark that usually seems to light her up from the inside seems a little dimmer, and her smile seems strained.

"Yeah, of course."

"What is with the clapping?"

I cock my head.

"Your mom." She slaps her hands together the way Mom does.

I smile. "Oh, that." I like that she's asking about my family. And I like letting her in on the private things that make us who we are. "She started doing that when I was little and she wanted me to listen. It's something my kindergarten teacher did to get our attention and Mom hijacked it." My shoulders push back, and I exaggerate my smile until I'm sure I look crazy. "One, two, three! Eyes on me!" I clap with each word, and she bursts out laughing.

"Did it actually work?" The soft curl of her lips has me wondering how they would feel pressed to mine. The way her eyes dance with amusement makes me desperate to keep her focused on me, to keep her laughing.

"Shockingly well." I shake off my teacher impersonation. "It devolved into a single clap by the time Mel was born. I don't think Mom even realizes she's doing it anymore."

"Do you think they're okay?"

The sudden shift in conversation confuses me. I point to Theo and Mel, who are moving even slower than before. Perhaps they're working together. "They're almost here."

Naomi shakes her head. Her curls brush her shoulders and I want to reach out and touch them. "Our moms. They were fighting earlier."

My eyes narrow. "About what?"

"Maybe fighting is too strong. But my mom said your mom was pushing her to talk and then your mom stormed off."

"That sounds about right. My mom tends to charge directly through whatever stands in her way and often fails to see that not everyone is comfortable with that." My gaze drops to the ground between us. "It's why I still haven't told her I'm thinking of transferring. I'm afraid she's going to say I shouldn't worry about her and Mel and should just go after my dreams."

"Meanwhile my mom said she envies the fact that I already know what I want in life. Even though I don't." Her hand swings at her side, then settles on her hip, then she crosses her arms over her belly.

"Did something else happen?"

"I got another email." She faces me, her eyes wide. "I have to return the contract by tomorrow or they're moving on to the next soon-to-be famous podcast." Her chest rises with each breath and tears shine in her eyes.

I wish I could help her in some way. "Have you talked to Theo yet?"

She shakes her head.

"What does your gut say?"

She smiles. "That's my line."

"It's a good one." My voice is soft, almost a whisper. "You'll figure it out." I move ever so slightly closer until our hands bump, and when her pinkie hooks through mine, I feel like she's the only thing keeping me from floating away. "And whatever you decide you want, you'll be amazing at it."

That earns me a smile that reaches her eyes, but quickly fades.

"I thought I knew what I wanted—or didn't want." My voice sounds scratchy, and I swallow hard. "But now I'm not so sure."

Her head tilts to the side and her brows furrow, not following what I'm trying to say.

I shift still closer. Pull her hand fully into mine.

"There you are!" Theo's voice interrupts whatever might have been about to happen.

Naomi turns, letting go of my hand. "Yeah, we've been waiting for you for ten minutes."

"It's barely been seven." Mel smirks at me and gives me a wink. I shrug and shake my head and she rolls her eyes.

"How far are we going?" Theo asks. "I have to pee."

I wave a hand at the terrain around us. "Weren't you the one who told me the world is our urinal?"

Theo reaches for his zipper. "If you all don't care." He runs back down the path and positions himself behind a scraggly tree. When he returns, Mel claps her hands like Mom and Naomi snickers.

"Everyone else okay to go farther?" Mel asks, and we all nod.

We walk for another half hour, Naomi still leading with the pokey twins behind me, and when we reach a bluff that overlooks an endless expanse of land, Naomi stops. "This seems like a good place to take a break." She drops her sling bag to the ground and sits next to it.

I'm over caring what Theo or Mel think, especially since every time I catch Theo's eye he nods and gestures at his sister, so I sit next to Naomi, leaving barely enough space between us to rest my hand. She pulls snacks out of her bag and tosses small packages of trail mix at each of us. Instead of throwing mine the three inches, she hands it to me, her fingers grazing mine in the process.

"I wasn't really sure what to expect out here." Theo's standing at the edge of the trail looking out over the horizon. Deer graze in the distance and a pair of hawks circle beyond them. The sun nears its highest point in the sky, warming the dry air. He turns to face us, tossing a handful of nuts in his mouth. "I'm used to trees and green. That's nature to me. But this is so open and big, it kind of hits you right here, you know?" He taps his fist to his chest. From anyone else, I'd think they were being pretentious, but from what I've learned of Theo, he doesn't say anything he doesn't mean. And his words usually have multiple meanings.

"Mom came here as a kid and always dreamed of coming back when she could fully appreciate it." I air quote the last part.

Mel sighs. "Does this mean I have to come back here when I'm old?"

I laugh through my nose. "Only if you want to." I stretch out my arm to poke her side. "Don't you like it here?"

"I do, but I'm more of a sidewalk and manicured lawns kind of girl." She exchanges a look with Naomi that I'm not going to pretend to understand.

"Hey," Naomi says to Mel. "I had an idea while we were hiking. What do you think of making science-y videos?" Mel scrunches up her nose and Naomi rolls her eyes. "Not like Bill Nye. Something fun where you'd talk about the stuff that interests you and *why* you like it. You could even tie in fashion, like a cross-over thing."

Mel purses her lips, thinking. "That could be interesting. Nelly might even help me if I tell her she can still talk about clothes."

Something in Naomi's eyes darkens. "What about Jessica? Would she want to do it?"

My gaze bounces between the two of them as I try to decipher what's left unsaid.

Mel flicks a raisin across the ground. "I don't know."

"Just something to think about."

"So, Hunter," Theo says, sitting on my other side. "Has Naomi convinced you to be on our show yet?"

A peanut lodges in my throat and I sputter for air. Naomi and Theo both smack my back, which not only loosens the nut, it makes me knock over my water bottle. "No," I choke out. "She hasn't."

Theo rubs his hands together. "I thought it'd be cool to get the college perspective. Three Good Things About Dating Without Your Parents Around."

"Don't you think that's a little risqué for our audience?" Naomi asks.

Theo lifts his brows. "That all depends on Hunter."

"I wouldn't exactly call my life risqué." But suddenly thoughts of Naomi and me in an assortment of scenarios that could definitely qualify as risqué run through my mind. All of them involving kissing and her discovering my boring underwear.

Naomi holds out her water bottle. "Cheers to that."

I choke again but wave her off when she moves to hit my back.

"But for real, how long are we gonna be here?" Mel asks. "I have to pee."

"It'll take at least an hour to get back," I say.

"Come on," Theo says. "We can start walking now."

Mel looks to me for permission.

"Stay on the trail."

She nods, then scrambles to her feet and skips down the path after Theo. "See ya!"

And now we're alone. Sitting in a clearing where people can see us for miles, but alone. She turns ever so slightly toward me and the air between us shifts. My heart pounds. I take a sip of water. Run my hand through my hair, bumping my glasses, and realize too late that my hand's covered in dust. I pull them off to wipe on my T-shirt and Naomi makes a weird noise.

"Did you want to head back?" Her voice is soft, almost a whisper.

I shake my head. I'm near-sighted, which means I can't see far away. Which also means that I can see every freckle on her face even though my glasses are still tangled in my shirt. I want to set them down, but I was trained at an early age to never ever set my glasses on the ground and as we're surrounded by nothing but ground, I keep them tucked in the hem of my shirt.

She glances at my hands, then back at my face. Her pulse flutters in her throat and before I can stop myself, I reach for her. My thumb trails lightly over her trembling skin. Her lips part as she takes a quick breath and her lashes lower for a beat. She watches me watching her, as if waiting to see if I'll do what I haven't stopped thinking about since we met.

My hand slides into her hair so I'm cradling her head in my palm. "Is this okay?" I whisper.

She nods against my hand, her eyes never leaving mine.

"Can I put my glasses in your bag?"

She blinks, the spell broken. "What? Um, sure?"

I hand them to her, my skin practically igniting where our hands touch, and she twists away from me to tuck them in a zippered pocket. My pulse jackhammers in my chest. *I can do this.* I take a quick breath and when she faces me, I cup her cheeks with both my hands. She whispers a breathy, "Oh," and we're so close I feel it on my lips.

"Is this okay?" I ask again.

When she nods, our noses brush, and I lean closer until her lips touch mine. For a moment, everything stops. My pulse, my breath, my mind. Vanilla and honey flood my senses, scents that will forever remind me of this moment. Then a bird calls in the distance and her hand slides over my shoulder and settles on my neck.

And she kisses me back.

Kissing Naomi is everything I imagined. She's soft and intoxicating and doesn't wait for me to take control. Her lips move against mine cautiously at first, and as I respond, she shifts closer so our legs are pressed together as closely as our mouths. Her hand moves up my neck to my jawline. When her thumb traces my cheekbone, the part of my face usually protected by my glasses, my heart somersaults. My lips part and our tongues meet, tentatively at first, then more boldly. I want to hold her closer but like a snap, I remember how exposed we are.

I pull back, peppering her lips and jaw with kisses so she doesn't think I'm stopping because of her. She tucks her forehead against my neck and exhales. "That was... wow." I feel her smile against my chest, and it fills me with an emotion I've never felt before. Happiness mixed with relief and something more, something that goes much deeper. Which is ridiculous because we barely know each other. And yet.

My lips settle on the top of her head. "I've been wanting to do that for a while."

She smiles again. "Me, too."

"I'd like to think this would have happened without our siblings interfering, but I do appreciate their efforts."

"Theo's been encouraging me since the day we arrived."

I pull back to look at her. Her cheeks flush and her gaze drops to her lap. As much as I don't want to ruin the moment, it's in my nature to be practical. "Is this a bad idea?" I wait for her to gasp or yell or worse, get upset, but she just bites her lip.

After several beats she meets my eyes. "Does it feel like a bad idea?"

"Quite the opposite."

"Then let's not worry about what happens when we leave." She trails her fingers down my bare arm, sending my nerve endings into hyperdrive, then reaches for the back of my neck. "Now let's try that again."

My eyes close as our lips meet. She sighs against my mouth and that soft sound carries me back to the daydream of us living on the same campus, when we have all the time and privacy we could want. But something small and insistent reminds me that I've already made up my mind to transfer and that daydream will never happen. I push those worries further down and concentrate on this amazing—yes, amazing—girl.

We may be opposites in a lot of ways, but we balance each other. Maybe that's what I need in my life to feel complete. I thought it had to be school and career and nothing else, but how can this feeling that's gripping my heart be bad?

When Naomi ends the kiss, my eyes blink open to find her watching me with a soft expression on her face. "Definitely not a bad idea." Her smile grows wider. "Can I ask you another question?"

Anything. "Of course."

"Were you named after that famous writer?"

My eyes roll so far back in my head she laughs.

"I can't tell if that's a yes or no." She grazes the side of my face with her fingers and I lean into her touch, closing my eyes.

"It's a yes. My dad was obsessed with *Fear and Loathing in Las Vegas*, Thompson's most famous book, and somehow convinced my entirely rational mother to name me after the guy." I blink my eyes open and meet her gaze. "Fortunately, not many people our age are familiar with him, but my professors think it's hilarious."

"That's rough."

"Yeah." I inch closer and brush my lips against hers.

After a moment, she pulls back. "If it's really gonna take an hour to get back, my bladder might not make it."

"No world-urinal for you?"

"Hard pass." We stand and she slings her bag over her shoulders. "Oh, your glasses." She unzips them, but before handing them to me, reaches for my face and studies me.

I try not to squirm under her gaze. "Are you making sure you'll remember what I look like once I go back to being Clark Kent?"

She snorts. The sound shouldn't make me want to pull her into my arms, but it does. "There's this vulnerability to you without them. Like when you're wearing your glasses, you're all business, totally in control, but without them..." She trails off. "I'm just soaking it in."

I step closer until our bodies brush. The length of her pressed against me makes my breathing grow shallow. "I never feel like I'm in control around you," I whisper. I touch her cheek, letting my fingers tangle in a stray piece of her hair.

She pushes to her toes to kiss me. My arms wrap around her, holding her close, and she tucks her head against my chest. "If this is you out of control, I'll take it."

We stay like that for several minutes. With each breath, the connection between us grows stronger until I'm ready to do whatever it takes to make this work.

"Bathroom for real," she whispers, and we separate.

With my glasses back on, I blink at the horizon. The sun washes out the landscape, scorching the grass and dirt until everything turns a muted brown. A light breeze carries up the side of the hill, offering relief, but it's not enough. "We might need to go swimming when we get back."

"Please don't talk about water."

I smirk. "That bad?"

She nods and I grab her hand. "Well, let's go."

Naomi walks fast when she's on a mission, so we make it back in forty-five minutes. After the bathroom is handled, we put a little distance between us for the final approach to the campsite. We speak at the same time.

"It's probably best—" she says.

"I'm not sure if—" I nod at her to continue.

"We probably shouldn't say anything to the moms about..." She points a finger between us. "Right?"

"That's what I was going to say, too. I'm sure they would be happy, but—" I hesitate, not wanting to say something that will somehow screw up this thing between us before we've even figured out what this thing is.

"But we don't need them over-analyzing everything we say and do."

"I'm glad we agree." I press a quick kiss to her cheek before continuing down the path. It shouldn't be too hard to keep this from the moms. They expect us to talk and do things together, so as long as I can keep myself from touching Naomi in front of them, they shouldn't have a clue.

But when we step into the clearing, all that fades away. Something is wrong.

The door to the moms' yurt is open. Raised voices carry to where we stand, and the coolers sit in a row near the picnic table.

"What's going on?" Naomi says.

Nancy comes outside with her suitcase in her hand. "What's going on," she says, "is we're leaving."

17

NAOMI

We can't leave.

Not now.

Hunter and I look at each other. He seems as panicked as I feel.

"Mom, what's going on?" I ask again. This isn't like her. She's the queen of talking about things until there are literally no words left. Bonus points if everyone's had a good cry. And while it looks like she may have been crying, I guarantee she has more to say.

She sets her suitcase near the coolers and drags her arm across her forehead. "We'll discuss it in the car."

I hurry to her side. "What? No! Mom, be reasonable about this."

Her jaw clicks and her eyes close. She takes a deep breath. "I am being reasonable," she whispers. "I didn't come here to—" She shakes her head. "No. I'm not rehashing this now."

Margo steps outside and she and Mom lock eyes for a moment before Mom turns away. "Nancy, please. Let's talk about this."

"I'm done talking."

Theo and Melody appear from the other direction. He gives a subtle shake of his head and his eyes widen, telling me to let it go for now. Clearly they've already witnessed part of whatever's going on.

Melody isn't as calm. She's clinging to Theo's arm and tears run freely down her cheeks. "You can't leave!" she says.

Everyone turns to her.

"You promised six days and today is only number four." Melody crosses and uncrosses her arms and Theo rests a hand on her shoulder. "What happened to seeing things all the way through and not giving up and talking about our problems?"

It makes me proud the way she rattles off the same conflict management techniques that our moms have used with us. *See, we listen to you!* I want to shout.

Mom exhales slowly and I can see her resolve weaken.

I press my hand against her back. "Whatever happened, do you really want things to end this way? You two are like best friends."

"We are best friends," she says softly. She sniffs, then looks at Margo, who's still standing on the threshold of their yurt. "This was supposed to be a relaxing trip and instead I'm being attacked." She says this loud enough for Margo to hear, and Margo's face goes stricken.

"Nancy, I swear I'm not attacking you. And this is a relaxing trip, but also one where we work through some of the problems we agreed would be easier to discuss in person." She smiles weakly. It's the most uncertain I've seen her since we arrived. "You know I would never do anything to jeopardize our friendship."

Desperation pushes words out of my mouth. "Mom, you always tell me that whatever's going on, running away isn't the answer."

She kicks at the ground with her sandal. "I'm not running away."

I give her a small smile. "You literally packed up your things and declared we're leaving."

She sighs. "Okay, maybe I am." After several deep breaths, she looks across the clearing at Margo. "We'll stay, but I need a little space."

Margo holds up her hands. "I can do that."

Mom picks up her suitcase but doesn't move. "Can I bunk with you tonight?"

Her request surprises me. She must really be hurting if she doesn't want to sleep in the same room as Margo. "Yeah, of course."

She seems to deflate in front of us. "I think I'd like to be alone. Theo, can you—" She sets her suitcase back on the ground.

Theo hurries to her side and grabs her bag. "Got it." He and I exchange a relieved look, one I feel to my core. Because while of course I'm worried about Mom and don't want her and Margo to be mad at each other, if she can't keep it together, what hope do the rest of us have?

Mom trails a hand on both our cheeks. "Naomi, I'll be in your yurt."

Margo returns to their yurt, leaving the four of us scattered around the campsite. Melody wipes away her tears and dances in a circle around Theo, but Hunter looks shell-shocked.

"I've never seen my mom look so uncertain," he says.

"She was backpedaling pretty hard when we got here," Theo says. "I don't know what exactly set Mom off, but she was pissed."

"I'm glad we're not leaving early," I say. Now that the moms aren't around, I reach for Hunter's hand. This connection between us feels too fragile to say out loud what I'm thinking—that it would be beyond unfair to yank us apart when we finally admitted we like each other—but I hope the panic and surprise still lingering on his face are because he doesn't want to say goodbye yet either.

And now Mom's going to be sleeping in my yurt.

He laces his fingers through mine and gives me a wobbly smile.

Theo points at our hands. "So this is a thing now?"

Melody jumps up and down and claps her hands. "Yay! Naomi, you'll fit so perfectly in our family and like I told you, I've always wanted a sister, and no offense Theo, I of course like you too, but ugh! This is so great." She presses her fists to her chest and bats her eyes.

Words. I have no words. It's all I can do not to tug my hand from Hunter's.

He responds by squeezing my hand. "Mel, slow your roll."

I laugh through my nose. He usually speaks so formally, like he wants to make sure everyone knows how seriously he takes the English language, that the slang catches me by surprise.

She wags a finger at us. "You can deny it all you want but I'm never wrong about these things."

Theo raises an eyebrow. "You've predicted other teen marriages?"

"Not specifically, but I know what I know."

"Can we please change topics? This—" I hold up our clasped hands. "Is off the table for fireside chats. The last thing we need is the moms dissecting our every move."

Theo strokes the nonexistent stubble on his chin. "What moves are you planning?"

"Omigod, Theo!" I face Hunter and run my hand up his arm. Hopefully the smile I give him is sweet and doesn't reveal that I'd like to murder my brother right now. "I'm gonna check on my mom, then did you still want to go for a swim?"

His eyes dart to Theo and Melody, who are far too entertained by us. "Yeah, that sounds great."

I want to push to my toes and kiss him, but Theo might actually combust. Instead, I leave Hunter to deal with our siblings and go inside. Mom's sitting on the edge of my bed, her head in her hands. She looks up when the door clatters shut behind me.

"I'm sorry I've made this such a mess," she says.

I hurry to her side and sit next to her. The mattress squeaks with both our weight. "Mom, you haven't made anything a mess. This group loves analyzing emotional drama. You've just given us something to do." I nudge her shoulder with mine and hope it's not too soon to joke about whatever happened.

She sniffs once before looking me in the eye. "I can't get over how grown-up you are."

My smile falls. "I don't always feel it."

"Can I let you in on a secret?" She waits for me to nod. "I don't either."

A groan escapes me. "You mean this feeling of not knowing what the hell I'm doing never goes away?"

She shakes her head, a smile toying with her lips. "Nope. You just get better at hiding it. Until your friend picks away at the walls you've put up and suddenly you're fighting in front of your kids."

"Is that what happened?"

"At its core, yes."

I scoot closer and rest my head against hers. "Is there anything I can do to help?"

She wraps an arm around my waist and settles into the snuggle. "I'll be okay after tonight. I just need time to think without being forced to explain what I'm thinking. I hope I'm not cramping your style by crashing in here tonight."

"What style could you possibly be cramping?" My mind flits to Hunter. Nothing's been said about a curfew but she might feel differently if I'm sneaking into bed in the middle of the night.

"This is your vacation, too, and I want you to have fun."

"We talked about going swimming. You can join us if you want."

"I might just hide in here for a bit, if that's okay with you."

"You do you, Mom." I lean closer and press a kiss to her temple. "Are you sure you're okay on your own?"

She pushes a hand through her hair, which makes it stick out every which way—the same way mine does. "Yes, of course. Go swim."

I fire off a quick text to Sage to tell her I kissed Hunter, and when I'm changing into my swimsuit, a new worry twists my stomach. This won't be the first time Hunter will see my bikini, but the idea of strutting outside half naked makes me break into a sweat. Fortunately, when I peek my head outside, no one is there.

It's also quiet at the guys' yurt. "Theo?" I call as I approach the door, but there's no answer. I knock, and still nothing. My hand rests on the door, ready to push it open, but Hunter could be changing clothes and even though I can picture Sage nodding her encouragement, I back away. They must already be at the lake.

As if on cue, Sage texts back.
Sage: annnnndddddd??????
I fill her screen with heart emojis.
Me: amazing
She doesn't know the joke now, but she will soon enough.
Me: hoping for more
Sage: it's the stars. I tell you they're magic
I glance at the sky. The faint outline of the moon peeks from behind a cloud, but otherwise there's nothing to indicate the magnitude of what comes out at night.
Me: I think you're right
Several families have blankets and chairs spread out on the small beach. They must be new arrivals since we've hardly seen anyone since we got here, but it seems they're making the most of the warm afternoon, too. I drop my towel next to Theo's, kick off my flip-flops, and scan the shore for the rest of them. My brother is flung across the back of a giant inflatable unicorn while Melody's wrapped around the neck. Hunter somehow drew the short end of the stick because he's pulling them through the water. The unicorn head bobs with each step, and Theo's laughter reaches me.

Hunter smiles when he sees me. Not The Smirk or any of its lesser siblings, but a real smile. He's not wearing his glasses, so they must be tucked in one of the towels. I pull my shirt over my head, careful to keep my suit in place, then slip off my shorts and set them on my shoes.

"No more stalling," I whisper to myself. My body has never been an issue for me. In addition to Mom's hair, I also got her curvy hips and perfectly average breasts. Theo's metabolism is faster than mine, but we've always fallen into the not-too-thin and not-too-heavy category. But right now, as I'm walking across the sand, every insecurity I've ever felt comes rushing back. My pale freckled skin, the slight curve of my belly, the way my bikini covers too much or too little of my breasts, depending on who you're asking.

If Hunter's watching me, he's being subtle about it, and I'm grateful.

"Hurry up, Naomi!" Melody shouts from atop the unicorn. She's standing, holding the giant neck for balance, and as soon as my toes hit the warm water, she leaps into the air. It's ungraceful and childlike and I'm happy that she's happy. That the problems waiting for her back home aren't stopping her from having fun.

Her splash sends waves toward me, and I gasp as the water hits my bare stomach. Once I'm close enough, Theo dips a hand into the water and splashes me. "'Bout time," he says.

I bat my eyes and gesture at myself. "You think this happens in five seconds?"

"Oh please," he says. "You take as long to get ready as I do."

I laugh and splash him back. "That says more about you than it does about me." Hunter's lingering at the front of the unicorn, so I lower myself to my shoulders and move through the water toward him. "How'd you get stuck towing them?"

He nods at Melody, who's doing a handstand, and shrugs. Only her ankles and feet stick out of the water. "She asked."

"Fair enough. You mind one more?"

He presses a hand to his chest and dips his head in a modified bow. "Your chariot, madam."

My cheeks redden. One moment he's like any other boy I've met, then he says something like that, and I remember he's in college. The one year difference between us isn't much, but there's a maturity to him that makes him more interesting than the boys back home.

I push off the bottom, swing a leg over the unicorn, and somehow end up straddling the neck. Hunter reaches for the small rope attached to the front and his hand grazes my leg. Then my foot. Then my leg again. Ripples of excitement warm me straight to my core. I want to pull him closer and feel his bare chest, but instead I settle for gripping the plastic unicorn and pretend nothing happened.

Theo nudges my back and I brace for his chants of insta-love. "Do I need to give the big brother talk?"

"You're younger than me."

"Those few minutes are irrelevant. Look, it's been a while for you and I want to make sure you're prepared."

"Jesus, Theo," I whisper. "I'm not sleeping with the guy. We barely kissed."

"I'm just saying. You saw how fast things happened with Sage and Neb. Fresh air does weird things to people."

Not to mention that I don't know when—or if—I'll see Hunter again. If anything's going to happen, we've got two more days, but even though I encouraged Sage not to worry about convention and just do what felt right, I'm really not ready to jump into Hunter's sleeping bag. "That might be, but I don't think that's the case with us."

He seems to consider this, then his face grows serious. "Is Mom okay?"

My lips press together, and I nod. "She will be. I think she underestimated what it would be like having the self-help turned on her."

"Three Good Things about being besties with a therapist?" he says.

I need to tell Theo about the offer, especially since I only have one day left to decide. My stomach churns at not knowing what he'll say to my massive Twin Trust violation, but I can't keep putting it off. He's the closest person in my life and I hate that we have this uncertainty hanging between us.

He laughs. "Perhaps she's regretting giving merit to the dread."

I twist around to give him my Mom Look.

"Not the reaction I was going for." He stretches out a foot and pokes my leg. "What's going on?"

I love that he doesn't ask if everything's okay. Because it's not, and I'm guessing the sudden tears in my eyes make that clear. I take a deep breath. "We need to talk."

"But I don't wanna break up."

I give him another Mom Look for good measure.

He bats his lashes. "It's not you, it's me?"

"Twin Trust?"

"This must be serious if you're playing the Twin Trust card."

I roll my eyes. "You played it to get me to admit I liked Hunter."

He bobs his head. "And you did, so my attempt was valid."

Enough tiptoeing around this. "What are you doing after high school?"

The smile falls from his face and this moment feels like one I'll remember for the rest of my life. The sun's warming us from its spot among the stars. Hunter's still pulling us through the water. Melody's doing backflips a little closer to shore. And Theo and I are locked in a space where we both seem afraid to take a breath.

"Why are you bringing this up now?"

"Two reasons." I could make this about him, but that's not fair. I hold up a finger. "One, Twin Trust requires that we tell each other everything, even the stuff I wouldn't mind keeping to myself." I glance at Hunter. "You deflect every time the future is mentioned, and I hate that I don't know what you're thinking. It's weird that we don't talk about this."

His gaze drops. "Older sister wisdom is real."

"And two. Something's come up with me and now I don't know what I'm doing."

His head snaps back up. "What happened?" His brows furrow and the protectiveness in his eyes makes me hold up a hand.

"It's all good." I take a deep breath and glance at Hunter, who's slowed to the point that we're barely moving. He already knows so it doesn't matter if he's listening, but I still fumble over my words. "What have you been thinking would happen to the show after we graduate?"

He shrugs his casual everything's-okay shrug, but I can read him as well as he can read me. This has been bothering him too. "I figured you'd record in your dorm room and send the files to wherever I am."

"And where will you be?"

"What if I don't go away to school?" he says.

"Like not go away, or not go?"

He shrugs, and the openness in his face is the most insecure I've seen him in a long time. "I'm sure I'll go. I mean, it's not like I have another plan, but I don't know if higher education is right for me."

I scoot closer to him on the unicorn, careful not to flip us. "It's okay not to have it all figured out right now. We're still in high school. We've got years before we need to get real jobs. And look at Mom. She's turning forty and wants to change her career." My head falls against his shoulder. "You'll be good at whatever you decide to do, so give yourself time to figure out what that is."

"You still haven't said why you're bringing this up now."

I take a breath and finally confess what's haunted me. "I got an offer. For the show. From a company that wants to take Three Good Things to the next level." I air quote the corporate-speak.

"Naomi, that's fantastic!" Theo scrambles into a sitting position and reaches for my hand. "Who is it?"

"Auralacity. They're in Seattle."

His mouth drops. "Auralacity, as in *Bird Watching with Nate* and *Storytime with Gramma?* You wouldn't think a podcast about bird watching would work, but he takes it to a Blair Witch level and it's mesmerizing. And everyone loves Gramma."

"How do you know this?"

"I take my producing duties very seriously." He leans closer. "I did a lot of research when we first started. Auralacity is huge and getting huger." He nods at me, his eyes bright. "Finding obscure podcasts and bringing them into the mainstream is kind of their thing."

I scoured their website when I got the email, but didn't realize all this. "Maybe this is a bigger deal than I thought."

He smacks my knee. "I told you you're amazing!"

Hunter snickers from the front of the unicorn and I fight back a smile.

"You don't seem happy about this," Theo says.

"I don't know what to do."

"And take the offer is the wrong answer because?"

"It's a huge opportunity, but I'm scared." There's no sense hiding that fact from him. If he doesn't already sense it, he'll figure it out soon enough.

"Scared of keeping the podcast going while you're in college or scared of being successful?"

"Honestly?"

He holds out his hands as if to say 'what are we doing here?'

"I think you know why I'm scared."

He leans across the unicorn and props his chin on his fist. "You are not a hack."

"Then why do I feel like I'm faking my way through this?"

"Because you're suffering from imposter syndrome."

"You're making that up."

"It's a real thing. Most common among women, but it basically means you don't feel qualified to be doing whatever it is you're doing and believe it's only a matter of time before everyone figures you out."

Something in my chest loosens. "That's exactly how I feel."

He gives me a soft smile, one that reminds me of when we were little and he'd wait to eat his after-school snack until I was ready. "I know it is, but it's not true. You were made to do this."

Tears threaten to fall as I shake my head. Admitting that I don't know if I can do this without him is harder than I thought. "They require that their podcasters be in the Pacific Northwest so at first I thought if I took the deal I couldn't go to Berkeley. Now I know that might not be the case, but I'm reconsidering what I thought I wanted. Maybe I'll just go to community college, or something else close to home. Or take online classes at University of Oregon." And going to a less expensive school will help with things at home.

He shifts so he's leaning on his elbows. "That's a good plan. Get your pre-reqs out of the way without paying for a dorm."

I pull back. "What do you know about pre-reqs?"

"I know things." After a beat, he smirks. "Mr. College may have shared some wisdom."

"You two talked about this?" It shouldn't come as a surprise. He and Hunter *are* sharing a room and Theo can talk to anyone, but for a second the connection I've felt with Hunter feels a little less special. Maybe he's like this with everyone once you get past his prickly exterior.

"You know how I am when it's dark and I can't sleep."

Yeah, he can talk for hours. "So what did he say you should do?"

He rolls his eyes. "He suggested the military."

My snort is so loud the unicorn judges me.

"Yeah, that's what I said, too."

I look up and realize we've drifted a good distance from shore. "Speaking of Hunter, where'd he go?" I ask.

"Your boy ditched us."

"More like he heard what we were talking about and wanted to give us privacy." I scan the shore and spot him sitting at the water's edge with Melody. "There's another thing with the contract."

"They want your firstborn?"

"They provide their own producer."

"Did you ask if you can keep me?" He says it so matter-of-factly that I feel stupid for not thinking of it myself.

"No."

"No?" If Theo had a Dad Look, that's what he's giving me now. "Unless this is your not-so-subtle way of firing me, you should ask."

"What if they say no?"

"I'm not gonna lie. I thought I'd be producing your show for the indefinite future, but if I get replaced, at least it's by a company as cool as Auralacity."

My pulse roars in my ear and I reach for his hand. I can't do this without him. Without his magical touch everyone will realize that I'm fumbling my way through each episode. "Maybe there's another way you can stay involved. It's not just that I don't know if I can do the show without you—I don't know if I *want* to. This has been our thing since day one."

"When do they need an answer?"

"By the end of the day tomorrow."

"Tomorrow?" The joy slips from his face. Everything moves in slow motion as the realization that I've kept this a secret settles over him. A knot clenches in my gut, the hurt of my betrayal that's rippling through him gripping me as well. His voice is almost a whisper. "How long have you known?"

I press my lips together. "A couple weeks."

"What happened to Twin Trust?" His eyes narrow and he grows quiet. For as big as Theo's personality is when he's happy, when he's upset, it's like he tries to crawl inside himself and block out everything around him.

That's what's happening now.

Sometimes I wish he would yell and call me names, but he internalizes his hurt until he finds the exact compartment in his brain to tuck it away, then he moves on. But he doesn't forget.

"I know I'm only the Producer Twin, but I wish you would have talked to me about this sooner."

"Talking about the future felt off limits. You always change the subject, so I didn't know how to bring it up."

"Yeah, because talking to people is a foreign concept for you."

"Theo, I'm sorry."

His hair falls in his face, shielding his eyes.

"I didn't mean to upset you."

"I'm going in." He slips off the unicorn into the water, ending the conversation.

Desperation pushes me to my knees and the unicorn lurches. "You're leaving?"

He sinks until the water's up to his nose and watches me. The connection between us has always been the one thing I could count on, but right now it feels like one of the threads binding us together has been permanently severed.

My voice cracks. "I'm sorry."

He swims back to me and grabs a handle on the side of the unicorn, then stretches out his body and starts kicking, propelling us toward shore.

When he doesn't have anyone to show off for, Theo is the sweetest boy I know—even when he's more upset with me than I can remember. He doesn't look back, but he doesn't let go, and right now all I can ask for. Once it's shallow enough that he can stand, he moves to the front where Hunter had been and drags me to the sand.

"Theo, how can I fix this?"

Something seems to shift in him, like he's found the place to hide how I've hurt him. He smiles, but it's the fake smile from his middle school days, the one he pulled out when kids made fun of him. "You know I've got your back whatever you decide." His gaze shifts from the ground and back to me. "But you better decide to take the offer."

"How can you know that so quickly?"

"What does your gut tell you?"

I love that we all seem to use the same logic. "That I should take the offer." Figuring out Berkeley can wait.

"Well, there you go." He nods subtly at Hunter, who's close enough to hear us. "You let me know if I need to set him straight or give him a nudge. Whatever you want."

I force a smile, trying to hide the nausea swirling in my gut. "You will be neither my guardian nor my pimp."

"What's this about a pimp?" Hunter's voice is right behind me, and I let out a squeak.

"No pimps," I say, but Theo just shakes his head.

"Sorry I marooned you," Hunter says. "But it seemed like you needed some privacy."

I raise my brows at Theo and give him a look that says *I told you.*

Theo raises his brows back and mouths, *"Maroon?"*

It's killing me how hard Theo's trying to pretend everything is okay.

Hunter trails a hand on the unicorn's neck. "Were you done, or did you want to stay in the water a little longer?"

Theo exchanges a look with Melody, who's standing behind her brother, and they clasp their hands to their chests and make kissy faces at me.

I try to ignore them. "That sounds great." I pat the unicorn's butt. "I was on this guy most of the time so barely got wet."

Theo's eyes nearly bug out of his head.

I step toward the water, but Hunter stops me.

"Let's bring your friend." He's holding the rope and his expression is impossible to read.

"Okay."

We wade into the water. It's nothing like the ocean, which sometimes has waves so strong it's a struggle to get past where they're breaking. On this lake, the only waves I've seen are from boats and right now the unicorn is the only vessel out here.

My thoughts bounce from Theo to Hunter and back again. I can't remember the last time Theo's been this mad at me. I have to believe he'll forgive me, but I'll never forget the hurt in his eyes when I admitted I'd betrayed our Twin Trust.

When the water reaches my chest, Hunter swings the unicorn around so it's shielding us from shore, and it's like we're the only ones out here. Water glistens on his shoulders, drops running over the smooth muscles that flex as he runs a hand through his wet hair.

"How'd it go with Theo?"

"Not great. He's really upset I didn't tell him about the offer sooner."

Hunter tucks a piece of my hair behind my ear, his touch gentle. "Is there anything I can do to help?"

"Just what you're doing."

"And what's that?" His gaze pulls me closer until I can feel the warmth of him through the water.

Or maybe it's my temperature that's spiked. "Distract me?"

"I realize hanging out behind a unicorn isn't the most romantic, but—"

I close the distance between us. My hand finds his hip beneath the water and my heartbeat races. "No, this is perfect."

In one swift movement, his lips are on mine. His free hand slides up my arm to my neck, cradling my head, and my hand moves around his torso to his back. Our bellies press together and the feel of his bare skin against mine is a total rush. The noise from people playing at the water's edge and thoughts of Theo and our moms fighting and worries about future decisions disappear. His lips move gently, as if he's still learning how we fit together, and we sink lower so only our heads are above the water. My hands roam over his back, up to his neck, and when I grip my fingers in his hair, he inhales sharply.

I take advantage of his mouth opening, our tongues meeting in a shock of heat. The kiss deepens and without thinking, I hook a leg around his hip. His free hand—because he's still got the other hand on the unicorn—pulls up my other leg so I'm straddling him. My legs hold me against him as we devour each other.

He breaks the kiss, breathing heavily. His dark eyes search mine, making me feel exposed. "Do you have any idea how incredible you are?"

I trail kisses along his jaw, trying to ignore the growing hardness in his swimsuit. A braver girl, one less concerned with how quickly things seem to be happening, would tug her bikini bottoms aside and go for it, but I'm not ready for that. "Are you saying I've upgraded from amazing?"

He laughs against my cheek and I pull back, hoping to catch a glimpse of The Smirk. But the look on his face is something more tender and it makes my heart gallop.

Maybe he's not ready for that either.

"You've definitely upgraded."

My lips travel from his neck to his shoulder. "I must admit my opinion of you continues to improve."

He pulls me closer, and for a moment we just hold each other, locked in this moment in a place I never imagined with a boy I only dreamed existed. One who's smart and funny and has enough edge to keep me on my toes. He's not intimidated by my strong personality, as Mom likes to call it, and based on the pressure between my legs, he really likes me.

"I'm glad to hear it," he whispers.

Words catch on the tip of my tongue. To ask what this means. Or if it means anything. But even though I know the odds of us lasting past this week are not in our favor, I want to live in this bubble as long as I can. I lift my face to kiss him again and he catches my cheek with his palm.

"Hey, what's wrong?" His voice is gentle. His thumb caresses my cheekbone and I lean into his touch.

"I wish we had more time."

His eyelids lower, and I can't tell if he's looking at my lips or lost in thought. "Since I started college—well, honestly, even before that. Really since I knew I wanted to be an editor, I thought the only way to achieve it was to block out everything else. To stay focused on my goals." His gaze lifts and the mix of sadness and uncertainty makes my heart clench. "My parents got married young. My mom put off her dreams to raise me and it took her years to establish her career. I don't want to make that same mistake."

"Liking someone doesn't have to be a mistake."

"I swore off dating because I thought it would be a distraction."

I glance at our bodies, which are still pressed together. "You're not wrong."

He continues to caress the side of my face. "I think I was. How can something—someone—that makes me so happy be a bad thing?"

A lump catches in my throat. I've longed to hear these words since I first understood what it meant to have a boyfriend. Well, maybe not these exact words, but the intention behind them. "Three Good Things about our moms being besties?" The lilt at the end of my sentence gives away my uncertainty. Despite what he's saying, my past experience warns that anything that seems too good to be true probably is.

His hand moves to the base of my ponytail and he presses his forehead against mine. His breath tickles my lips. "I'm not sure what two and three are, but you are number one."

I snort against his lips, but he doesn't seem to care because he kisses me again. This kiss is gentle, unhurried, and my heart thuds so hard in my chest I'm sure he can feel it. Time seems to stand still and even while my heart wishes this could last forever, the voice in my head that sounds exactly like me—not Sage, not Theo—insists that I better not change my dreams for a boy I met four days ago.

Hunter pulls back. "We should probably head back." He kisses the tip of my nose, then my cheek, and finally the curve of my throat.

"That's not gonna happen if you keep doing that," I murmur into his hair.

He lifts his head and smiles at me. "Let's go."

I untangle my legs from his waist, and we wade toward the shore, him dragging the unicorn behind us.

"The real question is," I say. "Can we keep this from the moms?"

"My mom's like a hawk with secrets. I swear she knows when I'm keeping something from her."

"But she doesn't know about school." His brow furrows and I want to smooth it with my fingertips. "Sorry, I shouldn't have brought that up right now."

"Have you thought more about what you're going to do?" he asks.

"I don't think Theo's made up his mind, but it might work out for us to both stay home."

"So we won't be on campus together." His voice is flat, and I'm surprised at the disappointment lingering there.

"I thought you decided to transfer?"

He catches my pinkie with his and gives me a smile. "That doesn't mean I haven't thought about what it'd be like to be there together."

And with that, I'm in. No matter what happens or where we go to school—and despite the fact that I've known this boy for less than a week—he's permanently lodged himself in my heart.

— 18 —
HUNTER

The water from the shower runs down my back, reminding me of Naomi's hands and how they felt in the lake. Being that close to her has me rethinking what I thought I wanted. I meant what I said about reevaluating my priorities and allowing space in my life for a relationship, but what can we have, living in different states? My friends' girlfriends have always demanded a lot of time and attention, something I can't promise, especially if we're long-distance. And is it moronic to even attempt to maintain anything after this week? Naomi truly is amazing, but how long would that spark last once we're back in the real world and separated by hundreds of miles?

I'm no closer to an answer when I get back to the campsite. Mom's sitting near the firepit by herself and the look on her face makes me stop.

"Are you okay?" I ask. It's not something I've had to ask her often. Usually if something's wrong she's the one telling us, and telling us in a way so we know exactly where we stand, or in my case, what I did to upset her. But this quietness enveloping her is new.

I dump my shower stuff in an empty chair, sit next to her, and wait.

She clasps her hands and taps them to her lips, thinking. "Have you ever had a moment that's made you rethink everything you thought you knew about yourself?"

I laugh through my nose and immediately wish I could take it back. She looks appalled. "No!" I grab her arm to keep her from leaving. "I was just asking myself the same thing. I'm laughing at the irony, not at you."

She watches me for several breaths, as if deciding whether I'm telling the truth, and finally her shoulders relax. "What are you rethinking?"

"You first," I say.

She smiles from the corner of her mouth, and it strikes me how similar we are. Her intensity and motivation have always been intimidating, and I realize now that those same qualities are what's driving me to stay focused and get my degree in three years.

Her gaze flicks to her yurt. "You obviously saw what happened earlier." She waits for me to nod before continuing. "Nancy said some hard things. None of them untrue. And it's got me thinking."

"Is there anything I can help with?"

She stares into the firepit. It's like she didn't hear me. "I worry sometimes that I've been too hard on you and your sister. I know better than anyone what being demanding does to your psyche, but as long as no one pushed back, I was able to convince myself that it was all for the greater good."

"So Nancy pushed back and now you're second-guessing yourself?" I ask.

"Something like that." She loosens her hands and leans back in her chair. "My intensity comes from a place of good, I swear." She smiles but her eyes brim with tears. "Your father loved to tell me how difficult I could be. I blamed that on our failing marriage, but what if he was right?"

We're edging toward dangerous territory. "I wouldn't call you difficult. I've always known that you support me no matter what." So why haven't I told her that I want to transfer?

No time like the present.

"In fact," I say. "That's kind of along the lines of what's been on my mind."

"Don't use qualifiers," she says, and I'm back in seventh grade at our kitchen table trying to explain why I don't like sports without admitting that I'm not athletic like some of my friends. Kids I soon drifted away from. "State your opinion and own it."

We lock eyes for a moment.

"It's crap like that, isn't it?" she asks.

"You could tone it down a bit, yeah."

She closes her eyes. "I'm sorry. Please tell me what's weighing on you." She looks at me. "I want to help. Truly."

I do my best to maintain eye contact, but I don't want to see the disappointment in her eyes when I tell her. Instead, I focus on a leaf between my feet. "You know how much I love Berkeley."

"Yes." She says it slowly, cautiously, a thousand questions dancing in that single word.

"It's been everything I hoped it would be. But I think I need to be closer to home."

She reaches for my arm. "It's normal to be a little homesick. This semester is the first time you've been away for longer than a week or two."

"It's not that. I'm worried about Mel. She won't tell me what's going on, but I know she's having a hard time. And I feel guilty leaving the two of you."

"That's not a reason to drop out."

"No!" How can I be so good with other peoples' words but so bad at explaining my own thoughts? "I want to transfer. I can live at home and be there to help out. My plans for my career haven't changed."

Her expression softens. "It sounds like you've already made up your mind."

Pieces of my conversation with Naomi come back to me, followed by how distant Mel seems after only a couple months. Being home won't guarantee things will go back to the way they were, but I'll regret not trying. "I think I have."

"Please tell me if there's anything I can do to help."

The tension in my gut loosens and I can finally breathe. "I will. Thanks, Mom."

She lifts her hands. "I literally did nothing."

"You're supporting me and aren't making me feel like I'm destroying my future." Because that's what Dad would say. That I needed to focus on myself and my own dreams. That Mel would be fine.

"Hunter, you're eighteen. Aside from getting arrested for murder, there's very little you could do at this point to destroy your future."

This time I laugh for real. "I'll remember that."

Mom starts to get up, but I stop her.

"Is everything okay with Nancy?"

"It will be." She sighs and gives me a sad smile. "She's another person I'm realizing I've been too hard on. But I'm working on it."

"I'm glad."

A lightness that I haven't felt in months carries me through the rest of the afternoon to dinner. Naomi smiles when she sees me.

"Why do you look so happy?"

"Would it be cheesy to say because of you?"

"Yes." A blush creeps up her cheeks and my pulse speeds up.

"I talked to my mom. About transferring."

"Oh, wow. Based on your smile I'm assuming it went well?"

"She barely reacted. I've built this up in my head so much that I thought the ground would split beneath me, but she fully supports my decision."

"I'm really glad for you." She steps forward like she's going to hug me, then pauses. Looks around.

The moms are working on dinner, moving carefully around each other like they're afraid to make physical contact. They aren't paying us any attention, but I honestly don't care. Telling my non-earth-shattering secret has made me want to share more. Like how being near Naomi makes me feel like a different person. A better person.

I move toward her and pull her into my arms. Her head tucks against my chest and I inhale vanilla and honey. "Maybe we can go for another hike later."

"As long as we don't go too far. My bladder almost exploded earlier."

I look into her eyes, trying to communicate what I'm thinking without saying out loud that I want to make out with her.

Her smile tells me she understands. "Oh. Yeah. A moonlit hike sounds amazing."

We both laugh at her word choice. Another thing about her that will forever be marked in my brain.

After an awkward dinner because the moms barely spoke and Theo was quieter than normal, the stars perform their evening show, and I'm struck again at the wondrous beauty above us. I knew the stars were up there—I did the planetarium field trip and marveled at the galaxies that go far beyond the Milky Way—but I never imagined what it would feel like for them to literally cover the sky above me. And I mean literally in the literal sense. There isn't a patch of sky untouched by their magnificence.

I'm sitting between Mel and Naomi, and while the enormity of the stars fills me with a yearning to reach for Naomi's hand, I hold back.

Instead, I pull out my phone and text the same message to Shawna and Darren.

`Me: Shawna might have been right (not really, but a little)`

Then I shove it into my pocket and lean toward my sister.

"Hey, there's something I'm thinking about doing and I want to hear what you think," I say.

Her eyes dart to Naomi and the corner of her mouth lifts. "I already told you to kiss her."

I cut a look at the moms. The light from their cell phones glow in their laps—the no cell phone rule officially out the window—and they still seem to be ignoring each other.

"No, goofball, not that."

"But did you kiss her?"

"Yes." Thinking about Naomi's lips on mine brings a dopey smile to my face.

Mel presses her hands to her heart and bats her eyes. "Yay."

"I'm trying to have a serious conversation with you."

She blinks several more times, then leans closer, resting her hand on my arm. "Okay, I'm listening."

I take a quick breath. "How would you feel about me moving back home?" It doesn't feel as terrifying to say the words out loud now that Mom knows, but if Mel doesn't want me there, is there any point to me transferring?

Her brows furrow in a mirror image of Mom. "Like leaving college? But I thought you liked it there."

"I do, but—" Suddenly admitting the reason for coming home—because I'm worried about her—feels treacherous. The same things that have shifted in Mel's personality could make her take this the wrong way. I scramble for a way to soften my reasoning. "I worry about you and Mom being home alone."

Her head cocks, like she's trying to read between my words. "We have an alarm system."

"Not that kind of worry. You and I have always been two peas in a pod and I'm not sure I'm ready for that to be over."

"We're still peas." Her expression is uncertain, like she can tell there's more but isn't sure if she wants to know what it is. "Did Naomi say something to you?"

My phone buzzes in my pocket but I ignore it. I glance over my shoulder at Naomi, who's texting and probably listening to us. "I asked but she wouldn't tell me. I feel like you don't trust me anymore. Did I do something to upset you?"

She shakes her head. Her hair falls in her face and I have to strain to hear her. "No. I just—I don't know. Things *have* been different this year, but I guess I thought that's because I'm in middle school, not because you left."

The words 'you left' weigh heavy on me. When Dad left, my world upended and while Mom filled the role of both parents as best she could, I never really got over it. Is that what Mel's feeling now?

"Would you be okay with me transferring to a school closer to home and moving back in?"

She strokes her chin as if she's considering my offer. "That would be pretty cool."

"Pretty cool?" I tease.

She smiles. "I think I would like that." I stretch out my arm and tousle her hair, and she squeals. "I take it back! Stay at Berkeley!"

Suddenly everything stops. The moms fall silent and my heartbeat echoes off the stars. The majority of the people sitting around the fire already know my plan, but hearing it out loud makes it feel more real. Like I can't take it back.

Oh god, am I making a huge mistake?

Mom leans toward Nancy, no doubt telling her about my decision, and I feel an odd spark of pride that my outburst got them talking again.

The only person still in the dark is Theo, who's watching me from the other side of Naomi. "Tell the truth. You're joining the military and you were trying to recruit me."

My mouth hangs open. I don't want to say the wrong thing and inadvertently offend him, but then he smiles a big open-mouthed grin that shows his teeth, and I exhale.

"Dude, you need to relax," Theo says.

"Sorry, I'm still reeling a bit from—" I wave a hand at our families. "At all of this being out in the open."

Theo lowers his brows and gives me a serious look. "Trust me when I say that it's better to get things out in the open." He levels a look at Naomi, who flinches.

Instead of responding to her brother, she turns to me. "So no more Berkeley?"

"Looks like it."

"It would have been pretty ironic if I ended up there just as you left."

Naomi would kick ass at Berkeley, even if the thought of her there without me fills me with a longing for something that was never actually mine. "That would be ironic." Then I notice her word choice. "Wait, would have been?"

She smiles, and it makes my insides melt. "Your courage telling your mom has given me an extra boost of determination." She steals a glance at Theo and shakes her head. "He supports whatever I want to do, like I knew he would."

"So you've decided?"

"I know what I want, I just need to say it out loud."

Her pupils flare on those last words, and I hold her gaze. The fire pops but neither of us looks away. I want to pull her into my arms and get lost in her honey-vanilla scent, but it's too soon. Another hour and the moms will head to bed, and we can wander off without prying eyes.

I check my texts.

Darren: that requires an explanation

Shawna's reply is just a bunch of confetti emojis.

Since her text doesn't need a reply, I switch back to Darren.

Me: just kissing. But she's awesome.

"Are we really canoeing again?" Melody asks.

"'Fraid so, chica," Theo says. "You wanna buddy up with me tomorrow?"

Her eyes light up. "Can I?" She looks from me to Mom, but Mom's not paying attention to us.

I tuck my phone under my leg. "There's no rule about who rides with whom," I say. Mel rolls her eyes at my usage of whom, and I bump Naomi's foot with mine. "Will you be my buddy tomorrow?"

She nods, and if I didn't know better, I'd say she's nervous.

The conversation drifts from one inane topic to another, and it feels like time crawls to a stop. Finally, *finally*, Nancy stretches, and Mom yawns.

"Naomi and Melody, is it still okay if I bunk with you tonight?"

"You're still doing that?" Naomi asks.

I had hoped they would have made up by now, but there must still be some lingering tension.

"Just for tonight." Nancy and Mom exchange a look that I'm not going to attempt to decipher.

"Good night, kids," Mom says. "We've got a big day tomorrow, so be sure to get enough sleep."

"We're just canoeing, right?" Mel asks.

Mom smiles. "Maybe, maybe not."

"Do I still get to partner with Theo?"

Theo raises his hand. "Will I be required to exert physical effort?"

"Yes," both moms say, and he groans while Mel beams.

"You'll have fun, I promise." Nancy tousles Theo's hair and he ducks away from her.

"Be sure to get enough sleep," Mom says. "We're leaving by nine." She looks at me a beat longer than everyone else and I do my best not to fidget. If she knew what I'm thinking, she'd never go to bed.

It's another half hour before their light goes out. Theo and Mel are both lost in their phones, while Naomi's been staring at the sky so long her neck has to be stiff.

"I heard the stars are even more amazing down by the lake," I whisper.

The corner of her mouth ticks up. "I bet they are."

"Want to go check them out?"

She turns her head to look at me. "I thought you'd never ask."

"Are you swimming?" Mel asks. "I want to go!"

"No, we're not swimming," I say.

"Well, that sounds boring. I can look at the stars here."

Theo smiles. "What do you know about constellations?"

Mel crosses her arms. "Just the main ones, like the Big Dipper and Orion. But it's hard to see them with all the other stars getting in the way."

Theo gives us a head nod and I mouth "thank you."

Naomi grabs a blanket from the chair Mom had been sitting in and we make our way down the path. The occasional lamppost brightens the trail, but the stars are so bright they aren't necessary. It's like being out on a full moon but instead of the one bright spot in the sky, the entire sky is turned on.

I kind of know how it feels.

Our intertwined hands swing between us as we walk, and her thumb is doing some kind of magic over my knuckle. With every brush of her skin, electric pulses zip through my body until all I can think of is her. Of how lucky I am that our plotlines crossed and that she actually likes me. We reach the edge of the lake and stand there for a moment. Neither of us speaks. The sky felt impressive back at the campsite, but the scene before us is next level.

"It feels like we're standing at the edge of the universe," she whispers.

The water is completely still, reflecting a mirror-image of the stars. "I was thinking the same thing."

"When my mom said we were coming here, it sounded weird to drive all this way to see stars. But now I get it." She squeezes my hand and smiles softly. "This is one of those things that stays with you for the rest of your life."

She's talking about the stars, but the same is true for her. Meeting Naomi has changed how I think about my future. I'm not so naïve that I think we're going to spend the rest of our lives together, but the way she makes me feel, like I'm somehow more complete when she smiles at me, is something I don't want to lose.

"Do you want to sit?" she asks. When I nod, she unfurls the blanket. We settle next to each other—right next to each other—legs, hips, and shoulders pressed firmly together. "This feels like that episode of *Friends* when Ross and Rachel go to the planetarium."

"I'm sorry I didn't bring any juice boxes," I say.

She snorts, and I laugh. "You watch it?"

"Mel's obsessed and Mom never misses a chance to say that she watched the show when it was first on TV. I've absorbed it via osmosis."

"That's good enough for me." She snuggles closer to my side.

I rest my head on hers and try to control my breathing. "I'm really glad we're here together."

"Me too."

We stay like that for a bit longer. I want to kiss her, but I also don't want her to think that's the only thing on my mind. She's easy to talk to and makes me laugh—all perfectly valid reasons to spend time together—but her lips also feel amazing.

I laugh through my nose without meaning to. That damn word.

She twists so she's looking at me. Her forehead bumps my chin, but she doesn't pull away. "You're required to tell me what you're thinking about that made you laugh."

"It's really nothing."

"Disagree."

I catch my bottom lip between my teeth. There's no point lying, since being honest will probably hurry along the kissing part of the evening. "I was just thinking about how amazing you are."

She smiles. "We've ruined that word, haven't we?" Our mouths are so close I can feel her breath. One slight shift and our lips will touch.

My voice comes out a whisper. "It wasn't that great of a word to begin with."

Her gaze settles on my lips, then she stretches toward me. For a moment, neither of us moves, our lips pressed lightly together. Then she melts into me. I drop to my elbow, cradle her head with my free hand, and slowly move my lips against hers. Time seems to stretch before us, and I want to savor this moment. The heady scent of honey and vanilla, the way her fingers play with the ends of my hair, and the way her mouth opens when she sighs, inviting me to deepen the kiss.

My hand glides down her side until it reaches her hip. When my fingers catch on the edge of her sweatshirt, I toy with the hem. I don't want to rush things. Since we don't know what will happen once we go home, I'm okay with simply making out. But when her hand slips beneath my sweatshirt, her cold skin a shock against my lower back, I allow myself to do the same.

I shift on my elbow and the slight change in position jostles my glasses. "Can we pause a second?" I ask. She gives me a quizzical look and I remove my glasses. "Wardrobe malfunction. Hang on." I reluctantly untangle my hand from her sweatshirt, slip off my shoe, and tuck my glasses inside.

She raises a brow. "I'm flattered."

Now I'm confused.

"It's not funny if I have to explain it." She waves a hand at my shoe, which I've set at the edge of the blanket. "That you think we're gonna get so... I don't know—rambunctious—that your glasses need protecting."

My insides flip. "It's a habit from living with a hyperactive younger sister, but I like your explanation better." I hover over her for a moment, trying to look into her eyes in the darkness. A thousand galaxies shine back at me.

"Come here," she whispers before pulling me into a kiss that changes me forever.

— 19 —

NAOMI

When I open my eyes, the first thing I notice is the gray, starless sky above me.

Not black. Gray.

The second thing I notice is Hunter lying on his back, his arm outstretched beneath me, fast asleep. The fact that I can see him this clearly means we have to go. Now.

I sit up and rest my hand on his chest to wake him, and it hits me how intimate this moment is. Adrenaline races through me, and not just because we need to hurry before we get in trouble.

This is the first time I've fallen asleep with a boy.

"Hunter." I shake him lightly. His hand covers mine, but he doesn't open his eyes. "Hunter," I say again. "We fell asleep."

His eyes snap open. The growing sunrise seems to have the same effect on him. "We fell asleep," he repeats.

"We have to get back."

He reaches for his glasses but makes no attempt to smooth his hair, which sticks every which way. Memories of last night, of me gripping his hair as we kissed beneath the stars, fill me with heat. He must see something in my eyes because instead of standing, he brushes his lips against mine. "Good morning."

"Why aren't you freaking out?"

"Freaking out?" His voice is far too calm for the situation, and I want to shake him for real. "We fell asleep. We didn't rob a bank."

"But—but, the moms. They might figure it out."

He twirls a strand of my hair around his finger. "Would that be so bad?"

Who is this chill boy and what did he do with the neurotic one I fell for? "Mom will banish me to my yurt if she knows we slept out here. Together."

He exhales a sigh. "I forget you're still in high school." He runs a hand through his hair, the movement and his words effectively shattering the bliss of the past minute.

"Excuse me?" I push to my feet and pull my hair into a messy bun. Maybe he really is Mr. I Can't Be Bothered With High Schoolers. "What the hell does that mean?" My heightened emotions swing in the wrong direction but I'm not awake enough to slow my reaction.

"Wait, I didn't mean it like that." He scrambles to his feet, but I step away before he can touch me. "I just meant that it's different in college. You don't have parents waiting up for you and can do whatever you want."

"Unlike me, who needs my mommy to tuck me in at night." Anger rips through me. At him for being a jerk and myself for forgetting he's a jerk. This is what I get for being vulnerable with a guy. I point at the blanket, on which he's standing. "Will you move?"

He reaches for a corner, but I yank it away before he can help. Dust and dead grass cling to the bottom but I roll it into a ball and tuck it under my arm, not caring that my clothes will get dirty. Without looking at him, I slip on my shoes and head toward our campsite.

"Naomi, please wait. Naomi!" He whisper-shouts my name but I refuse to turn around. Footsteps sound behind me and I flinch when he grabs my arm. How could someone who makes me feel so wonderful one moment make me feel like a piece of nothing the next?

"I don't have time to listen to what you have to say. Right now I need to sneak into my bed before my mom wakes up or she might give me a time-out after breakfast."

He hustles next to me, matching my quick strides. "I didn't mean that the way it came out. I meant you don't act like you're in high school and therefore I forgot that staying out all night would get you in trouble."

My anger wavers. That does make sense. But I've already made a big deal out of this and I really do need to get back and there's no time for a big make-up scene right now.

"Please don't be mad." His voice is still thick with sleep and the pleading in his tone almost convinces me. "You're overreacting."

My fury spikes. "That's the wrong thing to say when someone's mad."

I hurry ahead of him and slip into my yurt, careful not to slam the door behind me. Dim light filters through the dome in the ceiling. The Mom-shaped lump in the bed above mine doesn't move, so I tiptoe across the room, quickly shed my clothes, and carefully climb into bed.

"Naomi?" Mom's voice is even sleepier than Hunter's.

"Yeah, Mom?" I whisper.

"You okay?"

"Just went to the bathroom." The lie rolls off my tongue and I wish I'd thought of that explanation five minutes ago. One benefit to not having bathrooms in our yurt: legitimate reason to not be in bed.

"I slept like a rock. Must be the increased elevation."

I laugh through my nose. Every now and then I'm reminded where Theo gets his sense of humor. She doesn't whip out her jokes often, but when she does, they're terrible.

"How are you feeling about... everything?" I ask.

The springs above me creak as she shifts positions. "I think okay. We talked a lot last night and we both apologized for being headstrong. Then I out-stubborned her by insisting I sleep in here tonight."

Kind of like I just did with Hunter. His apology made sense, but I didn't want to admit I overreacted, especially once he called me out on it. A fun thing *I* get from Mom.

"But she was right," Mom continues. "I keep saying I want to make this change in my life, and at some point I have to jump. No one else is going to make this happen for me." She lets out a long sigh that I feel in my soul.

"Speaking of making things happen..." I spit out the words before I can change my mind, and a sense of relief runs through me.

"Mm-hmm?"

"I got an email yesterday that I've been meaning to talk to you about."

The bed squeaks and her head pokes over the side. "Was it a dick pic? Do you need my help reporting it?"

If my pseudo-fight with Hunter didn't wake me up, this did. "No, Mom! Nothing like that."

"Don't scare me. No one shows my baby their dick until she's ready."

"Mom! God! No. This is a good thing."

Her head disappears and I take a deep breath. "Auralacity needs the contract back today."

"I thought you already sent it to them?"

Unease turns my stomach. "I was going to, but I kept second-guessing myself."

"Hold on, I'm coming down." She climbs down the ladder at the foot of the bed and burrows under my blanket. "Okay, keep talking."

"You know, this could take the podcast to a level I never imagined, and way faster." My lip catches between my teeth. "It's what I want, but once I agree I can't go back. And I'm running out of time to decide."

"Is this why you asked about your residency?" Mom asks.

I turn my head so we're nose to nose. "Yeah."

"That's not all you're worried about."

My eyes close as I admit another fear. "What if I can't handle the podcast getting bigger while taking college classes?"

"You can get a perfectly good education at another college. Berkeley isn't the only school out there."

"I know there are other schools that are just as good, but it's what I've wanted for so long that I'm having a hard time picturing myself anywhere else."

"If you want to stay closer to home, it needs to be because that's what you want to do." She presses her forehead to mine. "What does your heart tell you?"

My heart thuds and I feel like the wind's been knocked out of me. No, the reverse. Like the wind is back in me. I've been so stressed about being forced into a decision about Berkeley that I never stopped to ask myself if it was even what I still wanted. But without an outside force pressuring me one way or the other, it's like a weight's been lifted from my shoulders.

"You know I'll support whatever decision you make," she says.

"I want to work with Auralacity. And to stay home." Admitting it doesn't feel as earth-shattering as I thought it would. "Sage is staying in Oregon, so it'd be nice not being so far from her. And my studio's already set up so it doesn't make sense to leave."

"You sound like you're still convincing yourself."

I catch the corner of my lip in my teeth. My pulse races and sweat beads on my brow. "What if it flops?" I whisper. "What if everyone finds out I'm a hack?"

"Honey, you're seventeen and the biggest podcast producer in the Northwest wants to work with you."

"They're not the biggest."

"One of the biggest." She sighs. "Naomi, you are the opposite of a hack."

"Are you sure?"

"Theo's not the only charming member of this family."

The disappointment on Theo's face comes back to me. "Speaking of Theo, he's really upset."

"You finally told him?"

The word finally is like another kick in the gut. "He ultimately said he's happy for me and that I should take the offer, but I really hurt him by not telling him right away."

She wraps her arm around me. "He'll come around. As you get older, it won't feel as devastating if you don't share every detail of your lives with each other."

I can't imagine ever not needing my brother. "I don't want things to change between us."

"The bond you two have will always be there. It'll help you withstand bumps like this, and whatever else the future brings. Like you becoming a famous podcaster."

I want to believe her. "I don't know about famous."

"Look at the way Melody reacted to you. People love you. And now even more people will love you."

"You're just saying that because you're my mom."

"I mean it. You don't think I don't have those same concerns? The only difference is once you're an adult you become better at hiding that you feel like an imposter. But I admit it'll be nice to have you around a bit longer." Her brows furrow. "So explain why you haven't sent the contract back?"

"I meant to send it back sooner, but this is my first grown-up decision and I felt like I needed to make it on my own. But I still need you and Theo."

"We're not going anywhere, even if you do become a celebrity."

"Thanks, Mom."

"So you've made up your mind?"

A calm settles over me. "I think I have." There's still a tiny part of me that doesn't want to let go of Berkeley, but who knows what the future will bring. This change in plans will bring opportunities I never imagined were possible.

"I'm really proud of you. You aren't afraid to go after what you want, even though it's different from how you saw your life playing out." Tears shine in her eyes, and I feel guilty for lying to her about where I was all night. Not so guilty that I'm going full-on confessional, but still guilty.

"There's another benefit to this," I say.

She touches my nose with her fingertip. "What's that?"

"Taking the offer will help at home."

"What are you talking about?"

I close my eyes. "You don't have to hide it from me Mom, we already know."

"I repeat, what are you talking about?" She looks genuinely confused, which confuses me.

"I saw you crying. Over the bills. This could help so you can change careers."

"Sweetie, I'm not sure what you think you saw, but the only thing I've been crying about is my lack of self-esteem. Margo's trying to help and I haven't handled it the best. And as much as I appreciate you wanting to help, we're doing just fine."

Relief rushes through me, loosening some of the tension I've been carrying for weeks. "Okay, but it *will* help."

A tear slips down her cheek, wetting the pillowcase. "Yes, but I don't want that to be a factor in your decision. This is your future we're talking about. Things will work out for me one way or another, but you don't get offers like this every day."

"Thanks, Mom." I snuggle against her side, breathing deeply. She smells like home, even hundreds of miles away. "So what time are we supposed to be leaving?"

"Probably soon. You ready for another day on the water?"

"I can't wait." And now that I've made up my mind, I mean it. Hopefully Hunter will forget about my tantrum and we can enjoy our last day together.

Everyone seems tired at breakfast, and the car ride is quiet. I don't mean to ignore Hunter, but my mind is stuck in a loop about the podcast and how my life might change if it succeeds and it's not like he's going to influence my decision. Assuming we're still paddling together, we'll have plenty of time to talk— or not talk—then.

We pull into a gravel parking lot with a sign that screams 'Sports & Adventure.' Racks of kayaks and oversized inner tubes stand near the small wooden building, and closer to the river sits a large inflatable boat.

"I don't see canoes," Theo says.

"Mom," Hunter says. "Is this what I think it is?" There's an energy in him that I've never seen, like a little boy discovering a new bike beneath the tree on Christmas morning.

Margo parks, then twists in her seat to smile at him. "We never got to go after you graduated and this place popped up when we were researching the trip so—"

"We're *white water rafting?*" Melody shouts from the backseat.

"Wait, what?" My heart thumps. All I know about white water rafting is it involves rough water and requires helmets and there's a possibility of being thrown from the raft and hitting rocks.

Hunter's eyes practically glaze over. "I can't believe we're doing this."

Theo leans forward and grabs the side of my seat. "I refuse to do anything that requires a waiver."

Mom reaches for my knee. "Kids, we would never force you to jeopardize your safety." She looks at Theo and squeezes my knee. "Yes, there's a waiver, but the risk of actually getting hurt is very low."

"We signed up for the all-day trip," Margo says. "And I'm really excited that we'll all be together." She looks at Mom and some kind of understanding passes between them.

It seems like everyone is figuring out their lives on this trip.

We head inside to sign our waivers and Theo wanders over to the stack of tubes. "I vote lazy river instead."

"Dude, this'll be fun," Hunter says. "I've heard it's a total adrenaline rush."

Theo's eyes look like they might bug out of his head while I'm trying to wrap my brain around Hunter saying the words adrenaline rush as something he actively wants.

Mom puts an arm around Theo's shoulders. "Honey, they've assured us that the majority of the float is calm. There's lots of wildlife to see and we'll stop for lunch—"

"And then we plummet to our deaths!" Melody looks up from her phone and laughs. "I'm reading the description on their site."

Hunter pokes her. "Not helping."

"But it does say there's a big drop right at the beginning."

My stomach flips and sweat tickles my upper lip. I try to discreetly wipe it, but I end up just covering my mouth.

Hunter gives me a concerned look. "Not you too."

"I'm not a big fan of roller coasters or anything that makes me feel like my stomach's gonna fly out of my mouth."

Mom pulls me against her side. "How did I end up with a couple of worrywarts? We wouldn't do this if we thought you'd get hurt. This will be a fun way to end the trip and I guarantee you'll have a good time."

Theo's brows raise. "A wager?"

She rolls her eyes and walks away, but I'm hung up on her comment about the trip ending. Obviously, I know this, but today is the last full day. My eyes lock on Hunter's, who seems to be thinking the same thing.

He hangs back while the others head for the raft. "Please don't be mad on our last day together. Can you forgive me for now, we'll have an amazing day, then tomorrow you can be mad when we leave?"

I hold in my snort. "What kind of logic is that?"

"The kind that allows you to smile at me."

It takes all my self-control not to smile. He really does have a way with words. "I suppose I can do that."

He exhales, and I catch myself reaching for his face. On reflex, we glance at our families but they're busy choosing paddles. Then the next thing I know, Hunter's lips are pressed to mine. The kiss is quick, but it makes me forget my fears. "Let's do this."

Twenty minutes later, we're loaded into a bright blue inflatable raft that Chip, our muscley guide who looks like he fell off a sporting goods website, assures us will not burst if it hits a rock. After giving us the safety talk on how to paddle—"left" means the left side of the boat paddles, while "right" means the right side paddles—and generally avoid falling out of the raft, he shoves us away from the dock.

"The water's calm to start off," he says. "The first pitch is about ten minutes in. I'll give you a warning."

My fingers tighten around my paddle. Hunter's so geeked about this that he insisted on being up front, and since Margo wanted Melody in the middle, the moms wanted to be in the back together, and I refused to be in front, that left Theo in front next to Hunter. Chip's at the rear—the stern—and chatters about the surrounding area like he can't believe he gets paid to do this.

"This would be a fun job," Melody says. "You get exercise, you get to talk to people while bossing them around, and you're outside so you get a tan."

"I thought you preferred indoor activities," I say.

She dips her paddle into the water. "I don't like bugs and wild animals, and those don't seem to be a problem in the raft."

"Oh, we get plenty of spiders," Chip says. "We hose down the boats in the morning but there's always a couple that get past us."

Melody's eyes grow wide.

"Not helping, Chip," Margo says.

"Naw, they won't hurt you. They're probably still hiding from all the jostling around. If they come out, it won't be 'til later."

We glare at him. He presses his lips together and gives a little nod.

"Since it's our last day," Margo says, "I want to revisit our conversation about our expectations for this trip. Mainly, if everyone got out of this what they hoped." She pauses long enough for Theo to give me a pointed look that includes making kissy faces at Hunter, who seems too focused on the water to notice.

I resist the urge to kick Theo.

"I'll go first," Margo says. "Like I said the first night, the fact that our families have taken this trip together means so much to me. And while I know yesterday was a bit tense—and for that, I apologize—I feel like this went better than I imagined."

"You can say that again," Theo murmurs. This time I do kick him, stretching my leg across the raft to kick him in the butt.

"Hey!" He swats at me, but I jump back. His eyes narrow, just for a second, but it feels like he's the one who kicked me.

"I want to apologize, too," Mom says. "Margo and I worked through a lot of things, and we know you all got caught in the middle. We never intended that, and we're sorry if it made you uncomfortable."

Hunter twists in his seat to smile back at them. His gaze slides over mine and my heart flip-flops. "I'll go next," he says, and I freeze.

Is he going to tell them? I try to telepathically inform him that I'm not ready for us to be a group conversation, but the only person who responds to my silent pleas is Theo, who shares my wide-eyed look.

"You all know I've been torn between staying at Berkeley and transferring closer to home, and what that could mean for my future plans." Hunter continues paddling, throwing glances over his shoulder as he talks. "Talking to all of you has helped me come to peace with my decision—or at least get a little closer to peace."

I want to reach out and touch him to show my support and settle for a platonic fist bump to his shoulder. He catches my hand with his and for a moment we're sort of holding hands in front of everybody. The moms must be too wrapped up in the scenery to notice, but when he presses a kiss to my knuckles, I yank my hand away.

"It's a tough decision, Hunt," Margo says. "I'm sure there will be moments when you'll wonder if it's the right one, but you're following your gut and that's all I can ask of you."

"I'll go next!" Melody says. "Obviously I already knew that meeting Naomi and becoming friends would be amazing" — Hunter and I both snort, drawing a look from Theo— "but she helped me with some stuff that's been bothering me and now I have a plan for when I go back to school." She gives me a grateful look and I'm filled with love and pride.

This is why I do the podcast. For moments like this, when I know I've helped someone and given them hope.

"You okay, Mel?" Hunter asks, his gaze darting between his sister and me.

"Oh, it's just some stuff with my friends. You know how middle school is." She rolls her eyes and flips a hand as if to brush off her concern, but I've gotten to know her well enough to know it's an act. But she's a strong girl and while it might not be easy, I believe she'll get through this.

I give her an encouraging smile and she lowers her gaze. A blush colors her cheeks, and I feel a tug of protectiveness toward her. If this is anything close to how Hunter feels about her, I understand his urge to move back.

"Kids?" Mom says.

I expect Theo to give me a goofy look or crack a joke, but he doesn't turn around. His knuckles turn white as he grips his paddle.

"I-I'll go," I say. "I came on this trip hoping to make new friends, which I did." My smile stretches across my face and when I reach to poke Melody, tears burn my eyes. Something clenches in my chest, and I need to get all the words out of me before I burst into tears. "I'm not ready for this to be over. I know we have the whole day and it'll be amazing" —Hunter smiles softly at me— "but I'm already sad to leave. You all have become like family and I'm gonna miss you."

Tears shine in Melody's eyes. I glance at the moms and they both look like they're holding back tears. Heck, even Chip's lower lip is trembling.

"You better lighten up before you've got the whole raft crying," Theo says. His eyes are dry, but it's clear he's wrestling with something. "Three Good Things about not crying while paddling to our deaths?"

"We'll be able to see the rapids," I say.

"We won't hit the rocks," Theo says.

"We'll see the animals coming from a mile away," Melody says, and I'm hit with the sads all over again. She hasn't known us for long, but she already gets us.

"Okay." I clear my throat and try to shake off the tears. "I've decided to take the deal for the podcast and even though you all helped me realize I don't have to choose between them, I'm not ready to go away to school. I've dreamed of Berkeley for so long that it was a really hard decision, but one school will not define my future."

Hunter nods at this, and I'm gripped with a sense of loss over what we'll never have. No waiting for each other outside a lecture hall, no eating terrible dining hall food together. Instead, if we are able to make this work, it'll be video calls and texts and if we're lucky, monthly visits to each other's houses, where we'll both be living at home and surely forced to sleep in separate rooms.

"So while I may not seem like it now," I say. "I'm excited for what's next."

Theo grins at me, but it's unsteady. For once I have no idea what he's thinking. "Down to me, huh?" He studies his paddle for several beats before casually dragging it through the water. "The rest of you have used this trip to do some serious soul-searching, and while I was determined to do nothing but relax, it's hard to ignore all the life-altering revelations happening around me." He glances over his shoulder at all of us. "And believe me, I tried."

We laugh, but his shoulders tense. "Hunter got me talking about something I haven't been able to admit to my own family." He taps Hunter's shoulder with his fist. "Thanks for that, man."

"Sorry I suggested the military."

"Hey, you didn't know." He risks another look at Mom, then faces forward. "College has always felt like a necessary evil. Something I know I should do. I'm not necessarily opposed to higher education, I just hate the idea of going into debt when I don't even know what I want out of it." He clears his throat, and his jaw clenches. "So when my beloved sister confessed that she might be going to community college and keep producing the podcast from home, my options seemed a little clearer. And if her fancy contract bumps me as producer, I'll figure out a different way to help."

"Co-host!" I whisper-shout, trying to ignore the bitter edge to his voice.

He glares at me. "You know I don't want to talk on air."

"Silent co-host?" Hunter asks.

"As if," Melody says, and I laugh.

Theo rolls his eyes. "Regardless, staying home will give me time to figure out what I'm supposed to do with the rest of my life while my sister becomes rich and famous."

"Aww, Theo." If this is his offer of forgiveness, I'll take it. I crawl across the floor of the raft to wrap my arms around his waist.

"Are you supposed to be doing this?" Panic is clear in Theo's voice. "There's got to be a rule about hugging while white water rafting."

I keep squeezing. "The water's totally flat. We're in a hug-safe zone."

"Actually, the first pitch is coming up," Chip says, his voice calm despite whatever lies ahead in the river. "Everyone get ready."

I scramble back to my seat, ricocheting off Hunter's back before settling onto the hard bench. "Shouldn't this thing have seatbelts?" Sweat slicks my hands, making it hard to hold onto my paddle. Theo gives me a terrified look at the same time Hunter gives me the biggest smile I've ever seen.

"You ready?" Hunter asks.

"Not even a little bit," Theo and I both reply.

"Okay," Chip says. "Follow my instructions and we'll get through this just fine."

"Has anyone ever flipped?" Theo asks. He's got the same death grip on his paddle as I do, and he stares unblinking at the water.

"Not on my watch," Chip says. His jaw clenches twice before relaxing into a casual grin. "Okay everyone, this is what you signed up for. The river will do most of the work, but we need to stay close to the left bank, where there aren't as many rocks. The current's gonna fight to push us into the rocks, so we gotta fight back. Is everyone ready to fight?"

My brain seizes on how many times he said rocks—plural—and all I can think about is one of them smashing into my face. "I don't know if I can do this," I whisper to no one.

Theo catches my eye, the same fear clear on his face, and we both shake our heads.

"Kids, you're fine," Mom says. "Focus on paddling and we'll be through it before you know it."

Her words sound familiar, comforting, and I flex my fingers on the shaft of my paddle. "I can do this."

Hunter turns to look at me. "They didn't provide helmets, which means the odds of actually hitting your head on something are very, very low. Companies like this won't stay in business if people die on their attractions."

His logic is comforting, and so like him. He understands that I need more than just platitudes that everything will be okay. I need actual proof that my face will not get up close and personal with one of the angry, jagged rocks jutting out of the river. I whisper thanks, my gaze lingering on the spot on the side of his neck where my lips were less than twelve hours ago.

"Ohhhhhhhhmigodohmigodohmigod." Theo shrinks away from the raft's edge as the sound of thunder fills the air.

Except it's not thunder.

"Here she comes!" Chip shouts.

I want to yell at him for assigning gender to a body of water, but I'm incapable of doing anything but stare at the spot twenty feet ahead of the boat where the river just... disappears.

"How high is the pitch?" Melody shouts over the sound of crashing water.

"Twenty feet, give or take," Chip says.

I don't for a second believe that he doesn't know the exact height of every pitch on this river, which means he's lying and it's taller than twenty feet.

"Here we go!" Hunter shouts. He leans forward in his seat, paddle ready. From the corner of my eye, I register that the others are paddling—even Theo, whose low moan grows louder the closer we get to the drop-off. Then the edge of the river disappears and we're tipping, tipping, tipping until we're staring at the water beneath us and my stomach flips and ohmigod the water's churning and Chip's yelling "Right paddle! Right paddle!" and someone's screaming and just when I think I might throw up, the raft levels with a splash and it's over.

Everyone shouts and whoops and Theo actually high fives Hunter. Someone pats my back as Hunter twists in his seat to face me. He leans close—so close I forget where we are and who's watching—and touches my knee. "We made it." Excitement brightens his eyes and it seems like he's trying to calm himself for my sake.

I push my hair off my face, but my shaking hand betrays how scared I was. "Oh, I know."

Theo laughs. "Naomi, I've never heard you scream that loud."

My face flames. So the screaming was me. Great.

"It's flat for about thirty minutes," Chip says. "Plenty of time to catch your breath."

I feel mildly attacked, but my heart rate still hasn't returned to normal, so I let it go.

The next half hour is indeed calm, but as much as I try to do as Chip says and relax, my brain bounces between counting down how many hours are left before we go home and flat-out terror over what lies ahead on the river. Both beg the natural world to stop time.

The next rapids sneak up on us. A few rocks poke out of the water here and there, and by the time we're actually in what Chip calls a chute, we're paddling around the rocks like we actually know what we're doing.

We stop for lunch along the river and there's a legit buffet set up. Sandwiches and salads, chips and cookies, and some kind of fruit salad with all my favorite berries. We pile up our plates and settle in at the picnic tables. Chip compliments us on our paddling, then everyone falls into casual conversation about nothing, but I'm struggling to say anything. The fullness in my chest grows the longer I have to sit across from Hunter but can't touch him. Maybe agreeing to keep us from the moms was a bad idea. Because while they may watch us closer tonight, all I can think about is right now, and right now I'd like to feel his arm around me and see his face from much closer than our current three feet.

"You okay?" he asks quietly, and I shrug. His brows furrow. "Are you worried about the next rapids?"

I laugh, surprised. "Actually, I hadn't even thought about that."

His foot finds mine beneath the table. That small contact calms me. "So what's up?"

"It's really hitting me that this is our last day. It's like the end of summer camp when you don't want it to end, and you don't know if you'll ever see your new friends again. You promise to text but after a while, you drift apart." I didn't mean to put all that out there over lunch, and I watch my words land with a thud on the table between us.

"I promise to do more than text," he whispers.

A smile wobbles on my lips. "I hate that we live so far away."

His foot slides forward until our legs press together. "We'll figure it out," he says. It's the first time he's acknowledged that there could be anything for us beyond this week, and he seems as surprised by the admission as I am.

After lunch, his comment carries me back to the raft, where my nerves are waiting for me. "Okay, maybe I am scared about the next rapids."

"I've done this hundreds of times," Chip says from behind me. I turn and he's looking down at me, beefy arms crossed over his equally beefy chest, but his eyes are compassionate. "People with far less ability than you have made it through unscathed." He rests a paw on my shoulder. "So I know you can do it."

"Thanks." I'm still tripping over his use of the word unscathed—perhaps my earlier assessment of him was unfair— and settle into my seat behind Hunter. He slides a hand behind him, along the side of the raft, and I give it a squeeze.

"You've got this," he says.

"Can you hold my hand, too?" Theo asks. I yank my hand from Hunter's and throw my flip-flop at Theo. He catches it and throws it back at me. "What? I'm legit scared."

Melody pats his back. "Do you want to trade spots? I'll ride in front!"

"No!" Margo says.

"It's better if we have equal weight at the front," Chip says.

Melody huffs. "It's not my fault I'm twelve."

Hunter stretches across the boat to fist bump Melody's knee. "This won't be our last time. You'll get a chance."

She seems appeased—apparently a promise from her brother is something she knows she can count on. "Then let's get going!"

Chip pushes us away from shore and it's quickly apparent that the calm part of the river is over. The current rushes over rocks and fallen trees, and it's not long before Chip is warning us of another pitch. "It's not as big as the first one, but I need everyone to keep us on the right side of the river."

Hunter and I paddle hard, but the raft stays in the center.

"Theo!" I shout. "Stop paddling!"

"He said right!"

"Left side paddle!" Chip says, a little too late.

We manage to avoid whatever obstacles lurk beneath the surface on the left side of the river, and a baby spike of adrenaline has me smiling when we clear the pitch.

"Okay," I admit. "That was fun."

The river ebbs and flows between calm and mini rapids, and slowly, slowly, my death grip on my paddle loosens. The next time Chip calls out, "Right side paddle!" my breathing stays calm and I'm able to look at the rocks ahead without panicking.

Except the right side doesn't paddle. Theo and Melody are laughing, his head thrown back while she's doubled over, and both their paddles dangle uselessly over the side of the raft.

"Right side!" Chip shouts.

They stop laughing and look ahead, but it's too late. The rocks that seemed harmless moments earlier now loom too close and the water swirling beneath us seems to whisper my name. The raft collides with the rocks—thankfully it doesn't pop—and we all lurch forward.

"Paddles in!" Chip says.

My instincts insist we should paddle out of this, but I trust he knows what he's doing. Hunter and I tuck our paddles against the side of the raft as we hit another rock. But instead of bouncing off like we did before, the right side juts up and over the rock. My stomach flips as my weight shifts and I'm falling toward the water. My hip hits the side of the boat and I scramble for something, anything to grab onto. My fingers graze Hunter's arm but it's not enough and suddenly I'm underwater.

For a second it's impossible to tell which way is up. Water churns in my face, my ears. It's quiet and terrifying and for a split second I think I'm going to die.

But I'm not. I'm not a helpless girl who just rolls over and lets life happen.

I control my destiny.

My life jacket pops me to the surface, and I take a deep breath. Someone's screaming my name. I twist in the water and push my feet forward like Chip showed us, and my head bobs on the surface—my life jacket refusing to let me stay underwater. The current carries me alongside the raft, but we seem to be past the rocks and out of danger.

"I'm okay!" I shout. But I'm more than okay. The decision to stay home and work with Auralacity feels right, like this is what I'm meant to do, and I'm ready for whatever this thing with Hunter turns into.

A splash snaps me from my thoughts. Strong hands grab my arms. "Naomi! Omigod! Are you okay?" Hunter pulls me to his chest. My feet brush the ground and I realize the water's not over my head. I trip over the bottom of the river until I catch my footing, while Hunter stands rock solid, anchoring me to him despite the current.

The raft continues downstream, away from us.

"The raft." My voice comes out a squeak.

He peers down at me, his hands running over my face and shoulders, smoothing my hair out of my eyes. "Are you okay? I almost had a heart attack when you fell in."

"Yeah, I'm fine. But the boat." I point at our families, but he doesn't look.

"They'll wait for us." His finger trails along my jaw and the next thing I know, his lips are brushing over mine. Sage's voice in my head insists that the moms will see but my own voice tells her to shut up. This boy, who a week ago I didn't know I needed, is holding me like he doesn't want to ever let go and I'm going to enjoy the hell out of it.

Our lifejackets make it impossible to get very close, but we make do. He cradles my face between his hands, deepening the kiss until the current makes me lose my footing and I stumble out of his arms. He sinks into the water next to me and finds my hand. Together, we flip to our backs and let the water carry us downstream.

The raft sits at a bend in the river, far enough that we can't hear them but not so far that they can't see us. Chip's standing in the water, holding the raft in place. Theo and Melody are still talking, but the moms look like they might burst with excitement.

"I guess they're okay with this?" Hunter says.

"It seems so."

I lean my head back until all I see is blue sky. A bird glides lazily on a breeze, and Hunter's hand tightens on mine. When we drift close to the raft, Chip calls out, "Do you need help?"

Hunter waves him off. "Nah, we're good."

And without another word, we float past them.

We did eventually get back in the raft, and the look on the moms' faces was priceless. They managed to contain their curiosity until we got to the car, and now that we're back at the campsite, I brace myself for the conversation that has to be coming.

Naomi and I avoided touching each other after our kiss in the river, but considering how little time we have left together, I kind of don't care what they think.

Mom seems to be watching me more than normal, or maybe I'm just paying more attention. She finally corners me on the way back from the bathroom and steers me toward the ring of chairs around the firepit. A thin plume of gray smoke rises from the fire Theo tried to start, but otherwise the campsite is oddly deserted. She sits and indicates for me to join her, then clutches my hand. "I want you to be absolutely certain that leaving Berkeley is the right thing for you. Not me or your sister, you." Her eyes bore into mine and I try not to squirm. "You know I believe you can do absolutely anything you put your mind to, but I also believe the right education will help get you there."

I open my mouth to reply but she keeps going.

"You put a lot of thought into choosing Berkeley and I'd hate to see you give that up after one semester. Now, my quick search online showed that you can still take most of the same classes at Bakersfield, but—and I repeat this—I want you to be absolutely certain."

I study our interlocked hands. Mine are larger than hers but that sense of security I felt as a kid when my mommy held my hand washes over me now. I know she's worried and just wants what's best for me, so I brush away the irritation that she needs more than my words as reassurance. "I haven't talked to anyone at either school about transferring, so I don't even know if it could happen by next semester or if I'd have to wait until the fall. But this is what I want, and I'm even more certain after spending this week with Mel. I want to be there for her. For both of you. College and my career are still important, but I'm realizing they aren't the only things that will make me happy."

She presses the back of her hand to the corner of her eye. "Have I mentioned that I'm proud of you?"

I can't fight my smirk. "You may have said something in passing."

"I'll help however I can." She takes a shaky breath. "It will be nice having you both under one roof again, but I'm done doing your laundry."

I lean forward and pull her into a hug. "Deal."

A door clatters behind us and we both jump. Naomi's standing in front of her yurt, an uncertain look on her face. "Am I interrupting?"

Mom stands, giving my hair a tousle. "Oh goodness, no. I was just about to get dinner started. You kids..." she trails off.

"I beg you not to finish that sentence," I whisper.

She pinches my cheek. "I won't embarrass you. But do be careful."

"Mom!"

She skips away—skips!—leaving me semi-alone with Naomi, who takes the seat Mom abandoned.

"I started packing," she says. Her lower lip catches between her teeth and she blinks several times. "This has been so much fun, and I hate that now I'm sad."

"Hey." I move out of my chair and settle on my knees in front of her, grabbing her hands and resting them on her knees. "You can be sad tomorrow. We still have like fourteen hours before we leave." My stomach drops. "Okay, wow. That really isn't very long."

She sniffs.

"It doesn't matter. We're not spending our last day here worrying about the future."

"That's quite a statement from someone who only seems to be locked in on three years from now."

A flutter in my heart warms me. I want to pull her into my arms and kiss her senseless, to not let go of her for a single second of these fourteen hours. "I blame you for that."

She leans forward until her lips touch my forehead. "I truly am not sorry." My eyes close and her lips trail down the side of my face until they settle near my ear. Her breath is warm on my skin. "Living in the moment is my specialty."

I reach for her, my fingers sliding into her hair, my mouth colliding with hers. The kiss is fast and hot, and I push closer until her knees are on either side of me. Her hands move through my hair, over my back. We shouldn't be doing this, not out in the open where anyone can see. But if I want to learn to live in the moment, maybe I need to stop worrying so much.

Naomi decides for us by pulling back to take a breath. "Fourteen hours isn't enough time."

In my head, Shawna screams about my hideous underwear, but I doubt that's what Naomi means.

"Maybe we can go for another walk later?"

Naomi leans back in the chair. A flicker of emotion crosses her face, and she lets go of my hand. "You sure my curfew won't cramp your style?"

I run my hand over my face. Her legs still cradle my sides and I rest my palms on either side of her thighs. "I'm really sorry about that. I know it sounded condescending, but I swear I didn't mean it the way it came out."

She exhales. Her gaze drifts above my head and I hold my breath waiting for her response. "I know you didn't. But it felt like a slap in the face after waking up in your arms."

I inch closer until my belly is pressed against her. "I can't promise I won't ever say another stupid thing, but I can promise to not intentionally hurt you."

A smile plays on her lips. "I can work with that." She reaches for my face but freezes, looking over my shoulder. "Incoming."

I scramble back to my chair and brush dirt off my knees as Theo approaches.

"Don't stop because of me," he says.

"We most definitely will," Naomi says. "Did you pack?"

Theo cocks his head. "I'm sorry, have we met? No, I have not packed. If you must know, I was napping. All that excitement wore me out."

The others join us soon after that.

"Naomi, did you email the aural city company?" Nancy asks.

Naomi shakes her phone in the air. "I was gonna do it after dinner. I'm starving."

I don't use the expression *her eyes bugged out of her head* loosely, but Nancy's nearly do.

"But you said they need an answer by the end of the day!"

Naomi taps her screen so the time shows. "Yeah, it's not even six."

Nancy rushes toward her and smooths Naomi's hair from her face. "Sweetie, end of day in the business world means five PM."

Naomi's mouth falls open and she stares at her phone. "It's an hour earlier there. I've still got time." She races to her yurt, the door slamming behind her.

Theo runs a hand through his hair, all traces of his earlier smile gone. "Do you think they'll take back the offer if she doesn't send it in time?"

"It's hard to say," Nancy says.

Silence falls over us as the minutes slip by.

"Should it take this long?" I ask.

Theo chews the corner of his mouth the same way his sister does.

None of us move until Naomi bounces down the steps and lets out an exhale. "We're good! Got it in before five Pacific time." Then she smooths her hair from her face and winks at Theo. "I added a line about bringing on my own producer."

Theo straightens. "What if they cancel the contract because of that?"

Naomi shrugs before rolling her eyes. "I said it wasn't a dealbreaker, just my preference. Can't hurt to ask, right?" Her gaze lands on Nancy as if she's waiting for reassurance.

Nancy's smile seems forced. "I guess we'll find out soon enough."

Over dinner, we avoid all talk of the contract and recount the stories of rafting, laughing about Naomi falling in and me ineffectively trying to rescue her. She had already saved herself by the time I made it into the water, but my heroics seem to have impressed her, nonetheless. I catch her watching me more times than I can count, and when the dishes have been packed away and the stars come out and the moms finally, finally, say goodnight, I reach for her.

She moves from her chair into my lap, but instead of kissing me, she tucks her head against the side of my neck. I wrap my arms around her, holding her, wishing we had more time. Even though I said I want to live in the moment and not think about the future, that's all I can think about. The uncertainty of transferring mixes with these new feelings for Naomi and try as I might, I don't know how they fit together.

Mel tosses a stick in the fire and catches my eye. "So, are you two, like, together now?"

Naomi's head pops up. Her eyes meet mine but neither of us say anything. After several breaths that feel like an eternity, she faces Mel. "We haven't exactly talked about it." Her finger traces a nervous circle on the back of my neck. "We live in different states so..." she trails off, and I fight to keep the emotion off my face.

I've been daydreaming about the possibility of a future with her, and she's already written us off.

"You know," Theo says. "I've heard of this thing that might make it easier."

Naomi stiffens. "If you say sex toys, I'm disowning you."

I choke on a laugh. Mel's eyes go wide but Theo purses his lips and nods like he hadn't considered that.

"Not where I was going, but I'm glad you're thinking ahead." He leans his elbows on his knees and peers at us over the fire. "There's this newfangled invention called the internet. It lets you communicate with people in faraway places like California and Oregon. In fact—" he holds a finger to his chin—"I've heard you can make *phone calls* but with video and actually see the person *while you're talking to them*. Could be interesting with those toys you mentioned."

"Omigod, Theo!" Naomi twists in my lap. "I need something to throw at him."

I grab a twig from next to my chair and hand it over. She flings it at him, but it barely makes it to the fire.

"That was anticlimactic," she says.

Theo laughs but mercifully keeps his response to himself.

I pull Naomi against my chest. She snuggles into me and my heart pounds so loud it's all I can hear. Before I lose my nerve, I whisper in her ear. "Do you want to talk about what happens after tomorrow?"

Her palm flattens against my chest, right over my heart. I'm sure she can feel how fast it's beating. "I'm doing a really bad job of ignoring that we only have ten hours left. I think if I had some idea of what comes next, that would help."

I tighten my arms around her and inhale vanilla and honey. "Not here."

She nods. Without looking away from me she says, "Theo, you need to give us some time."

"I'm sorry, what?" he asks.

She untangles herself from my arms, pushes to her feet, and reaches for my hand. "We're occupying your yurt."

21

NAOMI

My hands shake but I'm not backing down now. Emailing Auralacity gave me an extra boost of confidence so even though I'm mildly panicked at how I just altered my future, I'm also feeling bold. I lead Hunter across the campsite without another glance at Theo and Melody. I don't want to see whatever look my brother is giving me—I just want to get inside where we can be alone.

To talk.

I swear.

I pause at the door. It is his room after all.

Hunter reaches to open it and gestures for me to go in first. In the faint light I can make out the shapes of the furniture. It's set up exactly like mine, but with clothes everywhere and the not-so-subtle scent of boy lingering in the air. Hunter closes the door behind us, and the faint click of the lock makes me turn.

"I'm not implying that anything—"

"I'm not ready to have sex."

We speak at the same time, me skipping the bush and saying exactly what I'm thinking.

He laughs and I imagine his smirk. Then he takes my hand and leads me toward one of the beds. We sit next to each other. "Is this okay?" he asks.

"I'm the one who dragged you in here. I should be asking you the same thing."

His head dips and I want to memorize the way the corner of his mouth curves. "This is more than okay. And no pressure to do anything more than talk." He meets my eyes. "If that's all you want."

Before I can second guess myself, I kick off my shoes and lay on the narrow mattress. He does the same, and once I'm settled into the crook of his arm with my head on his chest, I spit out the words that have been building since this afternoon. "Rationally, I know this is ridiculous because we're teenagers who live in different states and we're still figuring out what we want in life. But I like you. A lot. No one has ever challenged me the way you do while also *getting* me, and I don't want to regret not seeing what could happen. Maybe we'll try long distance with this newfangled internet thing Theo mentioned and maybe it'll fall apart before we even see each other again, but maybe it won't." I take a shaky breath. "Now you talk."

Hunter hasn't moved since I started talking, but his heart pounds beneath my ear. My head rises as he takes a deep breath. "I like you, too." Another breath. "Everything you said makes sense. Logically, we should say goodbye tomorrow and chalk this up to an extra-fun vacation."

I bite my lip, a mix of dread and hope burning in my chest. In my mind I hear Theo insist to not give merit to the dread, and I fight a smile.

"But I'm tired of being logical. I thought focusing on college and my career were enough to make me feel complete, but they're not. I want to be successful, but I don't want to be alone. And I no longer think the two have to be mutually exclusive." He shifts onto his hip and cradles my cheek in his hand. "I realize we barely know each other and as you said, it might seem ridiculous, but you get *me*, despite my bad jokes and questionable moods. You've made me imagine a version of my future I didn't know I wanted—that I didn't know was possible—and I want to see how our story unfolds."

For all the times I've given advice to people who aren't sure if they should go after the person they like, telling them to lay it all out there and be honest about how they feel, I've never done it myself. And I've never had anyone say nice things in return. But here's this boy who, until a week ago, wasn't even on my radar, and now we're talking about a future together.

"Now you say something," Hunter says. His thumb caresses my cheekbone, his touch featherlight, and it's all I can do to maintain eye contact.

"I'd really like you to kiss me now." I catch the edge of a smile as he hooks his glasses on the underside of the bunk above us. Then his mouth covers mine. This kiss is slow, unhurried, as if we're saying we may only have a few hours left in Utah, but we have our entire futures ahead of us. This trip—this week—is just the beginning.

Then he rolls on top of me, silencing my declarations about patience. He holds himself over me on his elbows, not resting his full weight on my body, his eyes searching mine in the darkness. I pull his head closer and he kisses me again, but this time we both admit through our touches that we only have a few hours left. He lowers himself until his chest presses against mine and my legs hook over his. When our bodies start to rock together, he pulls back.

"Does this feel rushed?" he asks.

"Time isn't our friend. We're kind of on a compressed schedule."

He brushes kisses over my cheek. "It's like those classes they cram into half a semester. You still learn everything but in a much shorter time."

My fingers trail down his back. "And what have you learned?"

His lips move over my neck. "That I was stupid to waste the first two days of this trip trying to push you away."

"And I thought you were smart."

"Momentary lapse of judgment."

His mouth finds mine again and I hold onto him like I might never let go. I meant what I said about seeing how this plays out, but he's with me now and I don't know when I'll see him again. A lump catches in my throat and I turn my face before I start crying.

"Hey, hey." His voice is barely a whisper. "What's going on?"

I sniff. "It's all hitting me. Again."

"That tomorrow is only a couple hours away?"

I nod, grateful that he gets it.

He rolls onto his side and pulls me into his arms, holding me like he's afraid of what happens after tomorrow. "I can't promise it will be easy or that it'll end up the way we want." His lips move against my hair. "All we can do is try. And promise to be honest with each other."

I tilt my head up until our eyes connect. "I can do that."

He smiles. Not The Smirk, and not the casual smile he's thrown around all week. This smile is soft and sad and hopeful. We hold each other for hours and years and when I feel myself falling asleep, I gently kiss his jawline.

"I should go."

"I'll walk you back."

He peeks out the door. "No one's out there."

"Not even Theo?"

"Maybe he's in with Mel?"

My twin-fu insists that's too logical. I grab Hunter's hand and lead him to the firepit, where I spin in a circle and will my connection to Theo to point me in the right direction. But I'm frozen by the sight above us. Galaxies stretch to the edge of the sky, lighting the world and shining on us like we're the only two people in the world.

"It's like we're in a snow globe, except the world is filled with stars," I say.

Hunter wraps his arm around me, his eyes on the sky. "I feel like I'll be chasing the stars for the rest of my life."

"What do you mean?"

He looks down at me. Stars shine in his eyes as he brushes my hair from my face. "This feeling. This moment. I want to hold onto it forever." Then he kisses me and the world tilts on its axis, the stars threatening to tumble from the sky.

"I. Could. Have. Died." Theo's whisper-shout makes us spring apart.

"Theo!" I rush to his side. "Where did you go?"

"There was a raccoon. You should be glad I didn't scream."

I rest my hand on his arm. "Thank you for being brave."

"Where were you?" Hunter asks.

Theo glances over his shoulder at the parked cars. "I needed to get away, but still keep an eye on the bastard." He raises a brow at us. "I don't mean to be crass, but are you done? Can I go to bed now? Or do I need to sanitize things first?"

"Omigod. Shut it. No." Heat flames my cheeks and I smack his arm. "You are horrible."

"Just looking out for you." He winks, then taps us both on the chin.

Hunter stifles a laugh. "I'll be there in a minute." Theo meanders to his yurt and Hunter pulls me close. "I don't want to say goodnight."

My heart can't handle this. It's not even tomorrow but I'm imagining repeating this scene in front of our families, complete with tears and whispered promises we don't know if we can keep. I press my head to his chest. "Me neither."

"One step at a time," he says. He leads me to my door, where he kisses me softly. "I'll see you in a few hours."

"Good night."

When he finally leaves, I tiptoe inside my yurt and collapse into bed, desperate to hold him just a little longer.

22

HUNTER

My pillow smells like Naomi. With my eyes closed I can imagine her next to me, waking in my arms like yesterday—before I almost ruined things with a thoughtless comment. I love the written word because you can take your time crafting the perfect sentence, paragraph, chapter, but talking exposes my raw, unedited thoughts. Although I did okay last night. Maybe I just need more practice sharing what I'm thinking.

There isn't much left to say to Naomi except goodbye, and my stomach hurts just thinking about it. When I go outside, the scent of bacon and potatoes draws me to the picnic table.

"Are you packed?" Mom asks.

"Mostly." If throwing things in my bag in the dark because I couldn't sleep after Naomi left counts as packing, then yes, I'm packed. Meanwhile, Theo's things are still where they've been all week.

Will it be awkward when Naomi gets up? Will she keep her distance for the moms' sake?

My heart skips when Mel and Naomi emerge a few minutes later, and when Naomi's eyes find mine, everything feels right in the world. And when she crosses the campsite and wraps her arms around my waist, I feel like I'm home.

"Good morning," she says into my chest. "Did you sleep okay?"

"If you can call what I did sleep, it was awful."

She looks up at me. Her eyes are a little red and their normal sparkle is missing. "Same." Then she pushes to her toes and kisses me lightly, then holds up her phone. "I do have good news. Auralacity okayed keeping Theo as my producer."

"Naomi, that's great!"

"I know it is, but I'm having a hard time being happy right now."

I glance over her head at the moms, who are watching us from the corner of their eyes. Based on their smiles, they seem okay with this—with us—and I want to kick myself again for being a butthead at the beginning of the week.

Theo's voice snaps me out of my head. "We're still doing this?"

"Theo, can you not?" Naomi's voice sounds as tired as I feel.

I give her a squeeze and step back and lace my fingers through hers. I don't know when I'll get to touch her again and I'm not stopping until Mom shoves me in the car.

Mel plops in a chair near the firepit. "Do we have to leave? I'm not ready to go back to my real life."

Naomi pulls away from me and sits next to Mel. I don't mean to eavesdrop, but I don't want to leave Naomi's side, so I linger awkwardly behind her chair. Naomi bumps Mel's foot with hers and when Mel looks up, tears shine in her eyes. "Hey," Naomi says. "It'll be okay."

Mel wipes her hand over her face and my gut clenches. I claim to be this amazing big brother who's making a huge sacrifice for his sister, and I hate that I'm not able to help her the way I used to. The jealousy I felt earlier when Mel confided in Naomi is replaced with gratitude that she has someone she trusts, even if it isn't me. Mel glances at me but doesn't tell me to go away, so I sit in the chair next to Naomi.

"Everything you said, about talking to Jessica and standing up to Nelly, makes sense, but it's a lot easier to say I'll do things when we're thousands of miles away."

"Hundreds." The word slips out of me before I can catch it and Mel glares at me. "Sorry."

Naomi gives me a wide-eyed look before turning back to Mel. "You're stronger than you think you are. If you ever wonder if you're doing the right thing, just listen to your gut. Mine always tells me the right thing to do. The hardest part is listening to it."

Mel sniffs. "You sound like Mom."

"Yeah, well, your mom's a smart woman." She grabs Mel's hand. "Call or text me anytime you need to talk."

"Really?" Mel says.

"You might want to put a restriction on that," I say, but this time they both ignore me.

"Anytime," Naomi says.

Theo drops into the chair next to Mel. "Are we finally singing Kumbaya? I can't believe we've gone the entire week without it!"

"You don't even know the words," Naomi says.

"True, but I've heard it's the thing to do on wholesome camping trips." He narrows his gaze at Naomi, then me, then back to Naomi. "But I suppose this isn't that kind of trip."

Naomi shifts to face me and sighs. "Are we far enough along that you can defend my honor?"

I grab her hand and brush a kiss over her knuckles. "Theo, I must protest your implication that I have been anything but a gentleman."

"It wasn't you I was implicating about."

"Theo!" Naomi grabs a twig from the ground and flings it at him.

He deflects it with his arm, laughing. "I'm kissing! I mean kidding! I like you, Hunter. You're a good guy, dude. And you," he smiles at Naomi. "I love you like a sister."

"Theo! Have you packed?" Nancy waves a spatula at our yurt.

"How does she *know*?" Theo says, rising from his chair.

"Because you've never been ready on time a day in your life," Naomi says.

He runs his hands over his hips then pretends to flip his hair over his shoulder. "What can I say? This takes effort."

Mel sniffles again. "I'm gonna miss you, Theo."

He drops to a crouch next to her. "This is not the last time we'll see each other. The moms will surely want to do this again, and then, of course, there's their wedding."

Mel giggles, and Naomi covers her face with her hands.

"Theo, I beg of you."

He pops to his feet and pinches Naomi's cheek. "I've gotta go pack!"

Naomi peeks at me from behind her hands. "I'm really sorry about him."

I tug her hand away from her face. "Don't be. So, I've been meaning to ask you—"

"Are you proposing?" Mel screams.

Everything goes still. The moms, the birds in the trees above us, my heart. "Um, no?" Then Naomi laughs, and the world spins back into place. "I keep meaning to ask about the podcast, and what this partnership means. How soon do you start with them?"

She relaxes into her chair, seeming grateful for the change in topic. "I don't really know. Their email this morning said they'd like to meet with me to talk logistics. They don't seem to care that I'm still in high school, just that my podcast fills a niche they were looking for."

"That's so fricking exciting," Mel says. "I was already planning to tell all my friends to listen, but like now you've got a legit company backing you."

"That gives me an idea," Naomi says. "What would you think about me covering your issue on the show? We could draft a letter and I wouldn't use your name, but then you could have your friends listen to it." She catches her fingernail between her teeth. "Or is that totally not helpful?"

Mel claps her hands together. Now that Naomi pointed out Mom's quirk, I realize how much Mel does it too. "That would be amazing!"

I snort, and Naomi whirls on me. "A, that word is ruined for me, and B, did you just snort?"

I don't know if it's the lack of sleep or my jacked-up emotions, but I double over laughing. "I...believe...I...did!" I gasp. She joins me laughing, and the tension in me loosens. This is how I want to end the trip. Not sad and worried about when we'll see each other again, but happy and laughing together.

But the laughter doesn't last. Everyone seems down over breakfast and while the moms make a valiant attempt to keep the conversation going, the sads, as Mel calls the way she's feeling, hit hard. I help Naomi carry her bag to her car, then pull her into my arms for a final hug. My heart feels too big for my chest. I try to memorize the feeling of her pressed against me, and when I lift her chin for one last kiss, tears run down her face.

"We'll figure it out," I whisper.

"The odds are not in our favor," she says.

"Fortunately for us, I'm not a numbers guy. I don't know if I told you, but words are my thing." That earns me a smile, and I grab the opportunity to kiss her. I only intend for it to be a quick peck, but her lips part and I'm not an idiot. After a moment, several "ahems" sound nearby, but she doesn't pull back, so I keep kissing her. We don't stop until the car we're leaning against rumbles to life.

"I hate to break this up," Nancy says. "But we do have to go."

Naomi smiles softly. "Talk to you tonight?"

I kiss the top of her head. "Yes."

We step apart to hug everyone else goodbye. Theo whispers, "You really are a good guy. You two kids can work this out." Nancy says something similar, then Naomi's getting in the passenger seat and my heart feels like it's going with her. I hurry to her open window and lean in for one last kiss. "Goodbye for now."

"Goodbye for now," she says back.

Then I step back and the dust kicks up as they drive away, leaving me both broken and more complete than I've felt in a long time.

⁓ EPILOGUE ⁓

Four months later

"Is that it? Is this the house?"

Theo glances between his phone and the street numbers on the houses. "There! The blue one on the right!"

My trusty Corolla lurches when I slam on the brakes. Margo's SUV sits in the driveway of a blue house that looks exactly like the picture Hunter sent. I park in the street and have barely turned off the engine when the front door flings open and Melody barrels toward us.

"I didn't think this day would ever get here but you're here you're here you're here!" She launches herself into Theo's arms, then races into the street to hug me.

"Did she come over?" I ask.

Melody nods, but if she says anything else I don't hear it because Hunter is standing on the front porch, The Smirk in full effect.

"He's been watching out the window for the past hour," Melody says.

"I don't think you were supposed to tell me that."

She shrugs, then pushes me toward the house. "Go say hi to your boyfriend." She drags out the word boyfriend so long that Theo chimes in with a kissy face.

But I don't care. After months of attempts—two of which were disrupted by freak snowstorms—Hunter and I are finally in the same state. In the same city. And now, as I walk up the sidewalk and he jumps down the steps and scoops me into his arms, we're breathing the same air.

"Hi." He smiles down at me and wow, I forgot how attractive he is in person.

"This is so much better than a video call."

He laughs, then his lips are on mine and the world resets on its axis. "I've missed you so much," he says between kisses.

I respond by kissing him again but stop myself before we scare the neighbors.

Theo bumps my legs with our bags. "Excuse me, some of us have to pee."

Hunter leads us inside, where a dark-haired girl Melody's age sits on the couch.

"You must be Jessica?" I say.

She nods, and the part of me that thought I was a hack, that doubted if I could really help people, grows a little smaller.

"It's so nice to finally meet you. Melody has told me a lot about you."

Her gaze drops to the floor. "I want to thank you. For what you did. With the show. And before that. It means a lot to me."

I settle on the couch next to her. "Well, Melody means a lot to me, which means her best friend does as well. I'm so happy things are better between you."

Jessica smiles at Melody. "It is."

Melody sits on the other side of Jessica, and I notice the rainbow-colored Three Good Things button pinned to her shirt.

"Where did you get that?" I ask, unable to hide my smile.

"And where is mine?" Theo asks as he sprawls on the floor in front of the fireplace.

Hunter tosses one to Theo, then places one in my hand. "They made them last week." He settles next to me on the couch and I lean against him, grateful to finally be in the same room.

"Can we sell them on your website?" Melody asks.

Jessica nods, her eyes bright. "The kids at our school love them. They love you." Her gaze drops and I nudge her knee with mine.

"I think that'd be pretty cool." I toss a glance at Theo, who salutes.

"I can make that happen." Theo gives Melody a pointed look. Her eyes go wide, and he nods at her. "Mel made another button just for you."

Melody avoids my gaze as she hands me a hot pink button that reads *Insta-Love is Real*.

I burst out laughing. "We're not selling this on the website!"

Melody smirks. "What if there's a collection of buttons?"

Theo pumps his fist in the air. "Sold!"

"I feel like I've been set up."

Theo nods. "Set up for success."

Auralacity is waiting until my second season to officially launch, which starts next month. When they found out I had planned to go to Berkeley, they didn't love the residency loophole but came up with a compromise: If Three Good Things hits all their projections in our first season together—I'm still not fully sure what that means other than getting lots of downloads— they're willing to bend their regional restriction so I can still go to my dream school. Being four hours closer to Hunter would be amazing, but I'm still not ready to leave home. Theo swears I can send him the files and he'll work his producer magic like always, but for me, part of the magic is having him by my side.

Hunter was able to transfer to Bakersfield right away, and based on the smile on Melody's face, it was the right decision. He's found a new group of friends and while his future's still focused on books, he's realizing New York isn't the only path to his dreams. Our future is more hazy, but whether I end up at Berkeley or stay in Oregon, I'm hopeful he'll be in my life.

I swallow the lump in my throat and thread my fingers through Hunter's. "Three Good Things about Falling in Like on Vacation."

"About that," Hunter says.

"Yeah?"

"I think the title needs a little editing."

"Here we go," Melody says.

I smile at him. "You realize it's a fictional title, right? I'm not actually doing a show about this."

He winks at me. "Maybe you should."

"Oh please end the suspense and just tell us," Theo says.

Hunter laces his fingers through mine. "It's about the word like."

My brows furrow. "Too overdone?"

"It's not that. But I think Falling in Love sounds better, don't you?"

─ TO YOU, THE READER ─

If you enjoyed Naomi and Hunter's story, please consider leaving a review on Goodreads or any online book seller's website.

Connect with Melanie online:
www.melaniehoo.com
MelanieHooyenga@gmail.com
Newsletter: www.melaniehoo.com/hoos-letter
Facebook/MelanieHooyenga
Twitter & Instagram: @melaniehoo

Or if you prefer pen and paper:
Melanie Hooyenga
PO Box 554
Grand Haven, MI 49417

ACKNOWLEDGEMENTS

Writing a book during a pandemic is not so different from writing one during normal times (aside from the existential dread and worry that you and your loved ones will get sick and the world will fall apart): you still hunker over your laptop at odd hours of the day, laugh and cry with your imaginary friends, and emerge every so often for sunshine and sustenance.

I'd like to thank:

My early readers, who encouraged me to dig deeper, share what the characters are thinking, and add more family drama: Nancy Matuszak, Stephanie Scott, and my mom, Judy Hooyenga.

The Twitter writing community for both encouraging and distracting me along the way.

Taylor Swift, for releasing the albums *Folklore* AND *Evermore*, both of which were desperately needed and appreciated while writing this book.

Sara Spock Carlson, for grounding me through the craziness of 2020, showing up on my doorstep when we bought a new house, and for encouraging me whenever things turn sideways.

And finally, my husband Jeremy, who turned out to be the perfect pandemic partner. *whispers* I love you.

Multi-award winning young adult author Melanie Hooyenga writes books about strong girls who learn to navigate life despite its challenges. She first started writing as a teenager and finds she still relates best to that age group.

Her award-winning YA sports romance series, *The Rules Series*, is about girls from Colorado falling in love and learning to stand up on their own. Her YA time travel trilogy, *The Flicker Effect*, is about a teen who uses sunlight to travel back to yesterday.

When not at her day job at a nonprofit, you can find her enjoying the great outdoors and playing every sport imaginable with her husband Jeremy.